NO HOME FOR KILLERS

OTHER BOOKS BY
E.A. AYMAR

The Unrepentant

They're Gone (written as E.A. Barres)

NO HOME FOR KILLERS

A THRILLER

E. A. AYMAR

THOMAS & MERCER

Published by Thomas & Mercer, Seattle

www.apub.com

Amazon, the Amazon logo, and Thomas & Mercer are trademarks of Amazon.com, Inc., or its affiliates.

ISBN-13: 9781662504563 (paperback)
ISBN-13: 9781662504556 (digital)

Cover design by Faceout Studio, Jeff Miller
Cover image: © The Good Brigade / Getty Images; © Tim Robinson / ArcAngel; © caesart / Shutterstock; © Cafe Racer / Shutterstock

Printed in the United States of America

For Nancy and Noah, always.

PART ONE

When the Smoke Clears

Where will you be?
Where will you stand?
When the smoke clears?

What will people see,
Held in your hand,
When the smoke clears?

Will you be on your knees
Or in a police van
When the smoke clears?

Will we be free
In this land
When the smoke clears?

Excerpted lyrics from "When the Smoke Clears"
Written and recorded by Markus Peña
Blues for You Records

PROLOGUE

"Your brother's dead."

Everything in Melinda Peña's world disappeared for a moment. The light, chilly rain. The courier delivering dinner to the townhouse across the street in their McLean, Virginia, neighborhood. The tightness from her arms crossed over her chest. All she realized were those three stark words from the woman at her door and the painful, fist-like memories of her brother.

"You mean Markus?" Melinda's voice was strange to her ears, as if it belonged to someone else. Someone whispering.

"Yeah."

The stranger's disregard reminded Melinda of her own estrangement from Markus. The world slowly returned.

Melinda recrossed her arms, straightened her posture. Fought back the sudden press of tears and forced out a casual "Okay."

The woman looked a few years younger than Melinda, probably somewhere in her late twenties, wearing torn jeans and a gray hoodie, with a vape pen in her right hand, her left shoved in the hoodie pouch. Strands of wet blonde hair were stuck to her forehead like sloppily drawn *S*s.

She squinted up at the sky. "Can I come in?"

Melinda didn't move. "How'd you know Markus?"

The woman took a drag from her pen, turned the tip blue. "Same way women always knew Markus."

"I haven't talked to him in years." Regret flickered when Melinda heard her own words, a small moment when she wished she'd been more involved in his life.

Then she thought about what Markus had done to her.

The regret passed.

The stranger allowed herself a small smile. She took another hit from the pen. "You don't know shit about him, do you?"

"I know enough."

"Really?" Her smile turned contemptuous.

"What's that mean?"

"Hell, lady," the stranger said. "I just told you your brother's dead, and you don't give a damn."

Melinda ignored her, didn't feel the need to go into her family history with some stranger. Or return to her past at all. The past was like a dark stairway leading down to a secret room she'd locked long ago.

"What's your name?" Melinda asked to change the subject.

"Dani. With an *i*."

"Is that your real name?"

Another drag. Dani eyed her. "A lot of people give you fake names?"

The doorknob to that imaginary secret room was rattling. "They used to."

"Dani's real enough."

The silence between the women stretched like a rickety wooden bridge.

"How'd Markus die?" Melinda asked.

"Someone killed him."

That surprise again for Melinda, but this time more abrupt. As if she had been running and tripped.

"What?"

Dani watched her closely. "Someone killed him."

"Who?"

"I don't know." Fear touched Dani's face, widened her eyes. "No one does. But I have an idea."

Melinda had assumed an overdose, a careless car crash, something tragic but not entirely surprising, given what she knew about her brother. But Markus had been murdered. And murder changed death, complicated it. Murder made Markus a victim, a helpless victim against violence and rage.

And it changed Melinda. Her guilt grew.

"Can I come in?" Dani was asking again.

She'd moved closer, only a couple of steps away.

Melinda smelled the alcohol on the other woman, noticed the uneven brightness in her eyes, heard her slur. Maybe the twilit rain and the surprise of the conversation had hidden it, but these were signs that, years ago, Melinda would have immediately noticed. When she'd worked with women like this.

Before she'd locked that secret door.

"No," Melinda said, her thoughts still helplessly everywhere, scattering like escaping convicts. "I think you need to leave."

"I just want to tell you something else." Dani glanced behind herself. "It's important. Let me in."

"Absolutely not."

Dani took another small step toward her. "They might be after me."

"Who?"

"I just need help."

And then Dani's body was pressed against her, pushing her, her hands reaching around Melinda, that dense smell of beer everywhere. "What's wrong with you?" Dani was saying. "Help me!"

For a moment, Melinda was too surprised to respond. She felt herself pushed back, her foot pressed down on the hardwood inside. She heard the television from the family room, where her boyfriend, Rick, was watching *Jeopardy!*

But the step back was a tightening spring, a physical memory of the times she'd stopped men who were angrily searching for the women Melinda was helping. Melinda pushed forward and shoved Dani out. The other woman tripped, fell, landed on her palms and butt. From the ground, in the rain, her eyes burned.

"What's wrong with you?" Dani asked. "Why won't you help me?"

"What's wrong with *you*?" Melinda asked back, shaken, quick breaths making it hard for her to talk clearly. "You can't force your way into my home."

Dani gathered herself, picked up her vape pen. Glared hard at Melinda. "You want to know what happened? You'll find out soon enough."

"What's that mean?"

No answer. Dani walked away, down the sidewalk, heading out of the little townhouse community. Melinda couldn't help glancing up at neighboring windows, wondering if anyone had seen what happened.

She closed the front door. Locked it.

Melinda's legs were unsteady as she walked to the bathroom to wash Dani's touch off her. As she thought about Markus, about what the woman had said.

You'll find out soon enough.

Melinda desperately needed to get in touch with Emily, their younger sister.

It had been two years since the three siblings had last spoken, two years since the awful incident that had led their separation to grow, solidify like sunbaked mud. But, despite this, Melinda had always felt a connection with Emily she hadn't felt with Markus, their older brother.

Melinda needed to warn her. She didn't know what Dani had meant, but Markus had a way of pulling the entire world toward him.

And if the troubles in his life had finally caught up with him, then Melinda knew darkness would soon follow. Even dead, her brother would still cover all of them in his long, relentless shadow.

CHAPTER ONE

"Oh Jesus, shut up shut up *shut up!*" Emily Peña screamed at the kidnapped man kicking inside the trunk of her car.

Mercifully, Jon Winters, the kidnapped man, quieted down.

Emily sighed and yawned and reached over to the glove compartment. She popped it open, fumbled past a plastic case filled with syringes, pulled out an energy drink. Unscrewed the top, downed it, tossed the empty canister into the back seat with the others as she drove down the interstate.

Caffeine filled her, tingled in her nerves, evaporated the exhaustion behind her eyes. Emily had barely slept this week, and that pissed her off because she *loved* sleeping. She was always tired. Probably, she reflected, because of all the fighting. She almost always needed naps. Although her enthusiasm for naps made her feel a lot older than twenty-eight.

But it hadn't been fighting that had kept her up this week.

It was Markus's death.

They hadn't been close. There was always distance between them—Markus was single-mindedly attached to his music, and Emily would rather gargle marbles than listen to jazz. But there were moments, as the oldest and youngest siblings, when Emily and Markus had enjoyed camaraderie, a playful rebellion against dutiful Melinda or their strict parents. Laughing at their parents' demands while Melinda urged them to listen, getting drunk while Melinda resolutely stayed sober.

And then everything had split apart at their mother's funeral two years ago, the family sent flying in different directions. No one had returned.

Emily heard Jon Winters kicking again from inside the trunk and turned on her music, let "Rage" by Rico Nasty fill the car.

He kicked harder. Either the drug had completely worn off or Jon hated rap.

"I like this song!" she shrieked.

He stopped kicking.

Emily glanced in the rearview mirror. There was no good place to pull over on Interstate 66, the long road leading straight through Northern Virginia into DC. No place where privacy was promised.

Which meant she had to work quickly.

Time to put Jon Winters back to sleep.

Emily slowed the car, pulled over to the side. Left her emergency blinkers off, just in case someone saw them and decided to help. She grabbed her brown canvas mask with three vertical black stripes painted down the front, pulled it over her head, tucked her dyed-blonde hair inside.

Emily reopened the glove compartment and retrieved a syringe filled with midazolam.

She'd read online about the drug, a member of the benzodiazepine family used to sedate patients for surgery, to calm seizures and agitation, even occasionally administered in executions. Emily had gone to a small pharmacy, wearing large sunglasses and a big floppy hat, waited until the pharmacist was called to help someone searching for flu medicine. She slipped behind the counter, found what she was looking for, slipped out.

It had happened so fast that it didn't even feel like breaking the law.

Besides, as Emily often told herself, she was plunging the syringe only into men who deserved it.

Markus had once made a batch of weed-filled brownies during her senior year of high school and eaten them with her. The ensuing high, confusion, and loss of control had left Emily sobbing and begging her laughing older brother to take her to the hospital. Since then, she'd never done a drug stronger than alcohol. But even though she hated needles, she'd known the midazolam needed to be tested. The last thing Emily wanted to do was send criminals into comas, or worse.

She wasn't a killer.

She'd tried the drug on herself in her apartment, tense as she injected a mild dose into her shoulder, sitting cross-legged on the bed and watching an anxious couple search for a new home on *House Hunters*. She was asleep a commercial break later. Woke groggy and confused after an hour, annoyed that she'd missed which house the couple had chosen.

But the midazolam had worked.

Emily glanced in the rearview mirror again, saw a break in oncoming cars, crawled into the back seat. She kept her head down as she popped a latch, pulled the seat down to reveal the inside of the trunk. Heard a whimper. Smelled piss.

She positioned her thumb over the syringe's plunger.

No light from inside. Emily had taken out the trunk's bulb, disabled the emergency latch, removed everything else. Nothing was in her trunk except Jon Winters, his mouth gagged and wrists bound.

His eyes widened in fear when passing headlights illuminated her mask. He cried against the gag, tried to jerk his body free from the restraints.

Emily ignored him, squinted at the syringe. Tapped the tip to make sure no air bubbles were present. Pressed the needle against his bicep.

The back of her head smacked into the driver's seat.

His kick had come out of nowhere. Left Emily's world lopsided. Nausea briefly threatened to rise.

Oh, Emily thought. *His feet.*

Didn't tie his feet.

Another kick to her chest sent her sprawling into the front seats.

Emily shook her head and sat up, trying to see clearly. Jon Winters was still in the car, his bound hands scrabbling at the back door, looking for the handle.

"Rude," Emily said and reached toward him.

He opened the door and spilled outside.

Jon Winters was fortunate he'd opened the door leading to the woods and not the side to traffic, especially since a semi chose that moment to barrel past her car, so close the Civic shook. Emily saw Jon race into the woods lining the interstate, disappear in the trees.

She pulled herself together, climbed out of the car.

Took a second to think, then followed him into the woods.

She'd planned to question him. Might as well do it here.

It was dark, but Emily was learning to see in the dark. And she could hear him rushing through trees and bushes. Jon ran quickly, even with his hands bound. She wasn't surprised. Emily knew he was athletic, had watched him in his apartment through binoculars for a week, seen him sweating through an impressive cardio-and-weights routine. And she'd noticed his confidence with the men who visited him, ominous men who barely spoke, men used to intimidating others. Men who, when they passed her on their way into his building while she loitered and chatted gaily on her phone, stared her down. Like they were daring her to remember them.

Emily remembered them. She made sure of it. As soon as they entered the building, she stopped pretending to talk and typed their descriptions into her phone.

She wanted information about every spider in the Winterses' web of criminals.

The ground turned more uneven the deeper they went. Still, Emily ran easily, effortlessly, toward the fight and away from the highway.

Away from civilization.

Jon Winters abruptly turned and swung his bound fists into the side of her head.

Emily stopped and stepped backward, cheek stinging, mask crooked. She pulled the mask straight, winced as her hands ran over her throbbing face.

Pulled out her baton, pressed a button. The steel extended two feet.

Jon Winters stood in front of her, breathing hard. He roughly yanked the ball gag off his face, threw it into the dark.

Emily spun the baton, kept it moving. A technique she'd studied on her own, practiced by Filipino stick fighters to distract their enemies. She'd first come across it when she'd stumbled on an instructional video on Instagram and was mesmerized by the circular swinging motion as the teacher progressed through his kata. She'd been determined to emulate him.

And she gleefully loved her baton. It seemed innocent, almost ineffective, but even a soft strike from the heavy steel shattered bones. Emily liked the weight in her hand as she slowly twirled it. The way a hit echoed in her arm, traveled through her body.

"Say friend to my little hello," Emily said. "Wait, that's not right."

"Who the hell are you?" Jon asked. "What's with the mask?"

"They call me Three Strikes," Emily told him.

"Who the fuck does that?"

Emily didn't think this was the best time to explain her vigilante identity. "Your family has to answer for their crimes."

"Whatever." Jon's face turned ugly. He lifted his fists.

Emily felt a stony sensation inside her, a feeling with which she was familiar. That grim resolve. The chirpiness in her voice and mind, the lightness of her personality, turned distant. Almost as if Emily had been watching herself on television, sitting inches from the screen, and now she heard its sound from another room.

All that existed was Jon Winters, weaving in front of her.

Emily lunged and lashed his right knee with the baton, restraining herself from hitting too hard. She knew from experience how easily she could shatter his kneecap, send him into shock. And she needed Jon to answer her questions.

He winced and reached for her with his bound hands. Clumsily stepped toward her.

Emily ducked out of the way and slammed the baton into his spine.

Jon shouted and fell to the ground. His body lunged up like an inchworm, but he couldn't rise.

"Your family's done a lot of bad shit," Emily said. "Sex trafficking, selling drugs, whatever money laundering is, probably. You're going to tell me all about them, otherwise Mr. Baton here is going to do the talking."

Emily paused.

"Metaphorically, I mean. Mr. Baton doesn't talk. I'm not crazy."

Jon was in too much pain to respond. He just writhed, groaned, tried to crawl away.

"Okay, awesome!" Emily exclaimed and raised her baton over Jon Winters's broken body. She hadn't expected a confession, knew they didn't come easy. "Let's do this the hard way!"

CHAPTER TWO

You'll find out soon enough.

Melinda pulled out the ignition key from her Grand Cherokee, quieting the engine. She wasn't ready to go into her father's house, didn't want to deal with the ugliness that she knew would ensue. Instead, Melinda stayed in her car as the motor cooled and ticked, pulled her phone out of her purse, scrolled through texts. Chats with friends planning lunches, an exchange with her hairdresser to schedule an appointment, an unanswered message to her sister, sales notifications from clothing stores. And a message from Rick:

> Everything okay?

She wrote back:

> havent gone in yet

She waited for the three dots, the indication that he was replying. Instead, a different message appeared.

> Mel, can we talk?

David Martin, her boss.

Her breath quickened.

Another message from David.

I miss you.

Melinda stared down at her phone, flushed. She could have replied *I don't think this is appropriate.*

Or she could have written *I miss you too.*

Both replies would have been true.

Instead, she deleted his message and checked to see if Rick had written her back. He hadn't. She wrote going in now to her boyfriend, slipped her phone into her handbag, pushed open the car door. Walked up the path to her father's house, loose gravel shifting under her feet.

She hadn't been here for years, but nothing had changed since her earliest childhood memories: she and Markus and Emily crazily running around the sloped yard, their mother admonishing them if they ventured too close to the street. The house was the same, a squat rambler with an upstairs addition that looked sloppily placed, its paneling at odds with the home's brick structure. But the neighborhood had changed. The end of the street used to lead to fields and forest, but a mix of factors—the cost of housing, steady crime, lackluster public schools, rats—had pushed people out of DC and into Virginia and Maryland suburbs, and the city of Manassas was one of those expanding communities. Now newer houses with manicured yards of evenly cut grass and square-trimmed bushes lined either side of a street that seemed to stretch endlessly.

Melinda walked up the porch steps, pushed the doorbell.

She shivered, more from nerves than the cold. Virginia winters had become much more mild than she remembered growing up, a childhood cheerfully buried in snow. But only a few days of snow had fallen the year before, and less was expected this year. Still, she was always cold. Rick teased her about it, about how she wore wool socks and thick sweaters and tights even inside the house.

Her father was quick to open the door. As if he'd been waiting for her.

"Couldn't make the funeral?" Frank Peña asked, leaning heavily on his cane.

She recognized his tone. It was the bitterness when men felt the world had turned against them. And only them.

Melinda shrugged. "I probably could have."

These were the first words they'd spoken in years, and they were an immediate return to her childhood, a petulant retort to a nagging question.

"I thought maybe I'd see you," her father said. "But I didn't expect to see you here." He turned and limped inside. Melinda followed him.

The house was as cluttered as she remembered—dusty displays of pictures and knickknacks, unfolded blankets sprawled across chairs, an overflowing laundry basket in the middle of the floor. Melinda walked through the living room and into the dark family room, where her father had gone.

He leaned his cane against the wall, settled into a recliner. He'd had the cane for years after hip surgery but, even so, the motion of sitting had never grown smooth. He reached behind himself, felt for the chair, collapsed into it. Indicated the couch across the room with his other hand.

Melinda was surprised at the whiteness of his small goatee, a stark sign of how much he'd aged. Her father had always had salt-and-pepper hair until he'd decided to embrace baldness and shave his head, but now his facial hair was full of silver. The wrinkles on his forehead had deepened like ditches. Despite his bearing, there was an exhausted pall hanging over him. The sharp, angry blue of his eyes was watery.

"How's the leg?" Melinda asked.

"It's fine," he grumbled and reached for the controller. Turned on the television. MSNBC. Rachel Maddow giving her audience a knowing look.

Melinda glanced at the photos over the fireplace. Her mom and dad in a side embrace, holding each other with their faces toward the camera. Her brother performing at different clubs, artistic black-and-white photos, singing his heart away. Emily dressed as Spider-Man. The dog of their childhood, an excitable beagle named Charlie, sitting on Santa's lap and staring curiously forward, head tilted.

No photos of her.

"What do you want, Melinda?"

"I wanted to see how you're doing," she said, not ready to tell him about Dani's visit. "You're in this house all by yourself."

"I've been in this house all by myself ever since your mother died."

"I know. But now Markus is gone." She pulled her phone out of her bag, felt better with it in her hand, a connection to a world outside of this house. Glanced at it and realized she'd missed a text:

I want you again.

David.

Shame made her involuntarily turn the phone toward her so her father couldn't see the screen. Not that, with his eyesight, he'd have been able to read it. But she still turned the screen off and laid the phone facedown on her thigh.

Rick didn't deserve this. And Melinda wasn't the kind of person to cheat on someone . . . although she had. She'd experienced betrayal as the betrayer, the person plunging the dagger.

And unwilling to let it go.

"You want to know how I was doing?" her father said, mercifully distracting her. "You should have come to the funeral." He abruptly switched channels, turned to sports commentators shouting at each other about how terrible the Washington Wizards were.

"I didn't want to go," Melinda said.

Her response came almost without thought, and she wondered if it was entirely true. She quickly spoke before he could reply.

"Was Emily there? I've been trying to reach her."

He ignored her question, asked one of his own. "You hated him that much?"

It was a goad, a way to have Melinda respond, *Of course I didn't hate my brother.* And then her father would seize that point. Try and make her realize the regret she'd face when her forgiveness eventually returned.

"I don't know."

Frank shook his head. "How can you even say that?"

"Markus was a manipulative abuser. Even now I don't know if I can forgive everything he did."

"Abuser? Your brother never hit a woman."

Melinda held her tongue.

The two sat quietly. She had thought her father would pursue what she'd said, but he stayed silent.

This room had been different the day of her mother's funeral. The shades open for light to breathe in. The furniture removed and stacked in Melinda's old bedroom down the hall. A long table adorned with photographs and candles and flowers. Her mother's two sisters flew up from Panama and spent days getting the house ready for the memorial service, speaking in grief-stricken voices as they bustled about, clearly distracting themselves from pain with work. Melinda had helped them.

Her father had spent much of that time in his bedroom, mourning heavily, occasionally emerging to watch what was happening.

"¿Estás bien?" one of her mother's sisters had asked Melinda.

"Sí," Melinda said.

"Carla nos dijo que no hablás mucho con tu papá."

"Cierto."

The two sisters glanced at each other, a glance Melinda understood. In Panama, families fought but didn't split.

"Me gusta la nueva canción de Marcos," one of them said.

"No la he escuchado," Melinda lied. She polished the table, watched her shadowy reflection emerge in the dark wood.

"Está buena."

Melinda shrugged.

"¿Estás trabajando?"

Melinda had known the sisters were looking for information about her; these were questions to which they already had answers. Until her sudden death from a stroke, the sisters had spoken to her mother daily. Melinda remembered when she was a young girl and she'd watch her mother on the phone, talking quickly and excitedly in Spanish with them. And then, in recent years, holding the phone's camera in front of her as she walked around the house, chatting and laughing.

The sisters already knew everything about Melinda and the relationships in this family. They just wanted to analyze her reactions. Gather gossip to take back to Panama. Indulge in something other than grief.

But this wasn't a conversation she had wanted to have.

And then her brother's voice was behind her, Markus standing in the doorway of the living room. His face dark. "Melinda!"

And everything had exploded.

"Melinda?"

Her father's voice brought her back.

"Sorry," Melinda said, blinking. "I just haven't been here for a while."

Melinda and her mother had always been the buffers in family dramas, the mediators, the ones who tried to see both sides of a problem. After her mother's death, the fight at the funeral pushed Melinda away, and Emily had wandered off. But Markus and their father still spoke warmly, weekly.

And now Markus was gone.

"Have you seen Em?" Melinda asked again.

Her father ignored her, stared at the television. She wondered if he'd heard her, if he was pretending he hadn't.

Melinda thought again about his beard, how he'd aged. A small stoop was curving his thin body. She wondered if he thought the same about her, if they were changes he'd even notice. Her shorter hair. The weight she'd put on.

The affair that haunted her so much that, at times, she wondered if Rick could see what had happened in her faltering eyes.

"Were there a lot of people at the funeral?" Melinda asked.

Her father responded to that. "Seemed like the whole city came."

"They loved him up in Baltimore."

He smiled a sad smile. "They played 'When the Smoke Clears.'"

Melinda knew the song, slow, hypnotic, and sparse, nothing but a guitar and her brother's voice, written during the police protests of 2020.

"They played it six or seven times." He paused. "It was a bit much."

Her father's humor, nothing ever too sacred.

Melinda did miss it.

"You're just not meant to live long," he went on, "when you live like Markus."

"What do you mean?" Melinda was unsure where that statement was leading.

The drinking?

The carelessness?

Or the violence.

"You can't perform music the way he did and live a long life. Not many do. Maybe Dylan or Duke or Miles. Artists die young, especially relentless ones. I've seen people on TV comparing him to them."

Melinda had also seen the comparisons on television, online, flooding social media. Fans and celebrities offering their tributes, calling her brother a fighter and a champion, a voice of truth, people he'd never met weighing in as if they'd known him. It was distressing for Melinda to read these testimonials, to witness how gullible people were, to see those who knew Markus the least insisting the most on his character.

"The more he got into music, the more I knew this was his fate. An early death." Her father kept talking, his voice grief choked. "You hope that's not what's going to happen. Same way you hope your child won't pedal in the street when you show him how to ride a bike. Get into an accident when you teach him to drive. It's all hope."

"There was only so much you could do," Melinda said emptily.

He nodded, wiped his eyes. "I know. And keeping Markus inside any kind of boundaries was never going to work."

Talking about Markus made Melinda feel like a rubber band, stretching until she might snap. Especially since her father insisted on praising him.

You'll find out soon enough.

That woman's words came back to Melinda.

"Hey, Dad, did you know a woman named Dani?" Melinda asked. "A friend of Markus's?"

"No."

"She stopped by my place. She's the one who told me Markus was . . . who told me about Markus. She said she'd dated him or something, and she was worried *they* were going to come after her."

"Probably just some crazy fan."

"Maybe," Melinda agreed. "But when I asked her more, she said I'd find out what she meant soon enough."

Now her father seemed interested. He sat up in his chair.

"When was this?"

"A few days ago."

"Nothing since then?"

"No."

He settled back down. "Like I said, some crazy fan. Probably just trying to get money or something."

"I guess." Melinda was unconvinced. Dani hadn't asked for money. And Melinda remembered the way Dani's eyes widened with fear when she'd said Markus had been murdered, the desperate way she'd tried to force herself into her home.

"I just want to know what happened to him."

"The police said it was a random robbery. His death . . ." Frank cleared his throat. "They said it was an accident during the struggle."

"Yeah, but the police weren't his biggest fans. Especially after 'When the Smoke Clears.' Do you trust them?"

This was something they agreed on. "I don't think they're going to look too hard," Frank admitted. "But there was nothing suspicious about it. They showed me . . . they told me details."

Melinda thought again about Dani and the warning she'd given before she'd stalked off into the night.

"Have you heard from anyone in Panama?" her father asked.

"No one reached out to me." The words came before Melinda realized they sounded like an attack. She tried to backtrack, but Frank spoke first.

"Why would we? You said yourself you didn't care. Your brother was killed, and you and your sister didn't even show up to . . ." He stopped, wiped his eyes again.

"You don't know everything about me and Markus," Melinda said carefully. "Or Emily."

A silence had fallen over the room, like a held breath. She hadn't realized he'd muted the television.

"Like what?"

"Like stuff I don't want to talk about. Especially now."

Her father surprised her by agreeing. "You're right. I'm not ready for what you have to say."

Melinda felt like there was potential there, something to grasp. Some sort of reconciliation, a way for her father to share grief. Not suffer alone.

21

But he wasn't done talking.

"All your mother wanted was for the three of you to be family."

"I know."

"The morning she died, she was crying about it."

Melinda had heard this before.

"That stress you caused killed her." His voice was raw.

Pain and anger fluttered inside Melinda heavily, like stone wings. She struggled to maintain her composure.

"She was crying all that morning," Frank went on, "and I came into the room later that day, and she was dead."

"I know, Dad."

"Who did that to her?" His tears weren't held back anymore. This was her father's pit, the dark place that he'd sunk into and never completely left. Melinda had always suspected he'd loved their mother more than he'd loved his children. He'd taken her last name, abandoned Smith for Peña, a sign of his love and respect for her family. He was always helplessly lost in her, an emotion that struck Melinda as alternately sweet and troubling.

And after she had died and Melinda and Emily had left, all of his love had poured toward Markus.

"She was so sad about you." His voice a whisper. "Especially you, Melinda. She expected the most from you."

Guilt bit Melinda's soul. She wondered if this pain was why she had come.

Was she seeking blame?

"If I'd known Mom was going to die," Melinda said slowly, "then I would have tried to fix things. I would have talked to her."

"She'd be alive if you had."

Melinda's own sharp intake of breath surprised her. He'd actually said it.

She wanted to spring to her feet, say something cruel in response, irreparably wound him . . . but a part of Melinda believed him. Like an invisible hand on her shoulder, firmly forcing her to stay seated.

"Maybe," she said, quietly.

That was all she could offer.

It wasn't enough.

"She would be!" Frank was shouting now. "But you let her die without you. And you let Markus die without you. You need to stop being such a selfish girl and realize people need you. But you just abandon everyone when things get hard. You walk away because it's easier. You don't have what the rest of us do."

"I was sorry about Mom," Melinda said, struggling to control her voice, to keep calm, righting a rowboat during a hurricane. "I am. I always will be. But you don't know everything about Markus. Or me and Emily."

"I know enough!" Frank kept shouting. "And I know enough about you. Markus needed help, and you abandoned him. Just like you abandoned those women."

That was the push. That was what caused her to rise to her feet.

"You abandon everybody!"

Melinda didn't realize she was leaving the house until she was halfway out of the living room.

She didn't realize she was crying until she was unlocking her car door.

You abandon everybody!

Even as she drove away, those words from her father stayed with her.

Like the thought of her brother's body lying in a grave a few cities away.

Or the door to that secret room inside her opening.

Those women she'd left behind waiting for her, hands reaching out.

And dragging her back.

CHAPTER THREE

Emily left Jon Winters lying in the woods and headed back to her Civic, cheerfully whistling Wale's "Pretty Girls" under her mask. She climbed in, drove to the closest exit ramp, and parked. Traffic was sparse on the interstate, but she still wanted to move her car. The last thing she needed was someone seeing her Civic, pulling over, and following Jon's cries to where she was questioning him about his family.

Emily had heard a lot about the Winterses. She'd paid attention to them when Markus dated Rebecca Winters, heard her brother's slurred ramblings one drunken night about their illegal activities. She'd done further research and found suspicious connections between them and criminals, read about arrests made of their associates while the Winters family remained on the periphery. And she remembered how much money Rebecca had when she'd dated Markus, even though Rebecca had downplayed it.

People could rarely hide being born into wealth or poverty. Upbringing clung like a stubborn accent.

Emily remembered Rebecca's Chanel handbags, the way she had casually worn Louboutins, their flashy red bottoms winking up when she walked, the perfectly fitted silver sequined designer dress when Emily had seen her sing. She'd thought Rebecca was lovely on the few occasions she'd met her but could tell that Rebecca had never stepped off of her golden path.

The path her family's criminal work had laid.

Emily hiked back from her car through the woods, carrying a backpack filled with rope, bandages, her wallet, keys, snacks. The rush from her fight with Jon was gone, as if the fight had been an explosion, the moments afterward echoes. Emily was used to this feeling, the tiring loss of adrenaline. And she was prepared for the emotional shakiness, like violence was receding water, fear an incoming wave. The first time Emily had ever attacked someone, it had left her rattled, his cries and pleas striking her memory afterward like lightning, sudden and frightening and illuminating.

But it hadn't just been the violence of that first attack; it was the man. Younger than her, probably just turned twenty-two, wide eyed and soft spoken, with a wife he seemingly adored. Emily had heard the cops responding to the wife's distressed call on her scanner, the cop's resigned voice when he said the call had been a mistake.

At first it had seemed that way to Emily as well. She spied on the couple for a week, driving to their house in late afternoon, parking down the street in their Northern Virginia neighborhood. Quickly climbing the fence into their backyard and dropping clumsily, despite her efforts, to the ground on the other side. Then she would open her small backpack and slip her canvas mask over her head. Adjust it so she could peer through the mesh eyeholes concealed in the stripes.

Emily would stare through windows, following the wife from the kitchen to the dining room to the family room. She observed her go through daily routines of cleaning the house, preparing meals, watching Bravo reality shows, taking some sort of online college course on her computer in the dining room. The husband coming home from work, joining his wife for a dinner she'd made, the two of them watching nature documentaries for a couple of hours before retiring upstairs. From the backyard, peering through the bottom corner of a window, Emily would watch the documentaries with them, bored out of her mind. She seriously considered buying a universal remote to change the channel back to Bravo. Whenever the wife yawned, Emily felt solidarity.

During the days she studied the wife, analyzing her expressions, trying to see if her face ever conveyed fear or panic. But nothing seemed amiss, nothing aside from the moments where she looked up from her computer and stared into the distance. And then, as those moments lingered, Emily would see something flicker over the woman's face, a moment of pain that vanished with a shake of her head.

On the sixth day he struck her.

The wife had said something, and he'd spun toward her, his expression torn with sudden anger, arm clumsily raised like a bird's broken wing. Emily's fingers felt like they were indenting the steel of her baton as she watched.

The wife covered herself on the floor, blood running from her mouth. The young husband rubbed his eyes hard, pushed open the door from the kitchen leading to the backyard. Where Emily was hiding.

Waiting.

For Emily, there was no courage to summon, no resolve to gather. Her baton was in his ribs before he'd descended the last step. Her arm moved in a blur, the steel smashing his side, shoulders, leg, knee, chin. He shrieked, screams so high they almost broke through Emily's red haze, but it wasn't until his wife was pulling her waist, begging her to stop, that Emily was brought back. She raced out of the backyard and ran down the street.

An hour later a call of aggravated assault came over her scanner.

The couple claimed someone had attacked both of them. That the wife's bruise was from an assailant, and her husband had tried to stop the assault. Their false claim crushed Emily, as did her own sense of guilt. That man's screams haunted her, so much so that some part of Emily believed their accusation.

But she had kept going.

She knew he'd deserved it.

The reports of domestic violence on the scanner continued endlessly, the resigned voices of dejected cops reporting that charges wouldn't be pressed. That a bruised wife or scared child would stay silent. That nothing could be done until the next call, a next call that would likely require an ambulance or a hearse.

And so Emily kept driving to those houses. Sneaking onto the properties at night. Peering through windows. Waiting for that first hit.

And loosing her baton.

She still had doubts, moments of repentance like a lasso landing around her. Moments where the memories of her own violence stopped her.

Dreamlike memories where she was lost, fugue states of men begging her to stop, their hands raised as they wept. Emily stuck in those moments as if she were wading through mud, and sometimes sinking.

But then other memories would save her. The stories Melinda had told her about the scared, scarred women her sister had tried to help, the women who had been tortured and kept captive. The blackened eyes, broken arms, raw scars, burned skin, hair ripped from roots, skin indented with teeth marks, disfigured genitalia, women forced to smile bloody smiles through endless nightmares. The children whose wide eyes had witnessed a violence from which they would never completely escape, who would be forced to relive it in flashes for the rest of their lives. The dead these merciless men left behind, a vast mass grave to which the world cast a blind eye.

Or Emily would remember what had almost happened to her, that terrible night at a club. The night she'd never talked about.

And the baton would crash down.

Not all the men Emily went after were abusive boyfriends or husbands. She'd beaten pedophiles, pimps, the owner of a dogfighting ring. That last one had ended with Emily nearly mauled to death by an ungrateful pit bull when she'd opened the kennels to set the dogs free.

That wasn't the only time she'd been injured. She had a collection of small scars and lingering aches from men who'd fought back, especially in those early days, when she didn't know how to leave someone hurt and defenseless at the beginning of a fight. When, even with the element of surprise, the outcome was uncertain.

The only thing certain was her need to do this.

Emily slipped through the dark woods, stepping lightly. She heard Jon before she saw him, talking on his phone.

She cursed herself.

Way to take his phone, dumbass.

Not that she didn't still make mistakes.

He must have woken after her beating. Emily stopped just before the small clearing where she'd left him.

"I don't know who," Jon was saying. "They just attacked me." His voice was raw, like his throat had been rubbed with sandpaper.

Silence.

"Somewhere on 66. Heading east."

A breeze rustled. Emily leaned forward to listen better. "It was near Manassas," Jon rasped. "Around Bull Run. I saw the sign when I was running into the woods."

Silence again.

"I'll ping you where I'm at and you'll hear me moaning in pain! That's how you'll find me! That's why I'm paying you!"

He hung up and started crying.

Emily debated her options. She had no idea if she'd have enough time to question Jon before whoever he'd called showed up. Probably best, she reasoned, to find more leads. See who came for him, follow them wherever they went. She'd just need to find someplace safe to wait.

Emily glanced around, spotted a branch-heavy tree.

She climbed quietly even though Jon was sobbing too loudly to notice her. Emily reached a height she was comfortable with, about fifteen feet up. Perched her left foot in the V of a branch, her right foot

28

beneath her, knee close to her chin. Hung her backpack next to her. Looked down at Jon's body as he slowly, painfully tried to pull himself forward. She knew that, after the beating she'd given him, he wasn't going anywhere.

She took a plastic bag of Lucky Charms marshmallows out of her backpack, tossed moons into her mouth. Thought about doing some work from her day job on her phone, but a DC-based vigilante working right after beating up a bad guy seemed too depressingly reflective of Washington, DC, work-life culture.

She was jittery from the fight and the caffeine and the cramped position in the tree. Jon Winters had given up on crawling, was instead lying still and sobbing again as he waited for whoever he'd called. Emily pulled out a Lucky Charms marshmallow, aimed at his head.

Threw it down.

It noiselessly bounced on the ground a few feet away from his body. He didn't notice.

She pulled out another from her Ziploc bag, carefully aimed, tossed. Inches from his elbow this time.

Emily was going to throw another but was too hungry to waste food. She settled on slipping in her earbuds and started flipping through podcasts she'd saved on her phone. She was halfway into a true-crime podcast about the murder, three years earlier, of Baltimore County's district attorney when she saw flashlight beams zigzagging on the ground.

The flashlights stopped before Jon's body. The two men holding them were big and ominous, the kind of men Emily had seen outside of Jon's apartment building.

"What happened to you?" one of them asked. The night breeze shook leaves.

Jon's voice was ragged. "Got jumped in my garage. Kidnapped. I got out of her car, but she caught me. I think she broke my fucking back."

"She?"

A snort.

Anger from Jon. "The bitch drugged me, tied me up, and hit me with some kind of bat. It wasn't a fair fight."

Emily almost laughed. Despite the pain from a broken back, Jon still wanted to make sure these guys knew he had valid reasons for losing a fight to a girl.

She hadn't realized her baton was in her hand, that she'd quietly pulled it from her pocket and her thumb was poised over the release. She'd already come up with a plan to climb down the tree, wait for those two men to start carrying Jon out of the woods, and attack all three. Her mind had been doing this lately, constantly preparing for fights, her fists balling or legs tensing as she walked past strangers.

But she slipped the baton into her pocket.

At this point, fighting wouldn't get her what she wanted.

Fighting wouldn't help her find more information about the Winterses.

The two men were trying to carry Jon out of the woods. Every time they attempted to pick him up, he screeched.

"I need a stretcher!"

"Yeah," one of the men replied. "We didn't bring one of those."

Again, an attempt to pick up Jon by his shoulders. Again, a screech.

Emily covered her mouth to hide a giggle.

"Just ignore him," one of them said. "Let's get him to the car."

They staggered a few steps and he howled.

"Ow!" one of the men said and swore. "He bit me!"

"Don't pick me up like that!"

Emily watched the two men gaze at each other from either side of Jon's body. They stared for what seemed like minutes, and then one of them sighed and pulled off his shirt.

"What are you doing?" Jon asked. "Why are you getting un—" He didn't have a chance to finish the sentence before the man wadded up his T-shirt and stuffed it into Jon's mouth.

Jon's cries turned muffled even as their intensity increased. The men picked him up again and started carrying him through the forest.

They disappeared from her view.

Emily slung the backpack over her shoulders, shimmied down the tree. She tried to stay as silent as possible, hoped none of the branches would break underneath her. The sound of a snap would stand out in stark contrast to the silence of the night.

Emily touched ground just as one of the men stepped back into the clearing.

He stopped a few feet away from her.

Emily stayed pressed against the tree, not daring to move.

She watched his silhouette as he glanced around. But he must not have seen her, couldn't tell her figure from the tree behind her. But she was close enough to smell him, that dense, sweaty stench men got when they stayed outdoors too long.

Over the course of a dozen fights, Emily had rarely found herself in a situation where she didn't have the upper hand. But if this man discovered her, her chance for surprise would be brief. And his partner was only a shout away.

The beam from his flashlight stayed on the ground, inches from her boot.

The man grunted, bent, picked something up. Shone the flashlight into his palm, the light almost touching Emily.

A blue Lucky Charms moon.

Emily held her breath.

He dropped the moon, adjusted his crotch, kept walking back to where they'd found Jon. Scanned the clearing with the flashlight, apparently looking for anything they might have left behind. Turned and headed back toward the road.

Emily exhaled, pulled out her baton, quietly followed him through the woods to the interstate. She breathed softly and stepped carefully until she reached the edge of the trees, where that man's partner stood next to a van, pulling his shirt back on. Jon was on the ground, silent and still.

The two men slid the cargo door open, picked up Jon, gracelessly dumped him inside to his muffled cry. Shut the door, and one of them walked over to the driver's side.

Time to go.

Emily sprinted off, staying in the shadows of the woods, on the edge of the road and the trees. The exit where she'd parked her Civic was farther than she remembered. Small branches broke as she brushed past them; heavier ones clawed.

Emily finally saw the exit and ran down it, her legs hurting after being motionless for almost an hour. But she wasn't tired, and, despite the sprint, her breathing was normal. These were the times she was grateful for her robust conditioning, the brutal workouts that left her collapsed on the floor of her apartment, panting and sweaty, one hand over her chest to calm her heart.

But she had to hurry. Jon Winters was the best lead she had to the Winters clan.

Emily reached the Civic, tugged her keys from her pocket. Pulled off her mask and backpack. Slid inside and started the car in one motion, spun into the road and into a U-turn, heading to where she'd seen the van.

Gone.

"Shit!"

Emily sped up, passing cars on the interstate, her gaze fixed ahead. Finally saw the square shape of the van barreling down the road. She kept her eyes trained on it as she sped up, wove around a car.

Blue and red flashing lights.

"Shit shit *shit*!"

The cop car was swimming through traffic like a hungry shark. Emily glared at the van but knew she didn't have a choice.

She slowed and merged to the shoulder. As her Civic rolled to a stop, she stuffed her hooded mask and retracted baton under her seat. Took her registration out of the glove compartment.

Rolled down the window as the cop approached.

"How do you feel about bribes?" she cheerfully asked as the van disappeared in the distance, as the cop sighed and opened his notepad, as her thoughts raged under her smile.

CHAPTER FOUR

we need to talk about your brother

Melinda stared at the text, surprised at both the message and its sender.

Jessy Taylor, Markus's best friend. A woman Melinda hadn't spoken to in years.

"You can't let him get to you," Rick said.

"What?" Melinda asked, confused, and glanced up. She and Rick were shuttling a grocery delivery from the front door to the kitchen. Even though it was just the two of them, they each loved to cook, and the floor of their entranceway was buried in bulging brown paper bags.

"Your dad," Rick said. "You can't let him bother you."

"Oh." Melinda was still distracted. She slid her phone into her back pocket, picked up a bag.

"He's just lonely," Rick went on. "And now he's even lonelier. All he does is sit at home, right? Pretty much a shut-in?"

"Pretty much." Melinda opened the refrigerator, put a sealed package of drumsticks on a shelf. Peeled pink chicken always looked so helpless to her. She was the type of person who felt bad about eating meat, but not bad enough to stop. But thinking about the short, cramped life of a chicken, cow, or pig did make her sad, so she tried not to let herself ponder it.

Her phone buzzed again.

Just wanted to see how you're doing.

David, her boss.

Melinda put her phone in her pocket.

She couldn't text David now, not with Rick in the same room, dutifully stacking cans of soup in the pantry.

It was the same reason she'd downplayed the visit from the woman, Dani, who'd told her about Markus's death. Or, for that matter, Markus's death. Rick didn't need to know the messed-up depths of her family.

Or her.

"Are you going to try to talk to him again?" Rick asked.

"Who do you mean?" Her question came in a rush.

Had Rick seen the text from David?

"Your dad."

Melinda breathed, let her insides untwist. "Maybe in a few weeks."

She walked back to the hallway, trying to distance herself from Rick and her guilt.

"But does that make him right?" Rick called.

"Nope."

He followed her into the hall.

"But isn't this you running when things get tough?"

Melinda hoisted a paper bag to her hip, headed back into the kitchen. "I don't know what he wants," she said over her shoulder, and decided to turn everything in the conversation toward her father. Force thoughts of David and Jessy away. "He's never been happy that I got out of social work."

"But he knows how burned out you were."

Melinda slid open the vegetable drawer, started dumping in heads of lettuce, sealed packs of baby carrot sticks, tiny shiny red tomatoes. "My dad doesn't get burned out. He doesn't get tired. And he doesn't see how it happens in other people. He's sixty and thinks that if he can march and yell all day, then everyone else should too."

She finished, headed back to the hall. Saw Rick staring out the open front door, his hand in the air.

"Someone there?" Melinda asked.

"Well . . ." Rick turned toward her and frowned. "I guess not? I saw someone standing next to a car across the street, but they drove off."

They finished up the groceries, and Rick slipped into his home office to work, as he always did on Sunday nights. He was a patent attorney for a small private company, seemingly one of the few attorney jobs in the area that kept regular nine-to-five hours rather than stretching into evenings or early mornings. Even so, Rick still brought his work home. Melinda found that tireless quality alternately attractive and exhausting. It reminded her of everyone in her family. Everyone but her.

That wasn't something she wanted to be reminded of right now.

What Melinda wanted was to lose herself in something else, a simple distraction, like trashy television. A handful of strangers forced to live together. Fixed singing competitions. Quarrelsome young couples renovating an old home.

Escape the thoughts of Markus tugging at her, demanding her attention.

She'd gone on social media earlier that day, out of habit more than anything else, absentmindedly scrolled until she came upon a rush of posts about her brother. CNN had aired a tribute to Markus, and the show had caused another outpouring of support.

Markus PENA Absolutel KING!!!! a fan had written, and Melinda had closed the app and deleted it from her phone.

She went into their bedroom, the sprawling master that dominated the top floor of the townhouse. Sat on the bed, pulled out her phone. Stared again at the message from Jessy Taylor:

we need to talk about your brother

Was it grief, Melinda wondered, that had led Jessy to contact her? Did she expect Melinda to commiserate with her? She analyzed the phrasing. There was an urgency behind Jessy's words, one stronger than the slow ache of sadness.

Jessy needed her.

And Melinda felt that emotional tug, the desire to extend her hand and help someone scared, someone being pulled away, but she couldn't help Jessy. Markus was too much for Melinda to handle, his memory too massive.

She returned to David's message.

> Just wanted to see how you're doing.

She hesitated, her thumbs hovering over her phone. Then wrote:

> I'm ok, You?

His next message came quickly, as if David had been waiting for her.

> Same here. Hey thanks for that inventory check.

> No prob.

Essentials, the company David owned, was one of the first, and now most prominent, local food subscription services in the region. The company specialized in farm-raised meats and delivered weekly boxes of food directly to consumers.

David had brought Melinda on after the company's growth led him to seek someone else to help manage the day-to-day operations: the marketing, fulfillment, inventory, sales reports.

It was a complete departure from the social work she'd left behind, but Melinda approached it the way she did everything in life, determined to prove herself, relentless in her efforts. Taking classes in accounting and retail management to learn the ropes, researching similar companies, absorbing everything David told her like a sponge.

I need to see you again.

Melinda stared at his next message. She could have gone the entire conversation skating above its surface and felt like she might have preferred that. Although, had David *not* alluded to what had happened between them, Melinda knew she would have been left wondering.

Wondering why.

It was just so amazing, he went on.

She read that sentence a couple of times.

David, this doesn't feel right to me. I'm sorry, but it was a mistake. I shouldn't have done it. I do like you, but I'm with someone else, and I have to respect that. I'm sorry, but I can't continue with this. I understand it may change our working relationship, but it's a change I need to make.

That would have been the right thing to say. But it wasn't what she sent. Melinda wrote only two lines.

I know. For me too.

The wrongness of everything she was doing felt like it was turning her heart into rotted fruit. Melinda thought about Rick cheerfully working downstairs, without any idea what was happening in the room above.

She thought about her life, this lovely, oversize townhouse in upscale McLean, the happy security, the future's bright promise.

I can't stop thinking about it, David wrote back.

Me neither.

It was honest.

But it shouldn't happen again, she continued.

Melinda held the phone tightly in her hands.

A moment passed before David replied.

I know. But I want it to.

Melinda didn't want to make these plans, go forward with it, risk losing everything she had. She could understand affairs if something was lacking in a relationship, if there was a need in one person for love or sex or happiness that wasn't being met, but it seemed like nothing in her life lacked.

Even so, she wrote, When?

Melinda had purposely gone to sleep before Rick came up from his office, went for a long walk in the morning before he got out of bed, Eva Cassidy's voice in her earbuds, the dead singer wailing about the blues in the night. She came back when Rick was already working, tried to do the same.

But she couldn't work without thinking about David.

And now, the morning after their text exchange, Melinda's guilt was threatening to rise. She was terrified it would overwhelm her, overrun her conscience so relentlessly that the only saving salve would be confessing to Rick.

Which would mean losing Rick.

Melinda was used to keeping secrets—familial, professional, personal—but never anything like this. Those secrets had made her stronger, further defined her, not torn who she was in two.

In desperation for something to give her a sense of honesty, of pure purpose, Melinda went to see Jessy Taylor.

Melinda and Jessy had met during Melinda's days as a social worker, when she was helping victims of forced prostitution and sex trafficking. Jessy had brought a friend to the program, a small, shaken woman named Brooke who had been coerced into prostitution through love and drugs and ended up working the streets for her boyfriend, a pimp with women spread in different neighborhoods like the ends of a spider's legs. Melinda had helped Brooke as much as she could but struck a friendship with Jessy. Jessy would come by the safe house where Brooke and three other women lived and end up talking with Melinda as much as she did with Brooke. Eventually, she talked with Melinda more.

Melinda had liked her. Short and funny, with a mess of curly red hair. The kind of woman who was surprisingly open and giving, which was the kind that Melinda usually made fast friends with.

And then, one night over beers at a bar, Markus suddenly appeared at their table.

"Who's this?" he'd asked Melinda. Not even offering his sister a hello.

"This is Jessy," Melinda replied evenly. "She's a friend."

"And who's this?" Jessy asked back, matching Markus's abrupt tone. He reached out, shook her hand. "Markus Peña, famous singer."

"Okay, I was kidding. I know who you are." Jessy gaped at Melinda. "You never told me your brother is Markus Peña!"

"Don't say it like that."

"I didn't even know you had a brother!"

If Markus was offended, he didn't show it. Just pulled over a chair from someone else's table without bothering to ask, spun it around, and sat. Faced them with his arms draped over the back.

"It's cool," he said. "Nobody knows I have sisters."

"You have a sister?" Jessy asked Melinda.

Melinda and Markus didn't look at each other the entire conversation. Melinda quieted the more Markus and Jessy talked. Her friendship with Jessy was lost anyway, something Melinda knew the moment

Markus introduced himself, the moment she'd heard that awe-filled note in Jessy's voice.

Markus swooped over them like a magician's cape, and Jessy—at least the Jessy who had been Melinda's friend—had vanished when the cape was pulled away.

Melinda parked her car outside of Jessy's house in Silver Spring, Maryland, the smallest and newest in a neighborhood of old colonials, a 1970s rambler with an unkempt yard and dirt-smudged windows.

Her phone buzzed in her pocket. Melinda worried it was another message from David. She wasn't ready to respond to him, to continue where they had left off last night.

DONT COME IN!!!!

The text was from Jessy.

Why not?

No answer. Melinda climbed out of her car, confused.

The front door slowly opened.

Jessy stood in the doorway. She wore yoga pants and a gray hoodie with "Area Woman" written across the front. She didn't look that different from what Melinda remembered. Maybe a little older, a little more tired, probably from the grief framing her painfully red eyes, sorrowfully turned mouth, unbrushed red hair.

"I didn't know you were going to come here," Jessy said. "I don't—I don't think it's safe."

"Why not?"

Jessy glanced around. "Because I think I know who killed Markus."

Melinda glanced away from the intensity of Jessy's grief. "Someone stopped by my place a few days ago," she said. "And told me the same thing."

"Are you serious?"

"Yeah."

"Who was it?"

"A woman named Dani. I think she was a sex worker Markus knew."

The grief in Jessy's face grew. Or maybe, Melinda thought, it was jealousy. She'd never been certain about the extent of Jessy's relationship with Markus and preferred not to dwell on it.

"Did anyone follow you here?" Jessy asked.

"I don't know? I didn't check. Why?"

Jessy bit her lip, balled and relaxed her fists, a nervous habit Melinda suddenly remembered. "We need to talk. Maybe you should come inside."

"Why?"

Jessy's face was nothing but fear, whatever composure she'd had almost lost, like a dead bird falling from the sky, about to crash on the ground. "Because they're going to kill me next."

Melinda followed Jessy through a cluttered living room smelling of old paper and filled with clothes and boxes and magazines. This mess couldn't have been more representative of Jessy, Melinda realized, remembering the other woman's scattered thoughts and unpredictable behavior. Jessy had always been a bit peculiar.

Then Melinda noticed a standing cutout of her brother behind an open recliner in a corner.

A bit peculiar, and a terrible decision maker.

They went into the kitchen, which was just as cluttered. Cupboards half-open because of ill-fitted pots and pans, an island covered in unopened and discarded mail and notebooks and, for some reason, a bra.

They stood on opposite sides of the island.

"Did someone threaten you?" Melinda asked again, thinking about Dani's visit to her townhouse. "Did they show up here?"

Jessy was gripping the counter, squeezing and relaxing her hands. "No, nothing like that. No one's said anything to me."

Melinda was confused. "Then why—"

Jessy didn't let her finish. "Because there's something I want to do. And if I do it, they'll come after me."

Still confused. "Who?"

Jessy hedged, picked up an empty glass and set it in the sink. "Markus made a lot of enemies."

"You mean everyone who ever knew or met him?"

"Wow," Jessy said. "You two really hated each other."

You two really hated each other.

So Markus had said he hated her.

Melinda felt like dirt was being shoveled on her heart.

"I knew him better than you did," she said.

"You probably knew stuff about him I didn't," Jessy agreed. "But I definitely knew stuff about him you didn't."

And the stuff I knew, Melinda thought, *you accepted.*

Like Markus's cruel womanizing. His emotional and physical violence. That fucking ego. All while singing behind a facade of purity. Nobility.

"Like I said, he made enemies," Jessy went on. "Especially after 'A Song for Killers.'"

"What's that?"

"It was Markus's last song. I think it pissed off the wrong people."

"I never heard it." Melinda didn't add that she'd stopped listening to Markus's music years ago.

"I think it was leaked before it came out. *Someone* knew about it."

Melinda almost laughed. "You're telling me he was killed because of a song?"

Doubt shadowed Jessy.

"I mean, I thought he was, until you just said it out loud." Jessy skipped a beat. "Okay, I guess it sounds weird. But that's right when it happened."

"A *song*? Come on, Jessy. No one would have killed him for that. They didn't even come after him when he did the protest song that pissed everyone off. The police said it was a random break-in. Or, let's be real, some angry sex worker who'd finally had enough of his bullshit."

Helplessness in Jessy's voice. "But he died right after the song was recorded."

Despite Jessy's reluctance to change her image of Markus, a pang of sympathy thrummed in Melinda. The shaken state of her old friend did sadden her. "Have you been okay?"

Jessy started to answer but caught herself. She walked over to the fridge and pulled open the door, and a plastic bottle of water fell to the ground. She picked it up, twisted off the top. Closed the fridge with her hip and drank deeply.

"I remember getting the phone call that he was dead," Jessy said and coughed. "And then my hands and knees were on the ground. And I was so sad, but I wasn't surprised. There was something about Markus that didn't seem like he'd have a long life. Like a candle about to burn itself out. You know what I mean?"

Melinda allowed herself an assenting sound but didn't elaborate.

She didn't want to praise her brother.

Or acknowledge how much they'd once had in common.

The pursuit they'd shared, him with music and her with social work, a commitment to something greater than themselves. That sense of devotion that overwhelmed everyone in the Peña family.

"I want to release the song," Jessy said.

"What? 'A Song for Killers' or whatever?"

"It needs to be heard. I owe that to your brother."

"No one owes him anything."

"You're not being fair to him."

44

Something in Melinda flickered, a lighter rubbed to life.

"He made enemies," Jessy went on, "but he also had a lot of friends."

"Yeah, I knew some of those *friends*." Her cheeks turned hot.

"You mean me?" A flare in Jessy's tone, the anger under the conversation threatening to rise.

It was Markus's effect, Melinda knew. His shadow weighing down. And she still couldn't pull herself out from underneath it.

Anger inflamed her, a deep-seated resentment, a loathing turned both inward and outward. Melinda had felt it before, the kind of violence that heated her face, filled her with murder-red hate.

"You know what he did," Melinda told Jessy, "to the women I was trying to help. You know what he did to me."

There was an unsteadiness in Melinda's voice, a tremor that changed the tone of their conversation. That caused the flame in Jessy to lower.

"I'm sorry about that," Jessy said. "I am. I should have been different. It's just that Markus . . . nobody has ever needed me like he did."

Melinda knew exactly what Jessy was talking about. She remembered their friendship, the way Markus and Jessy had simply and wholeheartedly turned toward each other. There had been a time when doing anything without the other would have been unthinkable; even a trip to the grocery store meant pairing up, no matter the inconvenience. It would have been charming had Melinda trusted him.

Markus had always been good with women. From an early age, Melinda had noticed his difference from other boys. During the elementary years, when boys barely noticed girls, Markus's closest friends had been female.

That didn't change as he grew older. Markus always happily had a girl near him. Melinda watched the girls that hung out with him in junior high and high school, knew exactly when they'd fallen for her brother. She could see it in the aggressive ways they teased him, in how they dressed and did their makeup when they came over (too little clothing, too much makeup), the way their faces and mannerisms changed when Markus casually, innocently mentioned another girl.

Markus seemed oblivious to what these girls wanted, to how deeply they loved him. He'd had the maddening distance of boys that age, particularly when a girl was interested in him. A distance that, Melinda knew, only drew them deeper.

But the truth was simple and selfish: no woman could ever come close to Markus.

He'd never loved anyone.

"That's how he always made women feel," Melinda said. "He used you."

Jessy looked at her uncertainly. "I don't think he did."

"That's because he did it well." Melinda didn't see any point in staying, in continuing an argument neither of them would concede. "I'm done here." She took a deep breath, exhaled slowly. "And I'm done with him."

"I'm going to release the song," Jessy told her. "It might lead to the truth."

That gave Melinda pause. "So you think that's why he was killed, and you *still* want to put it out there?"

"He was my friend," Jessy said resolutely. "My best friend."

The worry in Jessy's face twisted something inside Melinda. She knew Markus's music didn't have anything to do with his death, but she did want to help this other woman out of her pain.

But then she thought about what Markus had done.

At how Jessy had accepted it. Refused to see the truth behind him. The pain he'd caused so many people. And how those who helped him had just spread the pain further.

"I'm leaving," Melinda told her decisively.

"Please, wait," Jessy called after her, but Melinda was already on her way out.

"Just wait! Melinda!"

Melinda was finished with Markus.

There wasn't anything about him she wanted to understand.

Walking away from Markus's memory, from his abuse and hypocrisy, was a sign of strength.

At least, that's what Melinda told herself as she left Jessy's house. As Jessy called to her, her voice increasingly scared, begging Melinda to stay.

CHAPTER FIVE

This wasn't the only time Melinda had walked away from those who needed her.

When she left Jessy's house, Melinda was vividly reminded of the smell from her client's houses during her days as a social worker.

Melinda would smell it from the porch as she approached the door of yet another disheveled home she had to visit, another despairing case. The smell of feces staining the air, diapers from the young and elderly that had been discarded and forgotten, thrown in a garbage can on the porch or tossed under it or, more commonly, left inside the house, festering with other waste. She would knock and the door would open and the stench would overpower her, embrace her against her will, stay in her nostrils long after she left. Melinda still smelled it, years later, haunting her.

Everything about that work haunted her.

The counselor she briefly saw called it "secondary traumatic stress," a disorder brought on by working with those suffering from PTSD. Melinda didn't know if that was quite right, and she wasn't interested in therapy enough to continue. The counseling had been at the suggestion of a colleague, a social worker who had found Melinda crouched on the floor of her office, utterly helpless in the throes of a panic attack.

It wasn't unusual to find someone in the Alexandria Department of Social Services overcome by sadness or anger, but that someone had never been Melinda. She'd graduated with a master's in social work from George Mason University and had been eager to start work, to help people. She was one of those rare individuals blessed with certainty, a sense of mission and purpose. She knew what she wanted to do, and what she wanted to do felt like what she needed to do.

That urge became complicated within days of her first assignment, when she started working with families beset by addiction, when she had to accompany colleagues to help parents who had just had their children removed. The work was chaotic—parents and others in the house sullen or yelling, her coworker offering tight-lipped instructions they ignored. Melinda had left that first house shaken, distinctly aware that she was the one they truly blamed for their child's removal.

It was a blame Melinda understood, especially when she stood in the middle of that blurred chaos and saw pictures of the child hung on the wall. And she imagined what it would be like for a parent to walk past those pictures throughout the day and wonder, maddeningly, where their child was.

Their anguish needed blame.

But this was something Melinda had been trained to handle. And her mentor, an experienced woman who had worked for the department for four years, helped her to recover and laugh over drinks and dinner. Months passed, and Melinda had grown used to the work, even had the enjoyment of rare successes. An addiction to drugs sated. A family finally at peace.

Until the afternoon of the panic attack.

That was when everything changed.

That morning Melinda had gone to visit a new home, work picked up from a beleaguered colleague who hadn't been able to come out for a week. A house in a distressed part of Alexandria, an area the vast wealth in Northern Virginia never reached.

No one answered the door when she knocked, but the door was unlocked.

And there was that smell, that rotted, fetid smell.

Melinda never knew what was waiting for her during a first visit, but she was never welcome. She'd been threatened by fists and once a gun, shoved out of houses, had her photo quietly snapped so they could "find her later."

The house was dark, blinds covering narrow windows, concealing a living room consisting of a sofa and an old square television set. Beer bottles crowded on a small table like a game of chess both players had lost.

"Hello?"

No answer.

Melinda knew she should wait outside, or leave and report that the subject—a single father, recently reunited with his young son—had failed to meet her at his property at the scheduled time. But something drew her deeper, a smell worse than the odor of shit.

She entered the bedroom.

A man was lying on the bed. A rope tied over his biceps, a metal chain on his wrist, a needle on the floor. Melinda assumed he was asleep.

She walked deeper into the room. That's when she saw the boy.

A small child, not older than five or six, lying on the floor next to the bed, his arm handcuffed to his father's wrist. His ankle tied to one of the bedposts. Alive, but barely. Melinda found the key, freed him. Held him in another room, the child hoarsely whispering to her that he needed to go back to his father.

That was the case that had broken Melinda, the one that gave her a panic attack hours later, the case she always remembered and never discussed.

Afterward Melinda had been given leave, then transferred to a new assignment where she worked with people who had contracted HIV or AIDS, but it was just grief compounding. Everything she did, even when she helped people, even when she confided in coworkers, even when she managed to laugh again, had an emptiness. Sometimes she cried into the night, and then she cried into every night. Depression was starting to overwhelm her, like a vulture perched over her body, its beak digging into her soul.

Something had been taken, and it remained trapped in that room.

Melinda tried another new assignment, working with women who had left sex trafficking. She listened to their stories, the rapes and the gang rapes and the abuse and the drugs and the neglect and the shame and the disease and the horror, and it was like insects crawling over her body, eating their way inside. Nightmares woke her at two in the morning and left her awake, and neither books nor television was enough of a distraction from what the next day would bring.

Sometimes the men came, pimps or husbands or boyfriends pounding on doors, shouting threats. Melinda would confront them, firmly, the way she'd been trained, waiting for the authorities to show up, refusing to allow admittance. She was afraid, but anger would begin to consume her fear, anger at what they'd done, at what these men were trying to do. And when that fury was just about to break through, those men always slunk away.

These encounters left Melinda exhausted, even physically ill.

She began to miss days of work, and she hated herself for this absence. But when she tried, when she met with these women, a feeling of utter hopelessness overtook her. She was still in that room, handcuffed to that father and son.

Melinda was nearly done, on the verge of succumbing to exhaustion and burnout, despite her desperate need to help these women who had been coerced. Women, often girls, who had escaped the maliciousness of sex trafficking. Women who, like a lot of people in the act of retreating, were vulnerable and raw.

That's when Markus had appeared.

Markus and Melinda had spoken infrequently, but he showed a genuine interest in her work, something that the social consciousness of his music often expressed. It was a welcome surprise. He became a regular at Melinda's shelters, accompanying his sister on her trips. It wasn't the kind of thing she normally would have advised, but she had cleared it with her clients first. And, truthfully, there was something he provided that Melinda realized she couldn't. She offered a way out, and counseling, and comfort . . . but Markus's fame meant more. A celebrity cared about them, took time out to visit and talk with them, and his instinctive charm offered a sense of hope. A chance to see that not all men were threats.

"Your brother is so great!" a younger client named Angela had told her. Unlike some of Melinda's clients, Angela was enthusiastic and chatty, with clear blue eyes that couldn't hide delight or, when she'd first come to the shelter, despair.

"Which song do you like?"

"I like all of them," Angela said resolutely. "All of them. But he's so much more than his music, you know?"

During those months with Markus, Melinda's relationship with him was the closest it had ever been. Their childhood had been nothing but quarrels, long periods of distance, scattered moments of love. That relationship, Melinda learned from her friends with siblings, wasn't unusual. Brothers and sisters defined themselves by their differences when they were children. As adults, they realized the importance of their similarities. At least that's what she hoped.

"Yeah?" Melinda had offered.

Angela's complexion turned pink, like dawn. "I probably shouldn't tell you this, but we went out last week."

Warning bells sounded within her. "What do you mean, you went out?"

Angela hesitated, and Melinda did her best to regain her composure, keep her face calm. "It's okay," Melinda said. "But what do you mean?"

"He came by last week and took me to dinner. He told me not to tell you, but it was just *so nice*. And then we sat in his car and talked."

It was a struggle not to let her emotions overwhelm her expression. "Just talked?"

Angela nodded. But those clear blue eyes couldn't hide a thing.

"Yeah, so?" Markus replied over the phone when Melinda confronted him.

"You can't do this!"

"Why not?" Markus's voice was distracted, like he was watching television at the same time that he was talking with her.

"She's in a fragile state, Markus."

Markus laughed, and it felt like Melinda was talking to someone she'd never met. He sounded drunk, dismissive.

"Whatever," Markus told her. "I'm just showing Tiff how good things can be."

"Tiff? Tiffany? I'm talking about Angela."

A pause.

It took Melinda a moment; then realization struck like a slap. "How many of these women are you seeing? What happened to Rebecca?"

A pained silence.

"Fuck off, Mel."

He hung up. Melinda's phone lowered from her ear. She stared at the wall.

After everything she was going through to help these women, everything that had haunted her career, now to discover that Markus had used her to find and seduce vulnerable women . . .

Melinda felt like her heart had been torn apart.

Especially when, after Melinda questioned those women, they defended him, stuck by him. Too enamored to care.

Melinda was done. She quit. Left those women and the debilitating anguish of that life behind.

Not that it had been easy, or something Melinda could ever accept. She couldn't forgive herself for leaving.

So when she heard Jessy's scared, calling voice, begging Melinda to stay, it was like the voices of those women, years past, the few who hadn't wanted her to go.

Like that boy's whispered call for his father.

Melinda still heard them all.

CHAPTER SIX

"What happened to your cheek?" Calvin Bell asked after he kissed Emily and closed the door to her apartment.

Emily's heart stopped like an axe stuck in a tree stump.

"My cheek?" She pulled out her phone, looked at her face in the camera. Saw a red bulge shining through makeup. It pissed her off. She always thought of her makeup skills as on point.

"I was pulling a box from the top shelf of the closet," Emily lied. "And it bounced off my face."

She walked away from Calvin and into her kitchen and leaned against the counter, her legs still stiff from the time spent crouched in the tree the night before. She picked up the speeding ticket she'd been given, waved it to change the subject. "Stupid ticket, man."

"How fast were you going?"

"Too fast."

"Sorry, Em. That sucks."

Calvin was still staring at her bruise.

"Are you hungry?" Emily asked, hoping to distract him. Food usually did it.

"I could eat."

Calvin followed her to the kitchen. There wasn't much to Emily's apartment—a large, square combined kitchen and living room with a bar and single stool she used for work. Separate bedroom and a single bathroom. It was a tiny apartment and far too expensive for the size, but that was the trade-off of living in DC, especially Woodley Park, the lofty area between the National Cathedral and zoo. A bigger apartment required a bigger paycheck, and marketing for the New Road—a non-profit dedicated to fighting unjust incarcerations—kept her finances right at the edge. Rent and groceries were nearly all she could afford but, even so, she never thought about working somewhere else.

Emily had worked for the New Road since graduating from college. Started as the small organization's only intern, eventually moved into marketing, and took over the marketing position once that person went to a bigger company. The work was constant but easy. Running advertising campaigns on websites, placing relevant tweets and Facebook posts whenever the organization had a notable success, assisting with public relations and media inquiries and drafting press releases and other repetitive tasks.

Emily had once heard that most jobs were, essentially, simply a matter of pushing buttons, but she didn't mind pushing buttons if they led to something worthwhile. These did. The videos of families waiting as a freed man emerged from prison gates always made her weepy. The women and girlfriends who'd held on to hope, all while raising a family and working and often educating themselves while their husbands or boyfriends were incarcerated. The young children who now had the chance to grow up with a father. The sense that, in a world where justice was far from guaranteed, it had actually happened.

But it was more than intrinsic value. Emily needed this work.

Although she and Markus and Melinda had been raised without religion, Emily knew the concept of penance.

And what she'd done required a lot of penance.

Her reflection in the door of the microwave yanked Emily out of her thoughts. A dab of concealer on a spread of foundation, plus a touch of powder, hadn't hidden the bruise on her cheek well enough. She bit her lip in annoyance. Amateur hour. She should have added orange lipstick, mixed it in with the concealer, turned both her cheeks a little redder. Even if Calvin had noticed the extra makeup, which was unlikely, he would have assumed she'd done it for him.

Her own bruises didn't bother her, but whenever Emily concealed a black eye or puffed cheek, she couldn't help thinking about women she'd known forced to do the same.

And that thought rumbled inside Emily like a wild animal pacing in a cage.

Calvin picked up her baton from the kitchen counter.

"What's this?" he asked.

Oh shit.

Retracted, the baton just looked like some indiscernible short metal tool. She hoped Calvin didn't accidentally press the button to extend it, end up inadvertently smacking himself in the face. That had happened to Emily when she first got it, eagerly opened the box, discarded the instructions, and punched herself in the boob.

"Don't, um, don't play with that," Emily said. She took the baton from Calvin.

"But what is it?"

"It's for work," she lied.

Another lie.

"That's one fat-ass pen." Calvin turned to peer into her pantry.

"I have a lot in common with it." Emily slipped the baton into her handbag, zipped it closed.

"Speaking of, you really eat this much rice?" he asked, staring at a row of Uncle Ben's boxes.

"It's nothing compared to how much rice I ate when I visited Panama."

"Serious?"

"Yea, verily." Emily had never been to Panama, but Markus had, and he'd once remarked in an interview about how much rice their family ate.

Emily didn't know why she'd lied about it just now. Or why she wanted Calvin to believe in some trip she'd never taken. An experience she'd never had. A person she'd never been.

Emily hoped to go someday. Their mother had wanted to take the family, but the timing and money were never right. Emily felt so disconnected from the small Central American country she shared blood with, the language she used to know so well fading like the feeling of a last kiss.

No one knew the real Emily, not even Emily.

Often there was a sense that she was watching herself, another person, the real person, lost somewhere inside her body or mind. Alone, it wasn't unusual for Emily to turn catatonic, confused in her thoughts, and then something would tear through them, a remembered scream from one of the men she'd beaten, a quick vision of his scared face, the disarming way she'd discovered that all faces seem young when scared.

Calvin pulled out a bag of salted potato chips from the pantry. "I'm going to motorboat this bag. Is that cool?"

"Just be nice to it in the morning."

Calvin tore open the bag.

Emily shifted. She was used to this soreness, pain persisting after fights.

And she was used to hiding it from people.

Hiding everything.

Twenty-four hours ago she'd broken a terrible man's back, and now she was in her apartment, a different person. Still feeling the slow throb of danger reduce inside her, lessen until she was someone else. The masked vigilante last night, sweet Emily Peña now.

Emily nodded in response to something Calvin was saying about his day, about the class he was taking to prepare him for the FBI's entrance exam. But she was too distracted to concentrate.

She missed her mask.

Emily had made it herself, following an instructional costume video on YouTube. She liked keeping it with her, despite the danger of someone seeing it and realizing who she was. She kept it in her bag, would sometimes slip her hand inside and run her fingers over the thin canvas material. She wore it when she exercised in her apartment, blinds drawn and door locked. Once she'd forgotten it was on and almost answered the door when a courier dropped off dinner.

Alone, she often slept in it. Woke with her hair sweaty.

Calvin wiped his mouth with the back of his hand. "God, these chips are good."

"I know, I'm just the best chef."

He nodded. "By the way, that bruise on your cheek didn't come from a box."

"Sorry?"

"Come on, Em." Calvin set the bag down, eyes suddenly hooded, face dark. "You know I've seen bruises like that before."

Calvin's father had been a relentlessly violent alcoholic. He'd repeatedly placed Calvin's mother in the hospital until he'd finally killed her.

"Yeah," she said, softly. "I know you have."

He glanced away, back at her, away again.

"But you're seeing something not there," Emily insisted. "This really came from a box. Honest! And then I flattened it and threw it in recycling. So, you know, I don't want to flex, but I kicked its ass in the end."

Sadness still haunted his eyes.

Like Calvin knew she was lying.

Emily wondered if something else was bothering him.

"Listen," she said. "No one's going to think you did this. Come on. Like you could take me."

"That's not what I was worried about."

"Okay. But, honestly, I'm good."

"All right." It was a reluctant acceptance.

She watched Calvin, her expression clear, though clouds covered his.

He deserved better.

Emily had met Calvin on Valentine's Day earlier that year at a DC bar named the Wonderland Ballroom that had dedicated its upstairs room to a "singles' night." She'd only gone because a female coworker had asked if she'd accompany her.

Emily had despised everything about it—shrieking dance music, men practically shouting as they told stories, women laughing too loud and eagerly in response. Bars and clubs made her nervous, something about the way people sized each other up, determining who was better. Emily didn't like being judged.

Her coworker had found friends, and Emily immediately stalked off to the bar, in search of the strongest drink possible. The jostling and impatience of the crowd nearly made her yank her baton out of her purse, use it to clear a path to the front. But Calvin ended up standing next to her, and he smiled, and she liked his smile. It relaxed her. And she liked his look—Black and thin, with a bit of stubble and a shaved head.

They talked as they waited, and Emily forgot about her irritation.

She had left her coworker with her friends and let Calvin accompany her home, although it had been a long time since Emily had worried about walking alone at night. Ever since she'd started fighting, that caution had receded. Emily had made men beg before her. Men stronger than her. Men others feared.

These days she whistled when she walked down dark streets.

Calvin took a swig from a bottle of water. Set the bottle on the counter, flicked the cap into the air with his thumb. Caught it with the same hand and quickly glanced at her, to make sure Emily had seen the trick.

His pride made her smile. It was cute. "Proud of yourself for that one?"

"Been practicing for a month now."

Emily walked over to the counter, leaned over it. Calvin met her halfway.

The kiss lingered. Her jaw ached more the wider her mouth opened, but she pushed the pain aside. He walked around the counter and kissed her again, one hand around her waist, another behind her head. She felt his body against her. Tasted the salt the chips had left on his lips.

She stepped back as Calvin's hands slipped under her shirt, his fingers grazing her bra. She tried to make the move less urgent than it felt, gently pushed his hands down.

"I do something wrong?" Calvin asked.

"I still want to wait."

"Got it," Calvin nodded, a little too eager, his head like it was loosening from his neck. "I understand."

Emily tried not to smile at Calvin's frustration. "Are you sure?"

"Oh yeah of course no problem." Still nodding. "We can just kiss, though, right?"

She studied him. "You think you can handle it?"

The loose nod turned into a loose headshake. "No."

"I love that you're so patient with me," Emily told him.

"After you told me what happened . . . I understand."

She let her expression falter.

"Sorry." Calvin's voice was alarmed. "I shouldn't have mentioned that."

"No, it's okay." She tried to remember exactly what she'd told Calvin. Had it been some made-up experience in high school? College?

So many lies, lies upon lies upon lies, like a rickety tower built on unsteady stones.

But they were lies to protect one important truth.

"What are you writing?" Calvin asked.

"What?"

"The notebook." He pointed to her journal on the other side of the counter, a pen pressed between pages, the pages forming a small wave.

Panic fluttered inside Emily like a startled bird.

She hadn't realized her notebook was out.

Usually she made sure to put all of her secret ass-kicking vigilante gear in the compartment in her closet, the compartment she'd made out of drywall and a latch and had hidden behind a shoe rack. But Emily had left everything out tonight. Almost as if she wanted to be caught.

She picked up the journal.

"Just some rough drafts for work," Emily lied. She walked into her bedroom, hid it under the mattress. Hid it next to everything else she kept under there: a second baton, brass knuckles, a stun gun, a book called *Ladder of Years* she'd never read that Melinda had sent her after their mother died, Markus's four albums.

Emily knew she was probably being too cautious about the journal. Even if Calvin had read it, he likely wouldn't have understood what the crossed-out list of names referenced, or the only name left.

Rebecca Winters.

Jon Winters's cousin. Markus's ex-girlfriend.

Emily's last connection to the Winters family and the evil they'd done.

And the person she was going to kidnap and question tomorrow morning.

CHAPTER SEVEN

Rebecca Winters pressed her phone to her forehead. Thought for a few moments and tossed the phone to a nearby couch.

And decided not to call the police.

She stood from the piano bench, lowered the fallboard of her baby grand. Walked to the large bay windows of her dark condominium, opened the blinds. Sunshine sighed into her living room.

Over a year had passed since Rebecca had last played the piano, longer than that since she'd sung. Music had grown distant to her, like a friend she meant to contact but never did. She'd always thought she'd miss music more, especially during her younger days, those days when singing seemed as necessary as breathing. When she imagined she'd die if she couldn't sing.

It still surprised her how easy it had been to walk away.

All this time, she'd thought it was love.

Rebecca looked down to Wisconsin Avenue in Chevy Chase, Maryland, one of the wealthiest towns in the country. Saks Fifth Avenue was to the right of the Rosemont, her condo building, Tiffany to her left. Later in the day this street would be filled with shoppers, but now, early in the morning, the neighborhood was empty, nothing but dark stores and quiet streets.

There was something about that isolation that Rebecca found beautiful, as if the world had turned from a movie to a painting. She escaped into that painting, the feeling briefly freeing, but then she thought about Markus.

Her black phone gleamed on her white leather sofa.

She didn't pick it up but feared she eventually would. Eventually she'd call the police. She couldn't resist much longer.

Rebecca turned from the window, from the sunlight hurting her eyes. Playing music in the dark was an old habit, something from her performing days, when Rebecca had first found her voice, realized there was sorrow in the notes that needed to be brought forth further. And so she rehearsed by candlelight, her voice intentionally wavering, unsteadily touching notes.

But none of that mattered this morning.

Her playing had been terrible.

Rebecca had expected her ability to fade, but not this dramatically. She should have known. She'd always given in to that constant desire to rehearse, used to feel lost if she skipped even a single day, like an alcoholic losing a year of sobriety to a single drink.

She'd stopped performing when her relationship with Markus ended. Instead, Rebecca had taken a job as a receptionist for one of her uncle's companies, more as a way to give herself something to do than anything else. She didn't need money and, when the job was furloughed, dipped into her trust account. Took out a few million and had a lot left.

Her friends knew she was rich. They often inquired, in subtle ways, exactly how much money she had. And Rebecca would demur, laugh it off, make a comment about how it only seemed like a lot and change the subject.

Her family's money wasn't something Rebecca could ever discuss.

She walked through the living room, passed the guest bedroom, entered her bathroom. Locked the door. Undressed and sat on the marble bench in the shower after water had warmed it, turned on the misting jets. Leaned against the glass, closed her eyes.

Despite the spa-like atmosphere, her teeth ground down. Tension ached in her body.

She knew her uncle had killed Markus.

Rebecca had been the one to end their relationship, to finally walk away from Markus's abuse. She still remembered that fear, the worry that Markus would show up in her doorway, face tight, fists ready. Her shaky phone call when she'd told him that she'd confessed everything to her family, that they were guarding her, that he couldn't contact or come near her again. It had worked. After that call, she never heard from him.

He had reason to believe her. Markus knew about her family. He knew her uncle wouldn't hesitate to put him in the dirt.

And her uncle wanted to act. Rebecca could tell when she revealed how Markus had been hurting her, when she saw his anger.

"Don't do anything," Rebecca had begged, gripping her uncle's arm, dropping to her knees as he stood. "Please. Markus didn't use to be like this. He didn't. It's . . . it's not all his fault."

Her uncle looked down at her.

"Please," she said. "I'm begging you. Keep me safe, but don't hurt him. Please."

"Someday."

That was all her uncle had said.

And now Rebecca wondered, Had someday come?

Was she responsible for Markus's death?

A buzz from the bathroom's marble counter, her phone vibrating. She ignored the call, pressed her palms against her face.

Guilt was like a high note threatening to erupt from her chest.

She'd met Markus in college, when she was studying vocal performance at the Baltimore Conservatory of Music, one of twenty-four students auditioning for the six open spots in Professor Alexander Hardaway's seminar.

Markus had walked into the room minutes before Hardaway, and, the moment he entered, the atmosphere changed. Everyone watched him. It was something about his lack of nerves, the way he barely noticed the other students, his lateness when every professor emphasized the importance of arriving early. And his look, dark and tall with hair that seemed intentionally messy and light-brown, searching eyes.

And, above it all, a calm confidence, a certainty.

Rebecca wondered if everyone was similarly mesmerized.

Then Hardaway entered.

The students were arranged in a circle of chairs. Two at a time would rise, each singing the first verse of "Saint Louis Blues," the jazz standard W. C. Handy had written over a hundred years earlier. After the verse finished, Hardaway would pick one student and the other would leave. There was little sense of celebration for the winner; this was only the first stage of competition, and those who moved on knew another elimination round was coming. For those that lost, a heaviness accompanied them out the door, often tears.

Now Hardaway, in the center of the students, pivoted slightly and pointed his closed fists at Rebecca and Markus. They rose, waited for Hardaway's fists to open. For the piano to start.

Rebecca felt the gazes from the other students, their curiosity, although most of their attention was directed toward Markus. She was grateful for that. Fear always had the potential of overwhelming her.

She smoothed her skirt. Closed her eyes as her mouth opened, picturing the music, the words, imagining the warmth of a spotlight.

The first line softly, lovingly, left her lips. Then the second.

"Thank you," she heard Hardaway say.

Someone laughed.

Rebecca's eyes opened. "What?"

Smiles in her direction, and, for the first time, Rebecca realized how cruel those smiles were.

"You mean me?"

"Thank you," Hardaway said, again. "Maybe next year."

"But . . ."

He waved her words away. And Rebecca realized Markus was still singing, in a pure, soft, calling voice.

She'd lost.

Rebecca left broken, in embarrassment and shock. Drove to her uncle's house. Explained what happened.

Her uncle did what he always did. Listened quietly, stoically.

He was a man who rarely spoke. And so, when he did, his words carried weight. And he told Rebecca something she'd remember for the rest of her life, through the hard years when she was rejected for opportunity after opportunity, when whatever path she followed arrived at a dead end.

"Don't forget who you are."

He paid for private lessons with Hardaway, and, for the next three years, Rebecca met with Hardaway twice a week, Tuesday and Thursday evenings for an hour.

And so, over the next three years, Rebecca was immersed in the study of music.

There was a chip on her shoulder. More than a chip, really—an entire fucking forest. Rebecca could never accept that she wasn't part of Hardaway's select program. She felt that rejection so intensely it became an intimate part of her, a thought prodding her mind during the days, keeping her awake nights. She couldn't lose the grudge; at best, she could assuage it.

Rebecca realized this anger helped her, motivated her. She never auditioned again, even if she was certain she'd have been selected. But, every semester, she asked Hardaway for a copy of the syllabus, the list of books and recordings that Hardaway's students read and listened to.

And she read through those books and hungered to learn more. Her hunger was bottomless.

This period, despite the difficulties of her studies and her burning jealousy of the students in Hardaway's program, was one of the best of Rebecca's life. Music had overtaken her.

Especially jazz.

She fell in love with Ella Fitzgerald's easy, cheerful style, the endless well of power she seemed to draw from. Sarah Vaughan's version of "Key Largo," just her low voice and the thrums from a bass, enthralled her; for weeks, Rebecca listened to nothing else. But where those two women displayed such effortless strength, Rebecca found herself similarly moved by the work of Astrud Gilberto, her soft hesitancy, the way she whispered words. She went through periods where different vocalists inspired her—if Rebecca didn't understand their mastery, she forced herself to keep listening, and in that way she was fueled by Nina Simone, Dinah Washington, Nat King Cole, Shirley Horn, Chet Baker, Billie Holiday.

By the end of their third year, shortly before he announced his retirement, Hardaway paid her a grudging compliment.

"I didn't want to work with you at first," he said. "No matter how much your uncle paid."

She had known, but the words stung nonetheless.

"But I'm glad I did," Hardaway said. "You'll never be as good as you want to be, but you'll be better than I thought possible." He considered his words. "That's quite an achievement. For both of us."

"Thank you?"

"I hope, a year from now, you're still practicing as ardently. But if you're not . . ." Hardaway touched her arm. "It's no fault of your own. You'll have progressed as far as you can go."

Rebecca knew what he was implying, that there was a limit she would reach and never surpass.

And because of that, Rebecca grew even more stubborn, more determined to keep music in her life.

Nearly a year after Hardaway's retirement, Rebecca had still been fervently practicing in the Highlandtown home her uncle had bought for her, sharpening her voice like a carpenter shaving splinters from a piece of wood.

Even though the success she sought remained elusive.

She had stopped, rewound the small voice recorder she'd set up on an easel, warily played the recording back. Took a seat on the couch, fingers steepled under her chin, eyes closed. And her face tightened and her soul hardened the longer she listened.

The longer she listened, the more she disliked it.

Rebecca had used to unashamedly love her own voice, the beauty of her high, lingering soprano, but now it grated on her. Sounded hollow, superficial. Showiness without depth. Skating away from complexity. There were notes she should have held longer, even if it meant a reworking of phrase. Crescendos that lacked an honest climb.

To be fair, there were some moments she liked. A couple. An occasional instance where her voice not only matched the note but defined it. But they were just moments.

Capturing an entire song to a level she respected seemed an impossibility.

A failure. Another failure.

Her doorbell chimed.

She rose from the couch. Opened the door and let in Markus.

He was carrying an umbrella, but, even so, rain had plastered his curly hair to his forehead. "You're lucky you're not wet," Markus said. He waited for her to acknowledge the innuendo, grinning.

Rebecca didn't respond.

He took off his coat, hung it on the hook by the door. "You okay?"

"Eh."

Markus pulled out folded sheets of paper from the back pocket of his jeans, unfolded and smoothed them. "I heard you outside," he said, "even through the rain. You sound good."

"Yeah?"

Markus scanned the papers. "Yeah," he said, distantly. "Anyway, you remember what we were doing Monday? I want to get that resolved."

His was the right approach. With her, it always was. Rebecca's mood couldn't be talked down.

All that helped was improvement.

He started singing scales, the easy way Markus's voice landed on every note like a well-thrown stone skipping across water.

He had everything she wanted.

As far as Rebecca knew, she was the only other singer Markus constantly saw. The private lessons with Hardaway had led to a few chance meetings between Rebecca and Markus, nothing more than awkward hellos that turned into walks to the bus and then trips to a nearby coffee shop. And then a friendship that was so natural and easy it surprised her.

They practiced together endlessly, coaching each other, sharing new music, discovering new depths. Rebecca would have expected him to work with the more accomplished students from the conservatory, but most of them had abandoned music, or soon would. The others had moved to Los Angeles or New York or Austin or Nashville, pursuing acting or turning to teaching.

Rebecca was the only one pursuing the same dream she'd had when she started school.

Rebecca, and Markus.

"You still on for that show tomorrow?" Markus asked.

She had a regular Sunday-morning gig at Miss Shirley's Café, a popular brunch spot in the Inner Harbor, one of the few restaurants in that location frequented by both tourists and locals. Rebecca sang with a guitarist while people ate, in a corner between silver pans of soft french toast and scrambled eggs and warm wrinkled bacon. Some liked the music, others glared at her and moved their chairs closer to each other to continue their conversations. Most ignored her. Once in a while someone asked if she had an album, and Rebecca gave them a copy of her demo.

Once someone paid her twenty dollars for it.

"You're going to be big someday," that person had told her, and Rebecca was ashamed at how much the comment mattered. How often she thought about it.

"It's less a show than it is brunch entertainment," she told Markus, distantly.

"Can I come?"

"I guess so."

Markus had never heard her perform, and she actually preferred that.

He was living the life she wanted. Markus was being approached by venues and event managers rather than having to approach them. *Baltimore* magazine had included him in one of their end-of-the-year listings of best local musicians, and the *City Paper* constantly promoted his events to its weekend readers.

It was his calling but didn't define him the way it had so many of the students in the conservatory. Markus sang, but he also drank and dabbled in drugs, and it wasn't unusual for him to get in fights. Rebecca remembered seeing him walk to her house once, grinning as blood trailed down the side of his face.

But when Markus sang, he was lost in the music, his hands held together, imploring. He became part of it, submerged in song, not the painter but the painting.

And that was something Rebecca reached only in moments. Like she was trying to shape water, the effort would slip from her hands.

At her brunch performance, she sang and watched Markus as he watched her, and it was truly the worst her voice had ever sounded.

Rebecca felt the deep sting of embarrassment, but she seemed to be the only one concerned. The crowd was more focused on their french toast and conversation than they were on her.

All her efforts, her years of study and sacrifice and hope and disappointment, and she was of less consequence than a side of hash browns.

When her set was over, Markus waited outside under an awning. She walked up to him.

"I think I'm done," Rebecca said. "That was awful."

"You had a bad day," Markus acknowledged. "You're just going to get better and better. Trust me."

Rebecca looked into his soft brown eyes. And she loved and hated his lies.

◆　◆　◆

Rebecca couldn't escape those memories of Markus, the beautiful or the bad.

She sat naked in the shower, held herself and wanted to throw up. Or cry and scream and beat the walls with her fists. All of those things.

Instead Rebecca gathered her emotions like armfuls of dirty laundry, trying to make sure nothing escaped. Breathed deeply and touched the tips of her fingers together in a rhythmic pattern, a calming device she'd used after she'd left Markus, the way her counselor had shown her.

She turned off the water, stepped outside, grabbed two towels, and wrapped one around her body, the other around her hair.

Flipped a switch, and the bathroom floor warmed under her bare feet. She applied moisturizer to her face, cool lotion to her arms and legs. Makeup.

Every time Rebecca looked in the mirror since she'd learned of Markus's murder, the haunted look in her eyes surprised her. The guilt.

She shook a Xanax out of its pill bottle.

Rebecca barely heard the doorbell over her bathroom fan. Turned it off and listened, then heard the bell again.

She put on her robe, cinched it.

Left the bathroom, crossed the living room, opened the front door.

Someone covered her mouth and pushed her to the floor.

Chapter Eight

From outside, the Rosemont was seemingly impenetrable. A set of deeply tinted double doors behind a watchful doorman. A sign stating that visitors needed to be ID'd and approved. Cameras on either side of the building, scanning the entrance. The lowest windows were two stories off the ground.

Emily had imagined herself cheerfully walking in, pressing the elevator button with her baton, whistling a happy tune as the elevator rose.

It wasn't going to be that easy to question Rebecca about her family.

Emily left the inlet of the closed coffee shop's entrance across the street where she'd been studying the building, walked down Wisconsin Avenue, turned on Jackson. She approached the side of the Rosemont and the shuttered entrance to its parking garage. A sensor and camera were mounted over the garage; otherwise, no door led inside. But a small alley between a yoga studio and upscale pet store was across the street. Emily slipped into the alley, reached into her handbag, ran her hand over her mask.

It took almost an hour of waiting, rubbing her palms together to warm them from the chilly morning, looking into the window of the pet store and idly wondering if she should get a cat, but a Lexus sedan finally turned the corner and the door to the garage slowly rose.

Emily peered out of the alley, glanced at the cameras on either side of the building, pulled on her mask. She waited for the car to drive into the garage and hurried across the street as the door began to close.

The garage door came down faster than she'd assumed it would, and she had to break into a run.

Emily thought about sliding, but she didn't quite know how to do that. Instead, she dropped to her knees and clumsily crawled as the garage door brushed her back, almost trapped her ankle.

But she made it.

From the ground, on her back, she gave herself a thumbs-up.

There hadn't been any information online about the Rosemont's layout, and certainly nothing about the parking garage. She was on a steep two-lane ramp that curved to the left. No other cars were in sight, just the distant red glare of the taillights she'd followed in.

Emily pulled out the handles of her bag, turned it into a backpack. Took out the baton and slipped the backpack's straps over her shoulders.

She trotted down the ramp, her steps light.

The ramp descended into a cavernous garage, each space filled. Emily saw the entrance into the building up ahead, someone waiting for an elevator. Probably the owner of that Lexus. She stepped into the elevator lobby after he left, pressed the button until it glowed.

The plan was to head upstairs to Rebecca's apartment, question her about her family, dig information out of her like a surgeon with a scalpel. She couldn't take the chance of Rebecca discovering her identity—Emily didn't know the other woman well, wasn't sure how close Rebecca was to the rest of the Winterses. She'd have to surprise her, drug her, question her in the dark once Rebecca awoke, keep the mask on. And, most importantly to Emily, leave her unharmed.

Rebecca shouldn't have to pay for her family's sins.

But something inside Emily bothered her, some firm feeling loosening from its anchor.

She'd never attacked someone who didn't deserve it. And she'd never attacked another woman. She couldn't convince herself that Rebecca deserved what Emily might have to do.

What Emily was willing to do.

She uneasily spun her baton as the elevator doors opened.

A security guard was inside. He took a surprised step backward.

Without thinking, as if by instinct, she whipped her baton to his face.

And, as if by instinct, he caught it.

"Well," Emily told him, "shit."

His other fist landed flush in her chest, pushed her out of the lobby.

Emily scrambled to her feet, breath ragged, chest aching. That stone feeling was settling inside of her, everything around her shrinking like the narrowing focus of a telescope, aimed at the security guard.

He followed her into the garage. He was both tall and wide, the kind of man who was probably asked a lot if he'd played professional football.

"Hey," Emily asked. "Do you play professional football?"

He ignored her. Unsnapped a walkie-talkie from his belt.

She lunged and smashed his hand with her baton. The walkie-talkie crumpled. Pieces fell to the floor.

The giant guard looked at her.

"Sorry about this," Emily said, and hit his shoulder with the baton.

Her body shook more from the reverberation than his did from the blow.

Emily came up with a plan B, and that plan was to run. She back-pedaled, turned, darted off. Heard his heavy footsteps. The guard didn't look fast, but she made it only a few feet before he caught her. One hand was around her waist, the other covering her face. He grabbed the bottom of her mask, began to pull it up.

His silence, speed, strength, the sense of how he was so unrelenting—all of it sparked terror deep inside her.

He easily lifted Emily off the ground.

"Please," she said, the word choked as his powerful arm squeezed her stomach.

The mask slipped up over her nose. She swung her baton wildly, hitting his arm, but he didn't stop.

Light began to leave Emily, darkness curling in from the corners. She felt her hits growing weaker, as if the baton was in someone else's hand. A child's.

He turned her around when she was nearly limp, her consciousness a flickering lightbulb. His body enveloped hers, her mouth and nose buried in his chest, the stench from his underarms everywhere. Her feet were high off the ground. His arm felt like a heavy chain. There was no escape, no cry for help. No more air.

Emily distantly heard her baton clatter to the floor.

"I know who you are," the guard said. He had the kind of voice a mountain would have. "That mask. Three Strikes. I've read about you online."

He adjusted his grip to pull off her mask, and her right arm slipped free. She pushed his shoulder, but it was like pushing a house.

He lifted the bottom of her mask.

And she stabbed his neck with the syringe.

Emily depressed the plunger, and the guard dropped her. Stumbled back.

"What the hell?" he cried, hands scrabbling over his neck. "What'd you do?"

Emily fell against the door of the elevator lobby, wondered if he'd broken one of her ribs. She stood as the guard slipped to the ground, his feet kicking like he was trying to run.

Emily picked up her baton.

Holding it was life returning.

Holding it was rage.

Another being was controlling her, guiding her to lift the baton and bring it down on the guard as he struggled to stay awake.

But that wasn't what she was here to do.

She left the guard sleeping and stepped into the elevator.

◆　◆　◆

Emily leaned against the wall, breathing hard as the elevator rose to the twenty-first floor, hoping it wouldn't stop for anyone else. She still had her mask on because she couldn't risk being seen. Not anymore.

She winced from the pain in her ribs. They weren't broken, she decided. Bruised at best.

She could work with bruised.

I know who you are, that guard had said.

Emily had read stories of her own attacks online, small DC-based papers and websites occasionally reporting about a masked vigilante. Others had done deeper research, started to suspect these attacks were all committed by the same person. Often this research was in remote corners of websites like Reddit or 4chan, obsessed users starting to put pieces together. She needed to be more careful.

Then again, something about the thought of people recognizing her mask brought her happiness. Almost made Emily smile, despite the pain whenever she breathed.

Although she wasn't sure about the name "Three Strikes." Someone online had given it to her, and the nickname had stuck. And Emily hated baseball.

She slowly spun her baton, thinking about the giant guard sleeping below. She didn't have a lot of time. There was the chance he'd wake up; more likely, a chance he'd be discovered.

Emily remembered when the second man she'd ever drugged had woken while Emily was searching for the photos she'd taken of him. Photos of him kneeling over his girlfriend, her hair in his hands. His free fist raised above her in one picture, hitting her in the next. His girlfriend crawling to the phone and him holding her leg, pulling her back. Emily had taken these photos from the roof of a neighboring building, fortunate that an unshaded bathroom window provided her with a vantage point. She'd printed them out, planning to leave them scattered around his body for the police to find.

But she couldn't locate them. She searched her backpack hopelessly, wondering if she'd left them in her car, and he'd grabbed her ankle.

"Please." He said the word through bloodied shards of teeth. "I'm sorry."

Emily didn't have the photos, but she had her baton. She'd smacked his hand away and then brought it down on his broken face.

On those shattered teeth.

The elevator doors were open to Rebecca's floor, surprising her.

She'd been submerged in memory.

Emily glanced out into an empty hall and headed toward Rebecca's condo. Her strength and certainty seemed to return with every step. The floors were hardwood, and she couldn't remember if she'd ever seen a hallway in a hotel or apartment building with hardwood floors.

She reached Rebecca's door and thought about the best way to enter. On a whim, she tried the handle. Locked.

She rang the doorbell and ducked to the side, away from the peephole.

When the door opened, Emily didn't wait to see who had answered it. Or even, she thought as she swung around the entrance and tackled the person and they fell inside, to see if she was at the right condo. Her mask was askew, and the floor was hard on her knees and her chest filled with fire from the collision. Still, Emily could tell she was on top of a woman, felt the small face as she covered the woman's mouth with one hand. Emily sat up on top of her, straddled her, straightened her mask.

Rebecca's frightened, familiar face stared up.

Emily brought the syringe to her neck.

And then Emily's arm was suddenly bent strangely and her body was rolling and she was on her back.

Rebecca wasn't alone.

Knees smashed down on Emily's shoulders and a hand pushed her mouth, rough and abrasive, her lips painfully pressed against her teeth. Weight on her ribs, too much weight on her aching ribs, bones that suddenly seemed brittle enough to collapse and cave.

A man peered down at her.

"Who the fuck are you?" he asked. "What's with the mask?" He glanced over at the floor, picked up something with his free hand.

Her syringe. Her last dose of midazolam.

"What's that?" Even now, years later and through pain, Emily recognized Rebecca's high voice. That weird way singers sounded like they were speaking in a different conversational tone, as if always preserving their natural voice for performance.

"No idea. But she must have been planning on sticking it in you."

Rebecca's face moved closer to Emily's, her sorrowful blue eyes big. Emily felt the sharp needle push into her shoulder.

"Is that safe?" Rebecca asked.

The man shrugged.

God, the pain from her crushed ribs, like thin sticks about to snap. The heaviness from the midazolam was nearly welcoming.

But there was one last moment of panic.

One moment when Emily felt the mask being tugged off her head. Rebecca looking at her. Emily saw her surprise. And then her confusion.

"I should have called first," Emily said.

She passed out.

Chapter Nine

Melinda had so many emotions swirling inside her as she drove to David's house that it was difficult to identify any one thing.

Thoughts of Rick, nibbling at her like tiny mosquitos she kept swatting away.

Unresolved feelings about Markus, and that relentless urge to learn what had happened to her brother.

The fading hope Emily would return any of her messages, and the concern whether her sister was okay. It wasn't like Emily to ignore her for this long.

Her heated fight with Jessy, and the pleading, heartbreaking way Jessy had asked Melinda to stay.

The lingering yearning to make amends with her father, and the heart-ripping image of him sitting alone in his house with nothing but his grief.

And underneath it all, this urge to see David again. This thrumming, anxious urge.

Melinda had been attracted to David since they first met, when he'd interviewed her at a coffee shop and hired her on the spot. They shared the same humor, an immediate flirtation that edged on daring. When they talked, they laughed. Conversations were hard to end. Phone calls continued into texts.

They worked together easily, the attraction consistent but comfortable, safely tucked away in each of their home offices, aside from occasional in-person meetings. It might have stayed that way if Essentials hadn't expanded, a move that necessitated a number of meetings with vendors, meetings conducted at David's house. He lived in a new colonial in Bethesda in the middle of a neighborhood full of homes from the 1950s, and his house looked like a misplaced model home of new construction. Bright white walls, gleaming fixtures, spare furnishing. The kind of home single men often lived in, one in desperate need of personality.

Seeing David in person, despite their flirtation, hadn't worried Melinda. The attraction made her happy, felt harmless. And it was only six meetings, hour-long presentations in which Melinda was immersed, taking copious notes about inventory and fulfillment. She was pleased to notice David doing the same. She liked his intelligence, how he rubbed his thumb over the right side of his chin as he spoke. The way he played with the gold button on the sleeve of his blazer.

After each meeting the hopeful vendor would leave and David and Melinda would eat lunch, a salad or sandwich at David's kitchen table. Their conversations made Melinda laugh, forced her to cover her mouth. The table was small and glass, and Melinda could see his shoes and her heels occasionally touch.

Sadness surprised her on the day of the final sales presentation. She'd grown used to these sessions, hadn't realized how much she looked forward to them. And now there was no need to continue seeing David in person, no reason they couldn't conduct their business over phone calls or online.

She wondered if David felt the same. He seemed fine, attentive during the presentation, cheerfully tipping the delivery man when their food arrived. She knew he'd been married and divorced in his early twenties and now dated occasionally. But as far as she could tell when he mentioned going out—and Melinda intently listened to those plans—he wasn't currently seeing someone.

Melinda wondered if that had changed.

Not that he had any reason to tell her.

And so she began to question, while they ate that last lunch, how much of their flirtation was in her imagination. Probably most of it, she realized, and there was a sadness there. And guilt. She hadn't known her attraction had so much depth.

They finished their food. David walked her to the door. She touched the doorknob. He touched the small of her back.

She felt the warmth of his hand.

Melinda turned toward him.

They were kissing in the hall, they were tripping up the stairs, they were fucking on his bed, loudly, desperately, her legs wrapped tightly around him, his hand tangled in her hair, pulling her hair, her nails digging into his back, their voices loud and hoarse.

She left in a rush. Dressing on the way out.

Guilt hit her in the car, halfway home. She pulled over and wept and wanted to confess to Rick. It had been a confusion of lust, completely inexplicable. But Melinda knew not to tell Rick, knew she'd lose him.

Rick had been cheated on before, had told Melinda about it, about how he'd immediately left that woman behind and never forgiven her. Almost as if it was easy.

And now, weeks later, Melinda knew what had happened with David would happen again. Knew she wouldn't be able to resist. She'd spend more than a rushed moment with David this time. It would last all afternoon, maybe into the evening. Her body and heart and mind wanted more, as if he was a land in which she wanted to wander.

It wouldn't be something she could explain as a single mistake.

Melinda wouldn't be able to keep it a secret. She'd lose Rick.

And she couldn't do that either.

Melinda waited at a stoplight, a few blocks away from David's house in Bethesda. Bit her lip, remembered his kiss.

She felt breathless, near tears. Unable to stop driving.

Melinda forced herself to pull into a parking space outside a coffee shop.

She wiped her eyes, took her phone out of her handbag, intent on canceling her plans. But couldn't bring herself to text him.

Instead, Melinda walked into the coffee shop. There was no line. Two women sat near each other at a table, staring down at a phone between them, their bodies curved around it like quotation marks. A man in a suit was perched in front of an open laptop, squinting at the screen. A bored cashier slouched behind the counter, checking her phone.

Melinda walked over to the register. "Coffee. Grande."

"Yeah, hold on," the cashier said without looking up.

She was young, probably early twenties, with green hair shaved on the right side of her head. A tattoo of two dolphins circled her ear.

Melinda waited.

After almost a minute had passed, Melinda asked, "Are you going to take my order?"

The cashier didn't look up. Kept texting. "Yeah, in a minute, Karen."

The DC-Maryland-Virginia triangle was so crowded that customers were constant, and it was a well-known secret that most businesses could afford to treat them terribly. There were always more customers waiting, and most people just passively accepted the disregard.

But for Melinda, not today.

She walked behind the counter.

"What are you doing?" the cashier asked.

"Getting my drink." Melinda took the coffeepot, poured herself a cup.

"Are you serious?" the cashier asked. "Put that down!"

"Nope."

"Put it down!"

"How about here?" Melinda asked. She let the glass pot drop to the floor.

In retrospect, Melinda realized, as hot liquid splashed the bottom of her pants and glass flew everywhere, this was a greatly flawed plan.

For starters, she should have just dropped the paper cup.

"What the *fuck* are you doing?" the cashier asked.

Melinda grabbed a washrag, rubbed it over her pants legs. "Getting my drink."

"I'm calling the cops."

Melinda left the store with her coffee, ignoring the stares of the other customers, their phones already capturing her every movement.

Then she ran back in, tossed a twenty-dollar bill on the counter, and ran back out.

◆ ◆ ◆

Melinda drove past David's house, out of Bethesda, and went to nearby Silver Spring.

To Jessy's house.

She was still going to see David, but she needed this first.

She needed to do something good.

And she needed to dry off her pants.

She couldn't believe what she had done at the coffee shop. It had happened like another being was controlling her, something inside her emerging, blinding her, leaving only afterward, when Melinda was forced to look at what she had done.

She hadn't felt that anger since the last time she'd seen Markus. And it scared her.

Melinda didn't know what she was going to say as she parked, as she walked to Jessy's front door.

She pursed her lips, rang the doorbell.

Rang it again, tried the knob.

It turned.

◆ ◆ ◆

Red and white flashes. Strong male voices issuing tense orders. The hard cold concrete beneath her. Curious stares from neighbors.

A blanket over her shoulders. A bottle of water in her hands.

A close voice. "She's in shock."

Piercing white light in her eye. Right, then left.

Other voices, farther away: ". . . kitchen floor . . ."

". . . Jesus . . ."

A tug-of-war in her brain, a pull between memory and nothing, as if her mind was trying to remember what happened.

"Ma'am?"

Melinda stared down into her lap.

"Do you need to go to the hospital?"

Melinda shook her head. "No."

"Are you sure?"

"I just need a moment."

She was grateful the cop gave her that moment. Grateful she wasn't alone, that this crowd of policemen and medics was here. Authority was here.

Rick would come soon. She trusted that about him, trusted he was rushing over after her scattered, broken phone call. Grateful for him too.

It seemed like hours since she'd walked into the kitchen and seen Jessy's face broken apart, her jaw nearly ripped off, head smashed into the floor. Blood like it had been flung around the room.

I'm going to be next, Jessy had told her.

She'd begged Melinda not to leave.

But Melinda had left.

Another person had been trapped in that secret room, and Melinda had refused her. Stayed on the other side of the door.

The sun sank and the sky darkened. The November cold was an unwanted hand caressing her cheek, the wind a rough voice whispering into her ear. Markus's shadow was the evening.

She couldn't escape its reach.

PART TWO

Us

When it was lost
And you were found,
Oh how I broke,
My soul thrown down,
And forever
I will never
Understand.

Oh my life was lost,
And we both drowned,
Lying together
When our lies allowed,
You kept my heart,
Made it art,
And I kept your hand.

Excerpted lyrics from "Us," from the album *Inner Demon*
Written and recorded by Markus Peña
Blues for You Records

CHAPTER TEN

Emily's eyes opened.

She lifted her head.

"Hey," she said, voice dry, tongue thick. "Sweet bedroom."

A woman rose from a chair in the shadows next to a bed. Walked toward Emily.

Emily squinted.

"Rebecca!" Her memory rushed, fragments of thoughts like rain suddenly turned into a storm. Emily tried to stand, but her wrists and ankles were tied to the chair upon which she was sitting.

"When did you get so good at knots?"

"She knows you?" A gruff male voice behind her.

Emily tried to turn, but the ropes prevented her.

She kept her eyes on Rebecca, the two of them staring at each other. Rebecca sat on the edge of the bed and, Emily had to admit, she still looked good. That enviably angular face with deeply expressive blue eyes. Short, fun blonde hair. Thin lips but striking red lipstick.

The recognition that had passed over Rebecca's face right after the needle had plunged into Emily was gone.

"I don't know how she knows me," Rebecca told the man. "I've never seen her before."

Interesting.

"Really?" he asked. He knelt in front of Emily, stared close at her face.

Emily decided he wasn't nearly as pretty to look at.

She felt oddly calm, even though she was tied to a chair with a criminal standing in front of her.

It was Rebecca, she realized. Rebecca had enough worry in her expression for two people.

And although Emily had no reason to trust this, and Rebecca hadn't stopped this man from drugging her, she had a sense that Rebecca wouldn't let more harm happen.

"So why are you here?" the man asked.

"DoorDash."

"Three Strikes," he said, ignoring her. "I heard about what you did to Rob."

"I wanted to go with something like 'Godslayer,'" Emily told him. "Because I can't tell you how much I hate baseball."

The man put his hands on his knees, stood.

"I need to make a phone call," he said. "You got her?"

Rebecca nodded.

He left the bedroom.

Emily looked around. A large king-size bed decorated with throw pillows. Gigantic bay windows on one side, covered by curtains. A set of double doors led to a bathroom, and another set opened to a spacious closet. Abstract art, slashes of red and black, hung from the walls. And on the nightstand were Emily's mask, baton, knife, and backpack.

"What are you doing here, Emily?" Rebecca's voice was low.

"You do remember me!"

"You were going to drug me?" Rebecca asked, anger burning her eyes. "Hurt me, like you did Jon? Is this who you are now?"

"I wasn't going to hurt you," Emily said, unsure whether that was true. "I just had some questions."

"About what?"

"About your family."

Rebecca sat up, her back stiff. "You know they killed Markus?"

Also interesting. "Maybe."

Rebecca stood abruptly, walked quickly to the door. Pressed her ear to it and listened. She returned to the bed and sat on the edge and leaned forward, hands clasped between her knees.

"I think they did too," Rebecca said. "I begged my uncle not to. But he was so angry once he found out what Markus was doing to me . . ."

Rebecca stopped talking as the man walked back into the bedroom, looking down into his phone. "Good thing Mr. Winters put me here to guard his niece after what you did to Jon." He sat on the bed, next to Rebecca. "What's your real name, Three Strikes?"

"Vengeance."

He smiled, placed his hands on Emily's knees, slid them up to the middle of her thighs.

"Try again."

He squeezed, and his fingers felt like nails driving deep into her bones.

Emily cried out and he stopped.

"I can go a lot harder," he told her.

Rebecca walked over to the window, peered through a part in the curtains.

And Emily wondered, suddenly and with fear, if she'd misjudged her. Fear was a wraith swirling in her, its claws scrabbling against her insides as the spirit rose.

But Emily wasn't just afraid. There was something else, something that the pain had dislodged.

Guilt.

Emily was suddenly wrapped in guilt and fear, remembering the lines she'd crossed, the people she'd hurt, the violence she'd utilized. Why would Rebecca help her . . . if Emily didn't deserve her help?

Mercy was a gift she wouldn't be given.

"What's your name?"

His hands back on her legs. And, despite how distraught she was, Emily couldn't stop herself.

She'd crossed too many lines.

"Medusa."

That pressure again, tighter now, painful even though Emily was expecting it. Her chin drove into her chest, eyes shut. Everything in her body was tight until the pain burst through and she heard herself cry out.

Emily could barely see him through the tears in her eyes.

"Please stop," she said, her voice low.

"What is it?" he asked.

"My name . . . ," Emily told him, her voice still low. "My name . . ."

He leaned forward.

Emily bit him on the nose.

"Fuck!" he screamed, but Emily didn't let go.

She forced her teeth together.

Emily fell on her side, still bound to the chair, grateful Rebecca's bedroom had a thick carpet. She spit out the tip of his nose and looked up.

Rebecca stood above her. With the knife.

She reached down and cut the ropes binding Emily to the chair.

Emily rose shakily, thighs throbbing, legs unsteady. Stumbled to the nightstand. Shoved her equipment into her bag.

The man was on his knees and crying hoarsely, facing the wall. His hands were pressed against his nose, the floor beneath him a pool of blood.

"What's *your* name?" Emily asked. "What can you tell me about your boss?"

He didn't respond. Just cried.

Emily had seen this before, the point where men were too overcome to be rational, to do anything but recoil into themselves. Fear was overwhelming him, fear from the pain and the surprise and the sudden possibility of death.

Rebecca pulled her out of the bedroom and into the living room. Emily had barely noticed this room when she first charged in. The black grand piano surprised her.

"You're so rich," she said. "I bet you get your groceries from Whole Foods, right?"

"You need to get out of here," Rebecca told her. "And you have blood all over your mouth."

Emily touched her lips, looked at the wet blood on her finger.

Wiped her mouth with her sleeve.

"He's not going to know I helped you." Rebecca spoke urgently. "I'll tell him you just got free. No one'll blame me for not trying to stop you. And he doesn't know who you are."

"But I have questions."

"We'll get answers later." Rebecca worriedly glanced back at her bedroom. "I'll find you. We need to talk."

She hurried to the front door.

"Tomorrow," Emily said. "Let's meet tomorrow night."

"Fine. Text me where and when. Can you remember this number?"

Rebecca quickly said her phone number. Opened the door.

"I'm sorry for what my brother did to you," Emily told her.

Rebecca froze for a moment.

And then unfroze.

"Markus's death wasn't just about me," she said, low and hurried as the guard in her bedroom loudly sobbed. "He and my uncle hated each other. Markus knew the truth about my family, how they made their money. What they did."

"What'd they do?"

Rebecca looked back again to the bedroom. "My uncle makes his money in commercial real estate, but his properties? They're fronts.

During construction he uses them for trafficking. Drugs, weapons. Sometimes people."

"Really?"

"He sold some of the same women Markus was involved with."

Emily blinked. "Shit."

"Bring your sister tomorrow night," Rebecca told her, just before she closed the door. "This involves Melinda too."

Chapter Eleven

Melinda remembered once opening the closet in her basement and seeing a small brown mouse in the corner. It stared up at her before darting along the wall, running between her legs, and vanishing. It wasn't the mouse that scared her; rather, it was the surprise of the moment. To this day, whenever Melinda opened that closet door, she always expected to see the same mouse inside.

That's what discovering Jessy Taylor's body felt like, a day later. Like Melinda would go into another room, any room, and see her corpse.

She'd overheard the cops talking to each other, describing the blunt trauma. When Melinda had seen her, Jessy's face looked like a giant's fist had driven into it, the center caved in. She'd felt the other woman's blood on her hands, so much blood that a trail of it dripped steadily from her fists to the floor.

She'd risen and run.

"Are you all right?"

Rick's voice came from somewhere distant, even though he was in the kitchen with her. She was perched on a barstool at the island. He sat across the counter, watching her attentively over his laptop.

Melinda tried to push the memory of Jessy's face away but couldn't. After talking to the police, she'd spent much of yesterday sleeping, her shock finally fading to exhaustion. She had woken this morning with a headache and spent another day in and out of harsh dreams.

Her eyes closed.

"Hey!" Rick's voice was alarmed. "Mel?"

"I'm okay," she said. Melinda was happier unable to see, blind to life. "I just need to clear my head."

She tried to remember what the counselor she'd briefly seen had told her the time she'd come across that child handcuffed to his father. Tried to remember the necessity of distance, the deep breaths to stabilize her heart and mind.

She sensed Rick standing behind her. Felt his hand on her back.

"I'm here."

As grateful as Melinda was that Rick had shown up so quickly at Jessy's house, now she felt the opposite. A deep desire to be away from him, one that had been growing all day. Melinda didn't understand it, this need for distance after the terror of what she'd seen.

But Rick standing behind her felt suffocating.

Her phone buzzed.

Melinda glanced at the sender on the lock screen.

"I have to take this. It's a friend of Jessy's."

She headed upstairs to the bedroom, closed and locked the door. Sat in a corner of the room behind a dresser and called David back.

"I was waiting for you yesterday," he said.

"I'm sorry." Melinda spoke softly, even though this corner of the room was nearly soundproof. Their bedroom was over the garage, and there were no vents nearby, so there was little chance Rick could overhear her conversation. Still, she was cautious.

"I stopped at a friend's house on the way to yours," she said. "I mean, a friend of my brother's."

"A guy?" David asked, his voice quieter.

His question reminded Melinda of how removed they were from each other. "No. A woman named Jessy."

"Okay."

"David . . . she was dead."

"What?"

Melinda was nodding even though David couldn't see her. "Her door was open, and I walked into the kitchen, and she was just lying there. Someone killed her."

A quick inhalation. "Are you sure? Maybe it was a heart attack or something?"

"Only if her heart attacked her face."

David paused, uncertainly, and Melinda wondered if her sharp response was misplaced, if she had come across as rude. She didn't want to push him away.

"Are you okay?" David asked.

"I will be." Her voice was softer now. "I just can't stop remembering what she looked like."

"Were you close?"

"No. I mean, we were at first. We drifted apart when she met my brother."

Melinda didn't understand her own emotions. Didn't understand why she wanted to talk with David more than she did with Rick. Why it was easier, or why it gave her the first true comfort she'd had in hours.

Rick was nothing but kind and supportive and loving, and it wasn't enough.

Sometimes Melinda wondered if *she* was enough. If, subconsciously, she felt like she didn't deserve Rick and everything he offered.

Or maybe David truly offered something she intrinsically understood, even if she didn't exactly realize what it was. Something that she more than desired, she needed.

"I wanted to see you," Melinda admitted.

"We don't need to talk about that," David said. "What did the police say?"

"They think it was a break-in. But I don't know how much it's going to be investigated. It's not like this area doesn't have a lot of crime. I mean, they barely looked into my brother's death, and he was famous."

"But the police didn't like him, right?"

"Not really. They hated the song Markus wrote about cops in Baltimore. I didn't think they'd lift a finger to find out what happened, and they pretty much didn't." Melinda felt like she was talking too much, words in a rush, tripping over each other. But it felt good, like gulping down water when she was parched.

"Do you feel safe?" David asked.

Melinda was confused. "From the cops?"

"From whoever killed your brother and his friend. Are they coming after you too?"

"Oh." Melinda reflected on that. "I really hadn't thought about that. But thanks for putting it in my mind."

"I'm sorry, I just wondered . . ."

"I'm fine," Melinda said. "My brother made a lot of enemies. He and I were estranged. Our lives didn't affect each other."

Everything about that last sentence felt false.

"You know, you can always talk to me," David said. "Anytime."

His words brought Melinda warmth. "I know that. And I do feel a little better. Thank you."

"Always."

Another pause.

"And, you know," David said, "it's totally fine to take a few days off from work. Really. Just let me know."

Well, Melinda thought as she hung up the phone, *that's always going to be weird.*

Melinda had already imagined a life with him, of course, wondered if it would be possible, if she could leave Rick for David. At first, it wasn't a notion she entertained. Then it grew in her mind and heart, and grew more when she realized he was just as attracted to her.

Melinda remembered stories she'd heard about affairs that turned into marriages; affairs that ruined families; more commonly, both. Famous books she'd read in college that dealt with wandering hearts, like

The Great Gatsby or *Madame Bovary*. A reality television show where one of the women was in her second marriage after leaving her prior husband for her new one. Melinda used to dislike that woman, everything about her—the way she described her new happiness and dismissed her first husband, her seemingly cavalier disregard for the children they had, the way she used too much makeup. But now Melinda saw her as a complicated figure, the woman's life like unsteady footsteps on a dim path, her overused makeup a reflection of her search for a new image.

A hand suddenly covered her mouth.

Melinda screamed, but the hand was tight. Muffled her voice entirely.

She was swung around.

Tossed on the bed.

Melinda looked up wild eyed and breathless into Emily's smiling face.

"Hey, Sis! Long time. Jessy's dead? Who's David?"

Chapter Twelve

"Fuck the hell shit? Emily?"

Emily raised a finger to her lips.

"How did you get in here?" Melinda asked, her voice slightly lower, still anxious. "Where were you? Were you spying on me?"

"I didn't come here to spy on you. Although I did end up seeing your boyfriend naked. I'm sorry about that. He was changing, and I was hiding in the closet and couldn't sneak out."

Melinda could barely process any of this. "What?"

"I mean," Emily corrected herself, "I'm sorry for seeing him naked. Not for what I saw. Is that weird?" She paused. "I saw his penis."

"What?"

Emily frowned. "You keep saying *what*."

Melinda put her hand over her chest to calm her breathing. "What are you doing here?"

"I came to talk to you. It's important."

"Why'd you sneak in? Why not just ring the doorbell like a normal person?"

Emily pouted. "I thought it'd be nice to surprise you."

Melinda shook her head. "It wasn't *nice*." She looked closely at her sister's face. "Are those bruises?"

"You can see that?" Emily pulled out her phone, glanced at herself. "I really need to get a better skincare routine."

"What happened to you? Did someone—"

"No," Emily said firmly. "You first. What happened to Jessy? And who's David?"

The sisters looked at each other.

◆　◆　◆

Melinda watched Emily climb out of the bedroom window, clamber onto a branch, and shimmy down the large eastern redbud that stood next to her house. She loved that tree, the reddish-purplish leaves blooming in the spring, fading afterward to a deep green. She'd never considered that someone could use it to climb up and break into her home.

"I need to go to the store," Melinda called out to Rick as she headed downstairs.

"Are you okay?" He stepped out of the kitchen, looked at her with concern.

"I'm okay."

One thing about her screwed-up family, Melinda realized: they were good at providing distractions. Seeing Emily had blunted the trauma of discovering Jessy's body. That memory was still stuck inside her, but the fear it brought was fading. Less solid, now shimmering.

She put on her jacket, grabbed her purse. Headed outside, zipped up her coat when she felt the evening chill. She climbed into her car, turned on the ignition.

Emily opened the passenger door, slid in.

"It's freezing in here!" Emily exclaimed. "Say sorry to my nipples!"

She turned the heater dial all the way up.

Melinda pulled out of the driveway and drove down the street to her neighborhood's tennis and swimming club. She was glad it was dark, glad Emily couldn't see the oversize houses and manicured lawns that defined the neighborhood. Her comfortable lifestyle, for some reason, embarrassed her.

This life was something that had seemed destined for Melinda. A handsome partner, upper-middle-class living, a pair of nice cars, the American fairy tale. Emily and Markus were different. Markus had managed to find success, surprising everyone but himself and their father. With his choices, Melinda had always thought, Markus was meant for either success or death. And he'd found both. But Emily would always struggle. It was apparent after the incident in college, when she'd lost the comforts given to her and been forced to take a hardscrabble path. And seemed suited for it.

Privately, Melinda couldn't see how Emily could ever be at peace.

Then again, she had no idea what Emily considered peace.

"I can't believe you're here," Melinda told her. "It's been years."

"I know, right?" Emily still had that strange gleefulness, that break from normalcy. She didn't look that different from what Melinda remembered. Still the same tall, thin body; those sharp eyes; blonde, nearly white, dyed hair; the sense that she was always about to smile.

But now, she had bruises on her cheek and forehead.

They parked at the neighborhood pool. This late at night, the parking lot was empty. "What do you need to tell me?" Melinda asked.

Emily was texting. She turned off the screen.

"You first," she said. "David?"

Melinda felt defensive. "He's my boss. I work for Essentials now. It's a food delivery service."

"And he brings the meat?"

Her sister's grin annoyed her. "Emily."

"How long have you been seeing him?"

"I'm not seeing him."

"Don't get mad," Emily chided. The smile was still there, but so was earnestness. An attempt at empathy.

Melinda didn't want to discuss David.

Emily must have sensed it, changed the subject. "I'm sorry to hear about Jessy. Who do you think did it?"

"I have no idea. I just talked to her the other day." Melinda didn't want to think about that either. "Why are you here?"

Emily glanced out the side window. Turned back toward Melinda. "You asked about my bruises."

"Yeah?"

"I'm Three Strikes."

A pause.

"Who?"

"Three Strikes."

"I—I don't know what that means. Are you in a softball league?"

"Three Strikes. The masked vigilante? Don't you follow the news?"

"You're in the news?"

"Kind of. Not the *TODAY Show* or anything. Yet."

Melinda rubbed her forehead. "So, wait, you're a masked vigilante? Is that how you got the bruises?"

"I go after people who deserve it," Emily said resolutely.

"Who deserve what?"

Something flashed in Emily's hand. Melinda saw a metal baton, suddenly extended. "Justice."

"What is even happening?"

Headlights bathed the Jeep.

The baton retracted.

"That's neighborhood security," Melinda said. "Thank God."

Emily's hand on her arm, stopping Melinda before she could put the Jeep in drive. "That's not security. It's Rebecca Winters."

It took Melinda a moment. "Markus's ex? The singer?"

The headlights flashed off. "Yeah."

"What's she doing here?"

"She's been waiting for me outside your neighborhood. I told her to meet us here. She wants to talk."

"Why?"

"Because she thinks her uncle might have killed Markus, and . . ."

The sentence trailed.

Melinda waited.

"Okay, look."

Emily took a breath.

"I went to kidnap Rebecca for information about her family but a security guard was there and caught me—well, there were two, but the first one I took out—and the second guard took off my mask and tied me up but I bit off his nose and then Rebecca helped me escape and he didn't seem to have any idea who I was and Rebecca didn't tell him but he saw my face and there's a chance he could identify me and if he does then the Winterses . . . Wintereeses . . . Winteri? . . . they might question you. Also Rebecca said she has something to tell me so we're meeting here and she asked me to bring you."

"Nose?" Melinda asked. She had a million questions, but that was the only word that came out, like a single bee confusedly floating out of a buzzing hive.

"Look, don't freak out," Emily said. "It wasn't his whole nose."

CHAPTER THIRTEEN

"I'm sure my uncle killed Markus," Rebecca told Emily and Melinda. She sat in the back of Melinda's Jeep, the two sisters each turned in the front seats. Rebecca was an only child, and she was always surprised at the similarities between siblings. Even now, Emily and Melinda were identical in the way they turned and looked at her, how they regarded her as she spoke, their slightly arched eyebrows.

"He did it because Markus hurt you," Emily said. "Right?"

"Markus and I hurt each other."

"But not the same way."

"I don't know," Rebecca replied quietly.

"I'm sorry," Melinda said. "I need to ask . . . did my sister really bite off someone's nose? I'm just getting caught up here."

"Not the whole nose," Rebecca said.

"See?" Emily told Melinda.

Rebecca noticed Emily's voice was childish with her older sister. Some things last forever.

"You really went to her place to kidnap her?" Melinda asked Emily, gesturing at Rebecca.

"More like question?"

"So why are you here?" Melinda asked Rebecca. "Why don't you just call the cops on your uncle? And, for that matter, my sister?"

"Hey!" Emily said.

"It's not easy to turn against my family," Rebecca said. "Especially my uncle. He took care of me."

This was the most Rebecca had told anyone about her family since she'd been with Markus. She took a breath. Tried to fight the feeling of betrayal.

"I don't blame Emily for what she did yesterday," Rebecca went on. "You two *should* hate me, especially because of Markus."

"We weren't exactly close," Emily said.

"But he's your family."

Again, Rebecca saw the similarity in the sisters. How they both glanced away.

"Look," Melinda said. "I don't mean to be rude, but why am I here? I know why you want to talk to Emily, I guess because of the whole Three Strikes thing, but why do you need me?"

"I promise I'll get to that," Rebecca assured her. "I promise. But I need to tell you about me and Markus first."

Rebecca could see that Melinda was about to resist, about to argue.

"Please," Rebecca added.

It took a moment.

"Okay."

"Markus and I had been dating for about a year and a half," Rebecca began, "when I found out I was late."

They had gone to the grocery store down the street from Rebecca's small home in Highlandtown, and Rebecca was afraid. Markus was excited, the way he'd been ever since he'd found out.

They studied a few different pregnancy tests, although Markus did most of the reading and Rebecca did a lot of glancing around, her hands palm down on her hips, as if trying to smooth her curves away.

An old man with thick eyebrows walked by and accidentally pushed his cart into a display of toothbrushes and then, in elderly confusion, apologized to the display. Markus laughed loudly.

"Will you calm down?" Rebecca asked crossly. She held up two boxes, each containing a different test. "Here. Pick between these two. Why are you so happy, anyway?"

She'd spent most of the past days crying while she waited for her period to come. "It's *never* been this late," Rebecca had said, over and over, sitting unhappily on the couch, a blanket wrapped around her lower body.

Markus, on the other hand, was overcome by a giddiness she never would have expected. Their relationship had begun a year and a half earlier, the evening of her brunch performance, a slight kiss at her door that turned into more, that turned into rushed weeks where everything else in their lives was forgotten.

She'd been happily swept away at the beginning, everything between them happening too fast when it started, the idea of love occurring in just days. Rebecca was always cautious with men, hesitant to trust, but Markus made her want to abandon that hesitation. He would look at her with such happiness, and the feeling echoed inside her. Normal things that had never meant much to Rebecca—the intimate closeness of Baltimore's row houses, neighbors communing on white marble porch steps, the beautiful blinding whiteness of those steps—delighted her. The world was enchanting.

"That box has a little brown baby on it," Markus told her. "I like that."

They paid and left. It was a hot night, and when they pushed open the door, it felt like the warm air was curling inside and carrying them out; Baltimore in the midst of a steamy summer. The sun had been setting late, and sometimes when they went to Rebecca's small house in Highlandtown, they'd pull chairs out onto the balcony, watch the sky blue then purple into blackness, look out into the neighborhood street, feed mobs of greedy pigeons, and talk about nothing in particular.

They walked up Eastern Avenue, quiet this time of day, and headed into her home. The night was dark and hot. Rebecca lit a thick aromatic candle on the balcony to ward off insects, sat down, took off her sandals.

"Do you think I am?" she asked.

"Hopefully," he answered.

"Aren't you scared?"

"Nah."

"That's amazing," she said. "Because me, I'm petrified."

"Don't be," Markus said. "It's wonderful not to be scared of this. I feel as happy as if we were already married and having a kid down the road, like this was a year from now or something."

"Already married?" Rebecca asked. "I didn't even know we were thinking about marriage."

"You weren't?"

"It's not that," she said. "I just want more time. If I get married someday, I want it to happen of my own choice. My own will. You know?"

"More time for what?"

"To know."

"To know what?"

"I don't know, Markus," Rebecca snapped. "Maybe to see if you're who I really want."

Melinda watched how regret overcame Rebecca's expression when she recalled those harsh words. Everything about Rebecca, Melinda realized, carried regret, a sense of being lodged in the past, her eyes often closed when she talked, voice low and monotone. It reminded Melinda of the way women who had shared violent memories with her seemed trapped in those stories, and even the shared act of confession didn't heal their pain. And then their fear afterward that this pain would persist, that it would never end.

Rebecca reminded Melinda of those women.

Those women who had tried and failed to understand why violence was done to them.

◆   ◆   ◆

"I'm sorry," Rebecca said to Markus. "I'm sorry. Come on, you know how I feel about you. You know how I feel. I'm sorry." Rebecca leaned over, her head nestled into his neck. He touched her hair.

"It's not that I don't want you," Rebecca said, breathing in the scent of his skin, the scent that made her smile when she found it on her pillowcases and couch. "All these doors have opened up for you. I mean, I know it's a small label, but they're legit, and I can't believe how much they love your demo. And I think things are getting better for me. But my family, my uncle . . . I told you about the paper-bag thing."

Her uncle had told her, once Rebecca started studying jazz, that he would never accept a boyfriend darker than a paper shopping bag. This wasn't unusual rhetoric from him, although it was the most blatant she'd ever heard his bigotry. Normally it was reserved, hushed, a quiet disdain with which he viewed other races.

"He'll get over it," Markus said.

"No, he won't."

Silence.

"I can't lose my family," Rebecca told him. "And any hope for my career."

"Why would you?"

"Be a mom," Rebecca said. "Spend all night walking back and forth with a baby. Feeding it every two hours. And we'd be strapped for cash.

We don't have any money problems now because we don't need anything. We'll *need*, then, Markus. I don't want to be in that position."

"But your family."

"My family will cut me off if I have a baby with you. They won't
care that you're half-white."

She said the sentences plainly.

"Do you care?" he asked.

"I wouldn't be with you if I did. I wanted them to get to know you.
To see you the way I see you."

"That's a lot to put on me."

"I know it is. And I was so happy I didn't care before. I thought
we had more time." Rebecca wrapped her arms around herself tightly,
squeezed her eyes shut.

A few moments later Rebecca left the balcony. She grabbed the
shopping bag and went upstairs, to her bedroom, to the bathroom
farthest away from Markus. Stood in front of the counter and stared
down at the pregnancy test box.

The test was in a white-and-pink box, with a curvy line separating
the words "Pregnancy Test" and "Early Response."

It wasn't the first pregnancy test Rebecca had taken, but it was the
first in years. She caught a glimpse of herself in the mirror, a moment
where she saw fear in her eyes, and hurriedly looked away.

She was having problems breathing, the same way she used to feel
when she'd first started performing, like air was hard to summon, the
burgeoning sense of panic that air would never come. She unbuttoned
her pants, slid them and her underwear to just below her knees.

Three to five minutes. That's how long she had to wait for results.

Rebecca was suddenly nervous, panicked, couldn't stay in the
confines of her bathroom. She wanted to leave, travel back in time,
ask Markus who he really was—the soft-eyed singer or the belligerent
drinker who, a week before, during a mild disagreement, had squeezed

her hand so hard it felt like the bones were snapping. "I'm sorry," he'd told her minutes later. "I'm so sorry."

She wanted two men.

That open, emotional, vulnerable man, the Markus who suffered hell after hurting her, who'd promised he'd never hurt her again. The Markus hopelessly excited about the possibility of their baby, sitting on her balcony, waiting for her to return.

And she wanted that angry man, the Markus who'd hurt her, who didn't care about her. The man she imagined who would hate the idea of a child with her. And wouldn't care what happened next.

Rebecca left the test on the counter and went downstairs. Slid open the glass door, stepped out into the warm night.

"He'd already hurt you?" Melinda interrupted.

"We hurt each other," Rebecca replied. "You heard what I told him."

Emily kept quiet. Her body still ached from the encounter at Rebecca's condo the day before, and her thoughts were growing uneasy the more Rebecca spoke. At the way Rebecca conflated love and pain, at how she accepted anguish.

Emily felt a desperate urge to leave the car. Breathe fresh air. Run screaming through the night.

But she forced herself to stay in her seat. To listen.

To let Rebecca's pain seep into her.

"I don't think," Rebecca told Markus, "I can do this."

"Do what?"

"The whole thing," she said. They sat above hilly fields full of squat massive trees, and they smelled grass and felt the heat in the late-summer air. They were sitting at the highest point of Baltimore's Patterson Park, at the base of the tall pagoda on Hampstead Hill. A few families sat around them, talking quietly. From here they could see a large slice of Highlandtown and the long Bay Bridge. Rebecca leaned back on the grass and looked at Markus, grimacing, the day's final touch of sunlight on her eyes and face.

"I think it'd be fun," Markus offered.

She laughed hollowly. "Don't be stupid."

Markus was quiet. Rebecca's words were sharp, as her words had been ever since her test returned positive, as had the second test, and the doctor's visit.

Shadows spread under trees like the way water grows.

"Would you care if I got rid of it?" Rebecca asked.

"I don't know. I think so. Yeah."

"I think I'd be scared." Rebecca paused. "I don't want it to mess me up for the future, if I do want to have kids someday. I've heard that can happen. And I don't want to end up, you know, thinking about it in the future either. Regretting it."

"Then don't do it," Markus urged her. "This is what I want. I know I've said it before, but it wouldn't matter if this happened now, when we're not married, or years from now, when we are."

Rebecca was pulling out grass and dropping it on the ground. She lay back and covered her eyes with her fists.

"Why do you want this so much?" she asked.

Rebecca felt his heavy hand on her arm.

She fought the urge to flinch.

"Because it's yours."

Chapter Fourteen

"I never thought Markus loved anyone but himself," Melinda said. "This is kind of blowing me away."

"He loved Dad," Emily put in.

"He loved me," Rebecca said.

Melinda was quiet. Emily looked around. She imagined the darkness beyond the lights of the parking lot as a black wave, one about to crash over the world.

A sudden light distracted her. Melinda's phone.

"It's Rick," Melinda said, glancing at her screen. "I have to head back."

"Can we meet up tomorrow?" Rebecca asked. "And keep talking?"

"Why?"

"Why?" Emily repeated Melinda's question, incredulous. "Because she thinks her uncle killed Markus."

"Meet us tomorrow," Rebecca urged, "and I'll tell you the rest. I'll tell you everything. I promise. I need your help, Melinda."

Melinda looked pensive but agreed. She pushed a switch and the Jeep doors unlocked.

Emily and Rebecca stepped outside. They watched Melinda drive off, the red taillights turning the corner out of the parking lot.

"You want a ride to your car?" Rebecca asked Emily.

"Hell yes, it's freezing."

They climbed into Rebecca's BMW.

"You and my sister have such nice cars," Emily said. She inhaled deeply. "You can almost hear the moos from the leather. Very classy."

Rebecca smiled.

"Thanks for coming here tonight," Emily went on. "And for talking to us. Especially after what happened yesterday. I really wasn't going to hurt you."

Emily still wasn't sure if that was true. She wasn't sure what she would have done if Rebecca hadn't volunteered information.

"I need to do it," Rebecca said, her eyes forward as she drove out of the parking lot. "I've been quiet for so long. After what happened to Markus . . . shit, Emily. You don't know how long I've kept quiet about my family. It's not forgivable."

"We can probably never prove the drugs or weapons. And I don't think we can even prove he killed Markus. But the trafficking? I know we can prove that. We just need to find one of the women."

"How do we do that?" Emily asked.

"We ask Melinda for help."

CHAPTER FIFTEEN

Emily woke the next morning exhausted, muscles aching; *Feels like a hippo spent the night chewing my body,* she thought to herself. She climbed out of bed, filled her bathtub with hot water and Epsom salts, stripped and sat and sank in the water until just her face showed.

It had been her experience that the salt didn't help her body, but the bath was a good way to clear her mind.

And her mind had been racing ever since her talk with Rebecca and Melinda, and Rebecca's revelations about her relationship with Markus, and the pregnancy . . . a pregnancy that must have ended. Unless, she considered, there was a baby Markus somewhere out there, beating up other babies.

Emily drained the bath, dried herself, wrapped her hair in a towel and her body in a robe. Sat in front of her laptop, typed some hopeful searches into Google:

Victor Winters + sex trafficking.

No results.

Victor Winters + prostitute.

No results.

Victor Winters + arrest.

His name in an article linked to a man arrested for money laundering. She'd seen the article before.

Winters + hooker.

Not the results she wanted. A bunch of images of barely dressed women on street corners in a snowstorm. Emily thought they looked cold. Grimaced in empathy.

Victor + sex trafficking.

Organizations that succeeded in shutting down sex trafficking operations.

Victor Winters.

She'd done this search before. A few articles about him and the businesses he'd opened.

He had an incredibly low profile for someone so wealthy. He'd built strip malls in DC and Maryland, and his name was tied to them, but not in a splashy way. There were no biographies of him online, nothing about his life or hobbies. Emily assumed that all rich people had an interest like horse racing or yachting or jumping into piles of gold coins, but Victor Winters kept his pursuits private.

She leaned back in her chair, chewed a thumbnail.

She could just wait until tonight. Wait until Rebecca gave her more information about Victor. Sit back and let her body recover and binge something on Netflix.

But even if she didn't have leads, Emily wanted to do something.

She opened her work email, idly checked her messages. The New Road was getting ready to announce another victory, a man named Simon Glowalter who had been accused of killing his wife and had recently been exonerated by DNA evidence. Emily had already planned out a marketing and promotional campaign to publicize their efforts, organic and paid posts on Facebook and sponsored tweets celebrating the organization's work, press releases to the *Washington Post* and *Washington Times* and the three DC Capitol Hill publications (The Hill, *Roll Call, POLITICO*), invitations for the local radio stations (WMAL, WTOP) to interview the New Road's executive director.

She gave all of it a quick glance, ensured the timing of the ads made sense, reread the releases for grammatical errors. Thought about working on a different project—a look back, through video and photos, at the organization's history for its website—but exhaustion was starting to hit her.

She leaned back in her chair, closed her eyes.

Emily's phone stirred her out of sleep.

She blearily lifted her head from the floor, realized at some point she'd either fallen off the chair or decided the floor was more comfortable. Or both. She climbed to her knees, grabbed her phone from her desk, stared at a text from Calvin.

Are you there?

Weird. Emily yawned loudly, grimaced at her awful sleep breath, rubbed her eyes.

Yeah Y?

I'm outside.

Emily rushed up to her feet. She had no recollection that Calvin was coming by today but knew they'd probably made plans. She always forgot her plans with him.

She hurried to the door.

Calvin looked good, which was distressing because Emily knew she looked awful. He wore black jeans and a brown mock turtleneck and an open jacket and carried a small bouquet of flowers.

He looked like a walking Neiman Marcus sale.

"Oh no," Emily said. She covered her mouth to hide sleep breath. "Were we supposed to go out?"

"Yup. And I even brought you flowers."

She took them. "Let me brush my teeth. I was asleep."

"So you didn't remember we had plans?" Calvin asked good-naturedly.

"I thought it was tonight!" Emily lied and rushed to her bathroom. Brushed her teeth, did what she could with her hair, added eyeliner to hide the tiredness in her eyes. Figured this was the best she could look on short notice. She took the flowers to the kitchen and put them in her only glass vase.

Calvin was leaning on the counter, jacket off, the turtleneck nicely tight against his chest and arms. He'd been working out for the physical portion of the FBI exam, and she'd noticed the difference.

"What do you want to do today?" he asked.

What Emily wanted to do, seeing him without his jacket, was undress him completely and gnaw on his body until her jaw was sore. But, as always, something inside stopped her.

"We could go out," she said, "but you'd have to wait, like, two hours for me to get ready."

"Yeah, no," he said. "Besides, it's cold outside. You want to stay in, maybe binge something on Netflix?"

Emily stared at him, transfixed. "That's *exactly* what I want to do. How'd you know?"

A cute half smile.

It was a blissful, peaceful afternoon.

One of the last Emily would have.

◆ ◆ ◆

"I have nothing to prove to you."

Brie Larson had just said that line in the climactic scene of *Captain Marvel* when Calvin asked, "Can I ask you something?"

They were lying on the couch, a blanket tangled between their legs. A sudden rush of intimacy had left them shirtless. He lay behind her, one arm somewhat uncomfortably under her neck, his other arm wrapped around her body and his hand cupping her left breast, his thumb slowly rubbing her nipple. The sensation was nice, enough to keep her eyes closed, to push her hips back into his, enjoy the slow grind.

She didn't mind missing the movie. Emily had seen it many times before.

But she hadn't expected him to risk interrupting the mood. She'd been wondering if his hand was going to lower to her pants, if she was going to let him unbutton them.

Or if something inside her would stop him again.

That feeling. That wall. The memories of those beaten men like an alarm's sudden shriek.

"What happened to you?" Calvin went on. "Back in college?"

Emily felt her body stiffen.

He wanted to know more about the lie.

Calvin sensed her reaction. His hand left her breast. "It's okay. We don't have to talk about it."

"Why'd you ask?"

"It's just . . . I feel something in you that's not, like, fully there. That's not accepting me. And I feel like, if you told me what happened, maybe we could get past that? Maybe you could trust me?"

The earnestness in his voice was heartbreaking.

Emily turned toward him, rested her elbow on the couch, propped herself up.

"Maybe you're right," she said.

She pulled the blanket to her shoulders.

"There was a guy in college," she told Calvin. "I was dating him my freshman year. I guess he was my first love."

There was a girl in college. Her name was Crystal Bloomsfield and she was tall and funny and gorgeous and she was Emily's roommate and she was Emily's first love. Emily couldn't tell back then, and wasn't even sure now, if the love was friendship or admiration or romance, but Crystal had entranced Emily. High school had been a caustic, lonely, ostracizing experience, a time when Emily felt the need to constantly change her personality because hers never seemed to measure up. Where happiness was subject to the whims of others. Emily had expected the same from college and been dismayed at the cheerleader-like looks of Crystal when they first met in their small dorm room . . . and then surprised by Crystal's enthusiasm and her acceptance of Emily. Crystal had moved from Colorado to Virginia and had a friendly western vibe that stood in stark contrast to the cultivated meanness of the East Coast. Other girls gravitated toward her as well, but Crystal kept Emily close. Even as they made other friends, they still returned to each other, sitting and talking on their beds at night, exchanging stories about friends and classes. Emily grew to love the intimacy of those nights, those soft, quiet conversations and sudden laughter.

"He was really out of my league," Emily told Calvin, "but he liked me. I mean, he loved me."

He's out of my league, *Crystal told Emily about her first boyfriend that first semester, an upperclassman who was the president of his fraternity and well known on campus. Emily knew he was handsome and popular, but the statement was ludicrous. Anyone would be lucky to date Crystal. That relationship didn't last long, but there were others, many others. Crystal had a type, Emily noted. The boys she liked were older and popular and lived off-campus or didn't go to college. There was a danger to that, something that crossed a line of familiarity. Crystal was seeking experiences outside of what Emily knew, and so Crystal became something outside of what Emily understood. She would climb on Emily's bed after returning to the dorm late at night and tell Emily about what she and her various boyfriends had done, about dinners and apartments and love and sex. And Emily would listen and smile and give the reactions she knew Crystal wanted, wide eyes and open mouth, and ignore her own jealousy. Ignore the question of whether she was jealous of the experiences Crystal was having . . . or if she was heartbroken.*

"He and I dated my entire freshman year," Emily told Calvin, "and it was really nice. And then our relationship changed my sophomore year."

Emily had a feeling that Crystal could sense her reticence, but neither of them ever mentioned it. Sometimes Crystal would stop her stories with an "Are you okay?" or "Is this cool?" and Emily would realize some shadow must have crossed her face and play it off. Yes, there was heartbreak, but Emily would rather suffer and hide it than risk the lovely intimacy she shared with Crystal. And there were boys Emily dated, boys she obsessed over and quickly fell in and out of love with and one she lost her virginity with, but no one replaced Crystal. That permanence made Emily happy, and she was delighted when, as their freshman year drew to a close, Crystal asked if they could continue living together their sophomore year. They spent that summer apart but talked two or three times a week, conversations that lasted all night and left Emily cheerfully tired the next day. Once Emily drove to Denver to see her as a surprise but was too shy to tell Crystal what she had done when she arrived. Instead, she saw Crystal with her family, through the window of their living room, her picturesque parents and sulky brother watching a movie together, Crystal's perfect posture on the couch, her long lovely hair. Emily left that same night.

And Crystal was even lovelier when she returned from Denver after that summer, her skin sun touched, her face faintly dotted with freckles, her hair silky when it accidentally brushed against Emily. She felt frumpy in comparison—awkward and brunette and, in her mind, pretty much the embodiment of the role of a comic sidekick. Not that Crystal ever considered her that way. And Emily began to realize that Crystal saw something in her, something she admired in Emily—her humor, her unpredictability. More than admired. Coveted. She saw it even when Crystal told Emily that she'd met someone new, an older man who excited her like no one else. Crystal had fallen in love, and love made everything in her shine. Emily was drawn to her in a way she'd never been, and Crystal seemed to realize that, to accept it. To want it.

As if Emily were her buoy and Crystal clutched her tight.

"I noticed he got strange," Emily told Calvin. "Like, became all possessive. Started getting moody."

Crystal needed Emily. She didn't say that, of course, but Emily felt it. Felt it the same way she felt her own love and the confusing complications of desire. They were friends and Crystal often said they seemed like sisters and Emily alternately loved and recoiled from that sentiment. She couldn't understand her own feelings.

Did she think Crystal was attractive? Obviously.

Did she want to be with her? Emily wanted to ravish Crystal's body . . . but with her eyes. Not her hands. At least she didn't think she wanted to use her hands.

Maybe sometimes.

Was she jealous of this new man who shared something with Crystal she never had?

That fucker, of course she was.

But nothing in their relationship left her as heartbroken, as shaken, as gutted and hollow and destroyed, as the terrible night when Crystal tearfully told her what that older man had done to her.

"And then," Emily told Calvin, "he hurt me."

Crystal crying against Emily's shoulder, her tall body hunched and broken, crying more helplessly than Emily had ever realized a person was capable of. She seemed to have turned from a woman to a child, scared and desperate and overwhelmed. Emily held her and cried with her, and her heart turned to a clenched fist. Fire danced in her mind.

"And I took it," Emily told Calvin. "I accepted it. I let him hurt me."

Sirens at their dorm a day later. Crystal sitting on the floor of their room, hands wrapped around the back of her neck, her head down in her lap. Tears, like she hadn't stopped crying since she'd first told Emily what had happened.

Emily's hands bloody and handcuffed.

He'd been easy enough to find—Crystal had his number thumbtacked to the corkboard above her desk. It was easy to call him and pretend to be Crystal and arrange a meeting. Easy to walk up behind him in that empty strip mall parking lot and stab him in the side.

He would live, and Emily's father would use what connections he had to help her avoid jail or any long-term consequences, but she was never allowed back to that campus. Or back into Crystal's life.

"It lasted years," Emily told Calvin, "until he finally left me."

Emily called Crystal, hoping to make amends, hoping that her friend would realize what she had done was extreme but necessary. But Crystal ignored her. Never replied. Eventually blocked her calls. Filed a restraining order after Emily showed up at her doorstep in Denver. It was the restraining order that did it, that and the scared look on Crystal's face when she opened the door and saw Emily on her porch. When Emily told her, haltingly, "I'm sorry . . . I just wanted to help," and Crystal closed the door.

But Emily saw her once, a couple of years later, when Emily was at a different school. Saw her in a restaurant, at a booth with that same man, the one who looked old enough to be her father. Watched Crystal talk with him, saw the way Crystal demurred to him, how she listened with rapt attention to what he said, how she smiled and laughed in response.

Emily realized she couldn't save her.

"He left me," Emily told Calvin, "and that was the only thing that saved me. And I can't go back to being that person. To needing someone. I'm sorry."

Calvin reached over, touched her dyed-blonde hair, let his hand tangle in it.

"Thank you for telling me," he said.

CHAPTER SIXTEEN

Melinda was tired when she woke the next morning around eleven o'clock.

It still felt like only moments had passed since she'd seen Jessy Taylor lying on her kitchen floor. The trauma remained rooted in Melinda's soul, despite all the distractions, despite the insight into Rebecca's relationship with Markus. She loathed the conflicting feelings Rebecca's story had stirred. For years Melinda had regarded Markus in one certain light, an ideal where whatever good he publicly showed was outweighed by the bad Melinda knew.

She heard the television downstairs, Rick listening to the pregame shows for the day of football. Melinda reached to the nightstand, took her phone to do her usual scrolling and distract herself from her thoughts. Text messages, email, Facebook and Twitter and Instagram (all where she mainly lurked rather than posted), a message from David:

Are you ok?

It wasn't much, just three little words, but they mattered.

Yeah. I'm getting better.

It took only moments for his next message to appear, those three blinking dots indicating that he was typing.

Good, I was worried. Do you want to talk? Come over?

She didn't pause.

Yes.

◆ ◆ ◆

There was something wrong about this, unforgivable, about choosing sin after someone had been murdered. Melinda knew it as she showered, as she applied her makeup and dressed and examined her face in the mirror.

Maybe that was why, when Melinda went downstairs, she stopped to talk to Rick instead of just calling out goodbye.

He was in the kitchen, wiping down the Foreman grill before putting its trays in the dishwasher. Wearing athletic shorts and a red T-shirt. An outfit that, adorably, reminded Melinda of a little kid's clothes.

She sniffed, smelled the warm savory scent of grilled meat and onions.

"Hamburgers?"

"Want one?" Rick offered. "I can make more."

"I'm good."

Rick smiled and kept cleaning the grill.

There was so much he didn't know.

Melinda had always had, of course, a private life and her own secrets, but never to this extent.

She remembered a quote she'd once read, "Everyone has three lives: a public life, a private life, and a secret life," and wondered if the same was true of Rick. If he really was the direct, plain man that stood before her, happily placing hamburger buns around a patty.

They'd met during the start of the pandemic, on a dating site Melinda had signed up for and checked on an irregular basis. He'd messaged her, and his message was a welcome departure from the other notes she'd received: pictures of straining penises, shirtless muscular men holding their phones in front of bathroom mirrors, messages that said nothing but "hey," others longer but filled with grammatical horrors. Rick's was a simple introduction:

> My name's Rick Walker. I wanted to know if you'd be interested in meeting for coffee.
>
> I mean, coffee six feet apart and in masks. :)

He'd worn a suit in his picture, a brownish-gray jacket with a blue tie. Had parted brown hair. Friendly eyes, but with an uncertainty in them Melinda found endearing.

She lived in the Mosaic District at the time, a town center in Fairfax, a neighborhood of apartments and stores expressly designed so residents would never have to leave, the kind of planned community suburbanites loved and urbanites loathed. The Mosaic was almost always packed, but the pandemic had thinned crowds and closed businesses. They met during a quiet Sunday afternoon, sat at opposite ends of an outdoor table, lowered their masks to sip drinks.

"It's crazy, isn't it?" Melinda had asked. "All of this?"

Rick nodded, turned away from her to blow on his coffee. "It really is. They're saying now it could last all summer."

"Hopefully that'll be it."

"Probably."

The conversation continued like this, natural and unforced and without sharp points. It was a relief to Melinda. The early days of the pandemic—the horror of what was happening in New York, the uncertainty of the disease—had brought a sense of comfort and unity, one of those rare moments of need shared by the public. It reminded Melinda of the day after the 9/11 attacks, when people overwhelmingly, unironically, loved each other.

"I just want to get back to the way things were," Rick said.

There was a sweetness to that, Melinda thought. Even if something about it, something she couldn't quite identify, had struck her as naive. Terribly so.

"Rick," she asked now, as he wiped down the counter, "do you have any secrets from me?"

He stopped like someone had pressed pause.

"Secrets?"

"Anything you haven't told me?"

Now his smile was gone. Uncertainty clouded him. "Why are you asking?"

He hadn't answered her question. "It's a friend of mine," Melinda lied. "She's having an affair. I'm meeting her now to talk about it."

"Who?"

She made up a name. "Bethany. I knew her in college."

"Are you asking if I'm cheating on you, like your friend?"

Melinda waited.

"I mean, no." Rick seemed astonished by her question. "Do you think I am?"

"I don't necessarily mean *cheating*," Melinda clarified. "Just, like, are there things you don't tell me?"

"I tell you everything."

"How often do you masturbate?"

"*What?*"

"I saw porn on the computer." This was true, although it had been close to a year ago when Melinda discovered it. And she hadn't really cared. She assumed all men looked at porn but chose not to talk about it, just like she chose not to think about it.

Rick was visibly shaken. "You did?"

"It was a lot of blow jobs, Rick. A lot."

"Well—"

"And vagina closeups. Like you're thinking about becoming a doctor."

Rick put his elbows on the counter, forehead in his palms. "It's too early in the day to talk about this. I don't know why I like looking at it, I just do. I'm sorry that I didn't think about telling you."

There was an embarrassed strain in his voice, one that plucked at Melinda. Plucked until it produced guilt.

"No, I'm sorry," she said, and she was. "It's my fault. We don't need to talk about this. I just—I was just worried after talking with Bethany."

"Okay."

She walked over to him, stood next to his tall bent body. Kissed the back of his head.

Melinda's phone buzzed, but she ignored it. She knew it was David.

But that afternoon, she stayed with Rick.

Chapter Seventeen

Melinda stayed with Rick until the evening. David texted once and she wrote back, Sorry, I can't today. He didn't write again.

Around six o'clock, she received a message from Emily with an address in DC and a note:

1 hr.

"I'm heading out for a bit," she told Rick.

"Dinner with your friend?"

"My friend?"

"Bethany. Who you were going to meet for lunch? She had to postpone?"

Melinda had forgotten the lie, even the name. "Right."

"Where are you meeting?"

"Someplace in DC."

"Drive carefully."

It was dark when Melinda left, and she longed for summer, her favorite season of the year. For winter Melinda wanted evenings when white snow glowed, turned black nights blue, rather than this cold, dry winter.

The drive didn't take long, the interstate for once not crowded. She didn't drive into the city often and always had a sense of guilt that she never took advantage of DC's museums and theaters and restaurants. Truthfully, the most Melinda had gone into the city was during her twenties, when she and her girlfriends went clubbing.

She and Emily were so different that way. Her sister was fun but had never been one for clubs or bars. Emily's nighttime activities during her twenties were, as Melinda had learned, decidedly different.

She felt a sharp pang of concern for Emily, something Melinda had felt when she first saw that bruise. And then anger flashing inside her, the beginning of a red rage, the overwhelming desire to hurt whoever had hurt her sister.

It took Melinda a moment to clear her head.

The address Emily had sent seemed familiar; Melinda realized, as she arrived, that it was only a block from Emily's apartment. She pulled up to a wide street lined with closed businesses, parked on the side of the road.

Another text from Emily.

c9374 u3b.

Melinda frowned at her phone, typed:

What are you talking about?

Emily shot her an emoji with a tense face.

Code 9374 unit 3b

Melinda sent her back a shrug emoji.

I have no idea what that means

Seconds passed.

ITS THE DOOR CODE AND UNIT NIMBER 4 THE STORAGE
UNIT BLDG RIGT NEXT TO YOU

Melinda typed back:

Are you serious?

JUST MEET US INSIDE. GOD MEL

Melinda left her car. A massive storage building was to her left. She locked her door and headed to the building. Looked up and saw the silhouette of a figure staring down from a window high above.

Melinda waved to Emily, or maybe Rebecca. She couldn't tell who it was.

She couldn't even tell that if was a man, not a woman, staring down.

"Welcome to my lair!" Emily sang out when Melinda arrived at the storage room. She extended her arm like a game show host revealing prizes.

It was a small dark room with boxes lining the wall opposite the door.

Rebecca sat on a box in the corner, arms crossed over her chest, looking cold and unhappy.

"Hi, Rebecca," Melinda said.

"Hey."

"So," Melinda asked. "What exactly do you do in your lair?"

"It's not really mine," Emily said. "My landlord lets me use it."

"We couldn't have met somewhere else?" Melinda asked. "Like, anywhere else?"

"No," Emily said. "You're here for a reason."

She pulled a large box out, then a second one. Patted the bigger one and looked at her sister. "Have a seat."

Melinda did, delicately, worried about the humiliation of the box crumpling underneath her, reminded again of the weight she'd put on over the past couple of years. She hated how thin Rebecca and Emily were in comparison. Fortunately, the box held.

"Why couldn't we have just met in your apartment?" Melinda asked.

Emily pulled a loose strip of packing tape from the second box. "I wanted the two of you to come here because of this. It's incredibly detailed. But it's important that I share it with someone now, before I present it to the cops."

She removed the tape, took a moment before continuing. "I've never shared this with anyone. It means a lot."

"Thank you," Rebecca told her. "Really. For trusting us."

"Yeah," Melinda added. She saw something different in her sister now, a determination, a seriousness. "Definitely."

Emily opened the box, pulled out a tube. She opened the tube and smacked the end, like a doctor with a newborn baby, until a rolled paper fell out. She picked up the paper, unrolled it on the ground, held the corners down with boxes.

The three women all stared.

"You want to show this to the cops?" Melinda asked her sister.

"Immediately."

"I'm sorry, is that . . . crayon?" Rebecca asked.

"Color coding, yes."

Melinda and Rebecca glanced at each other.

"What are we looking at, Em?" Melinda asked.

"An organization chart I made of the Winterses' syndicate!"

"It looks like," Melinda said, trying to find the right words, "like . . ."

"Like a Jackson Pollock painting," Rebecca said, "but with words instead of paint."

"You mean a masterpiece?" Emily cried out delightedly.

"Well . . ."

"What does"—Melinda squinted, bent to see better—"*Baldy out JWB SATSUN* mean?"

"Are you serious?" Emily asked. "That's referring to the bald guy who was standing outside of Jon Winters's building on either a Saturday or Sunday night. I forgot which when I wrote this down." She paused. "He was, like, super bald."

"And all the arrows pointing in two directions?" Rebecca asked.

"Well, I don't know who's working for who. So that's what that is."

"Uh-huh."

"You guys don't like it?" Emily seemed crestfallen.

Rebecca pointed to a drawing. "Is that a chicken?"

"Okay," Emily said, and she moved the corner boxes, rolled the paper back up. "You guys aren't appreciating this. But the point is, there's a lot of suspicious people associated with your family."

"Because they're bald?" Rebecca asked.

"This is what you brought me here for?" Melinda asked, before Emily could reply to Rebecca. "Your weird high school art project?"

"That's not why *I* wanted you to come," Rebecca told her. "My story is going to involve you. And I'm sorry about that."

"How?" An idea occurred to Melinda. It was implausible but, in light of everything that had recently happened, not an impossibility.

In fact, Melinda realized, it felt as real as a sudden, inescapable truth.

"Rebecca," Melinda asked, as a dejected Emily taped her box back shut, "did you have Markus's child?"

Chapter Eighteen

Rebecca had walked next to Markus with her head down and her arms crossed over her chest, as if she bore the solemn humility of a sorrowful monk. It wasn't cold yet, but it was chilly; the temperature had been dropping as the days grayed.

The Waterfront Fair, which seemed to encompass all of south Baltimore, from Little Italy to Locust Point, was in full celebration. Street vendors sold everything from carts or stalls or tents or blankets. Music in the distance. Children running ahead of calling parents.

"It's crazy what they did with this place," Markus told her, glancing at the manicured bricks, the green glass high-rise buildings, the bobbing ships, the endless people. "So much tourist stuff. You hear what it was like before. This is so different."

"Yeah, I know what you mean," Rebecca said. "It was crappy, but there was a kind of charm to it, I guess." She looked away, couldn't hold back her feelings anymore.

"I'm still scared . . ." Rebecca let the fragment drift before she continued. "I'm still really scared." And the sentence grew lighter as it ended, so the last word was said in a hush. They passed a small group of people standing outside one of the shopping pavilions, happily posing for a picture.

A kid dressed in black suddenly roughly bumped into them. He had long stringy hair and sunglasses and a skeleton earring and almost knocked Rebecca to the ground. She exclaimed and stumbled back. Markus grabbed the kid by his hair.

"Watch where you're going."

"Fuck, I'm sorry!" the kid exclaimed and squirmed.

Markus yanked the kid toward him, grabbed his ear. Pulled it until the kid cried out. People in the crowd turned toward them, nudging each other, lifting their phones.

"Markus!" Rebecca exclaimed, holding his arm.

The kid tore himself free, ran off.

Markus scowled after him, rubbed his hand against his jeans. He'd been more emotional lately, prone to anger, rage seething under the surface. The other day he'd yanked her arm during an argument. And there was that awful time, which Rebecca never liked to remember, when he'd slapped her. Minutes later he'd apologized profusely.

"You sure you're okay?" Markus asked now.

"Yes."

They walked on, following the festival's parade route down Pratt, heading away from the water and the harbor.

She was silent as they continued past Charles Street. It seemed like they'd been walking forever, the way it always feels after being at an event for hours. Only a few stalls were ahead, although the festival continued to Camden Yards. They slowed at one filled with charms and trinkets so Rebecca could look at jewelry.

"How am I going to have a career with a child?" Rebecca asked, not looking at Markus, pulling out a ring and staring at it.

"We have friends that can help. Family. It'll be easier than you think."

"No." Rebecca shook her head, set the ring down. "It'll be incredibly hard."

"But we'll be together."

"But it'll still be hard. And I don't want my life to be any harder than it already will be." Rebecca was still looking down into the tray of rings and not at Markus.

"We'll manage," he said.

They'd had this same discussion for weeks.

"But it's different for you. The label is so excited about your album, and it's really good. I've never heard anything like it before. The way they paired you with street musicians. It's so raw." Now she looked at him. "You seem like you've become a different person since this all happened."

This wasn't part of the discussion they'd been having.

"In a bad way?"

"Sometimes," she said hesitantly.

Markus didn't respond.

Rebecca wanted to say more. She couldn't say more.

"Maybe," Markus said, his expression tightening, "I'm trying to control as much as I can. But it's just too much."

"I know," Rebecca reassured him, hoping to tamp down his anger. "And it's mostly good, honestly. Like you're becoming who you're supposed to. Growing into this. It's just, sometimes you get so mad."

Markus didn't look at her, but his voice wasn't unkind. "I really am trying to control everything."

She had believed him.

◆　◆　◆

Telling her story was helping Rebecca, Melinda realized.

Yesterday had seemed like an attempt by Rebecca to explain Markus's behavior, to justify him, the same exasperating way Jessy and her father insisted there was something wonderful about Markus, even as they willfully ignored the truth.

This story was more than that, Melinda knew, and she knew it from her counseling days, when she'd held back her opinions and just let women talk, let them realize as they spoke how they'd been misled or abused. They'd needed to hear their own truth.

Rebecca already knew the worst about Markus, but his death had shaken that knowledge. And so this was something Rebecca had to relearn. She needed, Melinda thought, to return to honesty.

◆ ◆ ◆

Rebecca had walked over to the side of the stall, examining the good luck charms, tiny golden unicorns and horseshoes with attached loops and holes so they could be hung on ears or wrists.

Markus picked up the ring she'd been holding earlier and studied it, looking for the cost. The ring was slender and gold, with a small sea-colored stone.

The stall's salesman sat on the curb next to his booth and smoked.

"How much are these?" Markus asked.

"Five and a quarter."

He gave the stall owner six.

"'Gratulations," the man said, the cigarette poking out of one side of his mouth, squinting at the dollar bills before he shoved them into his pocket.

"You didn't have to buy it," Rebecca said as they walked away. "I didn't like it that much." She held her hand up. The skin around her fingernails was pink and chewed.

"I know," Markus said, "but you do like it."

"It is nice," Rebecca said. "Very cute."

A small crowd was gathered ahead, across from Camden, on the corner of Pratt and Eutaw. Markus and Rebecca joined in and watched a juggler at the center of the crowd's circle. He had flaming batons and was catching them and quickly throwing them back up in high, graceful circles. He caught the flaming batons in his hands, all at once, and blew them out quickly, and the crowd applauded. Then the batons automatically relit, and he yelped comically and tossed them, burning, high into the sky.

"So that ring," Markus said, watching the juggler catch the batons, "would make a nifty engagement ring."

"I think so too."

It seemed like the noise and commotion around them had all turned into a canvas of vague colors. The Bromo Seltzer tower, a tall brown brick building, so dark and ancient it wouldn't seem unnatural to see angels swarming up it, was lit now, near evening, and the top glowed a beautiful blue.

"Would you want to marry me?" he asked.

"I think so. But I don't know."

That sudden anger in his face, scaring her, trapping her like a snake tightening around her chest.

"Hey," Markus told her. "We need to talk." He firmly grabbed her hand, led her away from the sparse crowds to the side of the tower, near the entrance of the neighboring fire department.

"What's the matter?" Markus asked, close to her. "What are you doing to me?"

Rebecca watched him fight for control.

"I'm yours," she told him. "I promise."

She had been too scared to say anything else.

Chapter Nineteen

He quietly walked back down the hall, away from the storage room. Headed to the stairs, down to the first floor. Stepped outside the building and stopped next to Melinda's Jeep.

He pulled his phone from his pocket and dialed.

"Yeah."

He wasn't surprised by the abrupt greeting. Mr. Winters had been tense ever since the incident at Rebecca's apartment.

"Your niece went to"—he glanced up at the building—"E-Z Storage, down in DC. A blonde woman met her outside and let her in."

"You follow her?"

"Yeah." He spoke quickly so Mr. Winters didn't have time to swear at him. "And then another woman came and met up with them. They're all talking right now, in one of the units."

No response from his boss.

He spoke to fill the silence.

"I heard them. Your niece is telling the two women about her ex. Some pregnancy."

"You're not supposed to hear that," Mr. Winters said. "You'll need to forget it."

It felt like the cold night had seeped under his skin. Almost a child-like sense inside, like he wanted to cry from fear. "I'm sorry."

Silence.

"One of the women, Mr. Winters, I think she's the one who was in your niece's apartment. The one who bit off Dawkins's nose."

Nothing.

"She called herself Three Strikes. Said the storage place was her lair. I really think it's the same woman."

Fear was filling him like water, making it tough to breathe. He shouldn't have said anything about the niece's story.

He waited for Mr. Winters's next words.

"I'm in DC now," Mr. Winters said. "Send me the address."

Chapter Twenty

Markus had sat in a chair in Rebecca's kitchen like he'd been thrown into it. A kitchen witch hung in a corner, grinning feverishly and clutching a tiny yellow broom. A pair of scissors weighed down half the pages of a magazine open to a photo of some model thrusting herself into the camera.

"I'm so sorry," Markus told her.

Rebecca sat opposite him, her hands tightly together between her thighs, her shoulders hunched.

"What'd the doctor say?" Markus asked.

"He said it's common. That it happens to a lot of women. Especially their first time."

"Did it hurt?" Markus asked. "Do you need anything?"

Rebecca shook her head. "There was a little cramping, and then I went to the bathroom and I saw blood. So I went to the doctor, and he told me I'd lost it."

Markus lowered his head, covered his face with his hands.

"You're sure you're okay?"

Of all the ways he could have reacted, this was the most unexpected. Rebecca had expected disbelief, anger, Markus to jump to his feet and storm out of her house. Instead he was loving, and caring, and sad.

It broke her heart.

Rebecca had entertained notions of leaving him. Considered how scared she'd been during her short pregnancy as a warning sign, an emotional hint that their relationship was far more ruinous than she realized. But it was just a thought, different from how she'd felt the other times in her life when she'd firmly ended a relationship with some man. And she'd always firmly ended relationships.

Markus looked up at her. His eyes red with pain.

His sadness tugged at her.

"Do you want," she asked uncertainly, "to still be with me?"

Now something determined came to his expression, like a torch emerging from a dark cave. "I'll never leave you," Markus told her, his voice as sudden and definite as a struck bell. "Never."

And Rebecca would often think back to those words, the way she saw them then as a lovely promise but, later, a threat. She would think back to this afternoon, to how they'd eternally given themselves to each other.

◆ ◆ ◆

And again that unease nudged Emily, now at the concept of *forever*, the way Rebecca had described her irreversible connection to Markus. It was permanence, and that was something Emily actively sought to avoid. She liked living in transitional states—a rented apartment; a distant connection to family; a boyfriend, not a husband; a job that didn't consume her; a pair of identities between which she could switch.

But the connection she felt to Rebecca was more than that. Something else drew her in, and it drew her in with claws.

It was how Rebecca didn't feel worth attachment.

Emily often felt her own self-regard was playfully exaggerated, but with honesty underneath that playful surface. Objectively, she knew that she was pretty and smart and strong.

And, objectively, none of that mattered.

In the bricked depths of her soul, Emily knew she wasn't worth attachment.

She wasn't worthy of love.

Emily looked away from Rebecca as the other woman kept speaking.

"I'll never leave you either," Rebecca told Markus, distantly aware she was crying. Tears that would also haunt her later, that would cause her to wonder if she was crying because she was in love or guilty or trapped.

The last time she'd cried like that was when her parents had died.

Markus's arms were around her; his body knelt in front of hers. She smelled his familiar scent, the comforting warmth of his skin.

"I'm sorry," Rebecca whispered. "I am."

His lips moving against her neck. "I know."

Rebecca shook her head and wiped her tears. She stood and walked to the window, looked out at the line of row houses across the street.

She still felt that ache of sadness, but the tears had stopped.

"Do you ever feel," Rebecca asked, quietly, "like you've done so much wrong you can't do good? Like you're ruined?"

They were quiet.

"Rebecca," Markus asked, uncertainly, "did you tell me everything?"

"No."

Then she told him everything.

CHAPTER TWENTY-ONE

"I couldn't tell Markus I didn't want his child. But there was stuff with him I wasn't sure about, like how angry he got. The drinking." Rebecca's voice quieted. "How he hurt me. And then, especially afterward. I should have just let him believe it was a miscarriage."

"How he acted wasn't your fault," Emily said. "None of it."

"He wasn't like that before what I did. Markus wasn't that bad."

"Bullshit," Emily argued. "You can't blame yourself."

"Emily's right," Melinda said.

"I think I killed him," Rebecca went on. "My uncle told me he'd go after Markus when he found out what he'd done to me."

"Someone would have," Emily said.

"There's something else," Rebecca went on, "and it's why you're here, Melinda. There was a woman Markus was with after I left him. A sex worker named Dani. She came to see me after Markus was killed. She told me what she knew about my uncle."

"Dani?" Melinda asked. "She came to my house too. She's the one who told me Markus was dead."

"She did?" Rebecca asked.

Melinda assented, but uneasily. She didn't like remembering how brusque she'd been with the other woman.

"She told me stuff about my uncle that made sense," Rebecca said. "The rumors I'd heard and things I noticed . . . he's not a good man. I've known that for a long time. Longer than I want to admit."

"Did you work with Dani back in the day?" Emily asked Melinda.

The memories of those women were like a flood rushing toward a dam.

Melinda swallowed.

"I would have remembered. I remember them all."

"Can you find her?" Emily prodded. "Call your old contacts? Help us out?"

"Help you what? Put Rebecca's uncle in jail?"

"It's what Markus deserves," Rebecca said.

Emily didn't reply, but Melinda stood.

"Deserves?" she asked. "After what Markus did?"

"It wasn't all . . ."

"I'm not helping Markus," Melinda said. The words felt cold leaving her mouth. "I should have helped Dani. I really should have. And if she needs someone, I'll be there. And I'll do what I can if she wants to testify against your uncle. But I'm not doing this for Markus. I can't."

Melinda didn't like leaving the way she did, without another word, the silence resounding as she walked out of the storage room and down the quiet hall. She felt anger growing, knew it was an attempt to justify her actions and didn't care.

Melinda was angry at Emily for asking her to do this, to revisit these memories.

Angry at Rebecca for telling her about her past with Markus, for complicating how she saw him.

And, as Melinda climbed into her Jeep, she was angry at herself. Angry at the shaken feelings inside her, at the way it felt like Markus was manipulating her, even in death.

That's why, as Melinda started the ignition and slipped her seat belt over her shoulder, she was too distracted to notice the group of men walking toward the E-Z Storage building.

Chapter
Twenty-Two

"I really thought she'd help," Rebecca said, crestfallen.

"Melinda will come around," Emily told her. "She can be pretty stubborn. One time I signed her up for this dating site without her knowledge and set her up with this guy. I made plans with her for dinner and showed up with him. Once we were all there I told her what I'd done and introduced her, and then the dude kept telling us how hot his own sister was. Which, you know, weird? And it was a deal breaker for Melinda. She didn't talk to me for, like, a month. And we never did go back to that Chili's."

"What?"

"Anyway," Emily went on, "we need to find this Dani chick. Any idea where she is?"

"Maybe Virginia. Or DC. Or Maryland. I'm not really sure."

"Hell of a starting point, Bex."

"I'm sorry," Rebecca told her. "I'm not sure what to do. I don't even know if I should be doing this."

The lights in the storage room turned off.

"What happened?" Rebecca asked, panicked.

There were no windows in this room, nothing but cement walls around them.

Nervous energy coursed through Emily. "Did anyone follow you here?"

"I don't think so. Should I—should I have been checking?"

Emily knelt and reached for her handbag, somewhere on the floor next to her.

A sudden light.

The flashlight from Rebecca's phone.

"Oh, good," Emily said. "Shine that here."

Rebecca illuminated the handbag. Emily dug through it, pulled out her mask.

Slipped it over her head.

"Isn't that mask going to make it hard for you to see?"

"If someone's here, like your uncle's men, it'll make it harder for them to see me."

"Why would they be here?"

"Probably looking for the other half of that dude's nose." Emily pulled her phone and baton out of the bag, slipped the phone into her pocket, clipped the baton to her pants. Extended the handbag's straps, switched it to a backpack, swung it over her shoulders.

The light from Rebecca's phone shifted as she rose. "We should leave."

"I should leave," Emily said. "You'll be fine."

"How do you know?" The fear in Rebecca's voice slowed Emily, softened her.

"I'm thinking it's your uncle. He's the one who set you up in that sweet apartment, right? Probably did what he could for your career?"

"Yeah."

"He'll just, I don't know, take away your allowance or something." Emily's thoughts were rushing ahead of her. "Stay here. Let me see what's happening. It could just be a power outage."

Emily left the storage room, closed the door behind her. There were windows at either end of the hallway, next to the doors for stairs, and they showed the neighborhood around her. The neighborhood was still illuminated.

Only this building had lost power.

Emily looked out the window again. Melinda's Jeep was gone. Men were milling outside the entrance.

She trotted back to the storage unit. Rebecca's flashlight blinded her eyes.

"Okay," Rebecca said. "That mask is terrifying."

Emily ignored her. "Your uncle's men are here. Call the cops. I'm going to sneak out. You'll be okay if they find you. And I'll find Dani."

"But you don't know where she is."

"Hey, it's one of three states. DC, Maryland, or Virginia."

"DC's not a state."

"See you soon."

Emily stepped back outside.

Her nerves were starting to get the best of her. Her throat was sand dry, breath hard to come by. Emily tried to keep her panic from lunging up as she trotted down the hall, the backpack bumping the small of her back like a rapid heartbeat. She headed to the stairwell closest to the storage unit, reached the door, slowly turned the knob. Opened it soundlessly.

Beams of light rising up the stairs.

Emily closed the door and walked over to the window.

The window was just a sheet of glass without a way to open it.

Emily thought about running down the hall to the other stairwell, but there was probably another group of men climbing up it. And she had no interest in getting trapped in the freight elevator.

That panic rising.

Emily looked up and saw a ceiling grate.

It was within reach from the window's inside ledge.

◆ ◆ ◆

One of the best things about the mask, Emily decided as she crawled through the ceiling shaft, was how it kept dust out of her nose. The shaft was caked in dirt; she could feel the grime under her palms even if she couldn't see a thing. But with her allergies, and without the mask, she knew she'd be sneezing up a storm.

And that would be disastrous, given the group of men beneath her.

Emily had heard the stairwell door open moments after she climbed up, heard their low voices whispering instructions. She was surprised at how cautious the men were.

But Emily was garnering a reputation. She'd already taken out Jon Winters in the woods, another of their men the other day. There were stories about her circulating online. For all they knew, there could be a group of people called Three Strikes, taking down the Winters family one at a time.

Or she could have a gun. A grenade launcher. An entire fucking armory.

Or maybe Victor Winters was just that concerned about his niece.

Which made Rebecca even that more important.

Emily followed the men down the hall, silently crawling above them, softly cursing herself. It had been stupid to meet here. She should have brought Melinda and Rebecca somewhere unidentifiable, particularly since the men below stopped outside her storage unit.

Whoever had followed Rebecca here knew exactly where she'd gone.

Which meant they'd be able to find out who was renting this unit.

Which meant they'd be able to find Emily.

She needed to escape, but first she had to learn more.

Emily crawled to a small fan vent, peered through the grate. Stared down at Rebecca.

And, again, that worried thought. Could she trust her?

Or had Emily revealed every single thing about herself to the very people she was hoping to destroy?

CHAPTER
TWENTY-THREE

Had singing really been everything? That was something Rebecca constantly wondered, especially after Markus's death. Her music and Markus were intertwined, the same way he'd wrapped himself around her entire life.

Rebecca glanced at her phone. The battery was nearly dead.

But, still, she kept the flashlight on.

Music had been both a blessing and curse. Once people saw she had talent and drive, they sought to control it. Everyone in her life was desperate to own it. To own her.

She had seen that when, as a young girl, her mother had taken her to audition after audition. Painfully pinched a sliver of her skin between her fingernails whenever Rebecca told her she wanted to go home.

She had seen that in college when Dr. Hardaway put his hand on her knee, sitting next to her at the piano. And instructed her to keep her eyes on the music as his hand rose.

She had seen that when Markus told her that to get more gigs she needed to change her style, to sing something more contemporary than jazz standards, even as she tried to explain to him that jazz was where her voice belonged.

And her uncle. Determined to control her under a guise of concern. Emotionally distant and secretive but always present. He was the atmosphere in her world, the air she breathed and the environment in which she lived, and he quietly controlled where she roamed.

Rebecca had been controlled by everyone in her life. She'd known this for a while.

She remembered when Markus had told her they wouldn't need her uncle. They could have the baby, he insisted, and make their own way. She remembered her face turning into hard lines at his words, as if someone had asked the impossible. And he had.

And so Markus had realized, like everyone else in her life, that he could control her as well.

Rebecca heard the men outside the storage unit.

Her singing was better than she'd ever accepted, better than the confines in which she'd been kept. Markus had loathed that about her. That's what had driven his anger, those times when it seemed like she could almost see his resentment. That had been the root. Not her lies. Not her family. Not what they'd lost.

He had blamed it on all those things, never admitting to jealousy. But the worst nights, the brutal nights, the nights when she feared she'd be killed . . . those were the nights when she had sung.

Markus would drink and fume, fuck and beat her. Taunt her about the car accident that had taken her parents when she was a child, left her in the care of her criminal uncle. Tell her that never having a true family was why she didn't understand his true love.

Rebecca was aware that she'd become something else to Markus, a goddess to whom he assigned too much power. She knew he was ascribing too much blame to her, too much love, too much hate. But she couldn't leave him, locked by love and guilt. And even when she did finally leave, it wasn't complete. As if their hands were still around each other's necks, squeezing. Begging to be apart, always together.

The lock to the storage unit shook.

Rebecca wished she hated him. Wished that, for all those nightmarish nights and gasping sore days, for the parts of her that he'd savaged, she had the emotional reach to hate him. Maybe it was the Catholic Church from her youth, or some inner reluctance of will, but Rebecca simply couldn't feel the same disdain his own sisters did.

Markus had taken so much from her.

But he'd given her love.

Those moments of his love, the excited eyes, pure feeling. The times when he showed her the streets of Baltimore, the roads he'd wandered before her. In a neighborhood next to Bolton Hill, they'd kissed near a statue of an angel holding a laurel with one hand and a dying soldier with the other. She remembered the tickle of wind, taste of night.

Afternoon days, sunlight rising to cover them like a sheet. The sheer happiness and the audacity of happiness, as if they'd been given something that couldn't last, something nobody should be allowed to hold. They'd showered together at night, in the dark, without sex, just a romantic ease, like a summer drive through the country. He'd washed her hair, standing behind her, her eyes closed as water and shampoo ran down her bruised chest.

The voices outside were louder.

Like pulling away from a kiss, Rebecca slipped out from her memories.

It wasn't about Markus. Or her uncle, or music, or any of the other controlling figures in her life. They all wanted to push her in a direction. Wanted her to be something different from what she was, follow the path they thought was right.

Rebecca needed to make her own path. She'd left Markus. And now she'd leave her family.

A loud clang outside, and the door to the storage unit shook again. Rebecca stepped forward, unsure of what she was going to say to her uncle's men as the door swung open.

She lifted her flashlight. A gun surprised her.

Rebecca's last note left her lips.

CHAPTER TWENTY-FOUR

From above, Emily watched Rebecca die.

The phone had been in Rebecca's hand when the door to the storage unit opened, shining on the men as they rushed inside. One of the men had his hand high, shielding his face from her flashlight, his other hand firing his gun blindly when Rebecca screamed.

Her scream abruptly stopped.

Rebecca took two steps forward, breathing hard, as if incredulous, then sank to her knees. She put an arm out, and her body lay down, slowly, like a settling blanket.

Her phone's flashlight was still pointed at the men, illuminating the one who had fired, the others' shadows behind him.

"Miss Rebecca?" he said. His voice was young, with a southern accent.

Emily couldn't see him well.

"What happened?" he went on, his voice a cry. "Was that me?"

More flashlights snapped on, but there were no sounds from the men other than breathing. The one who had shot Rebecca asked again and again, "Was that me? Was that me?" Lights kept landing on Rebecca and moving away, as if guilty.

Emily stared at Rebecca, her body now an unmoving dark pile, hoping she would crawl, rise, that she had only lain down to recover her strength.

It was too jarring for Emily to comprehend that Rebecca had been relaying her story to her and Melinda and now, minutes later, she was gone. This was the way Emily had felt when her mother had died, when she'd learned Markus had been murdered, confusion and futility. Death always seemed like an impossibility, until it happened.

A shadow covered Rebecca. The flashlights stopped moving below. A hush fell over the men.

A giant figure leaned over Rebecca's body, entirely obscuring Emily's view.

"Who shot her?"

"I think it may have been me," the young man with the soft, scared southern voice said. "But it was an accident. I've never shot anyone before. I swear it, Mr. Winters."

Emily stared down into the dark.

Victor Winters was here?

"Hold out your gun," the deep voice commanded.

"Yes, sir."

Victor Winters's giant shadow moved out of sight, like the moon drifting out of orbit.

Emily listened intently, heard nothing but hard worried breaths.

"Your gun's warm," Victor Winters said.

"It was an acci—" And that was all the young man got out before his voice choked. He was suddenly lifted into the light, Victor Winters's giant shadow beneath him, his hands around the young man's neck, raising him like an offering to ancient gods.

The young man disappeared, swept away. Reappeared as Victor slammed his body down to the floor.

Gasps from the young man. A grunt from Victor Winters. Nothing from the men watching.

Victor moved to the side, and a flashlight illuminated the young man's face, curly brown hair and brown eyes and light skin and his mouth open, his face still, paralyzed by fear or the impact of Victor slamming him down.

Victor knelt, and his hand covered the young man's throat. Emily heard a low gurgling, not words, just whimpers.

The whimpering abruptly stopped.

"Find where she went," Winters said.

Men rushed from the room.

Emily also wanted to leave, to scoot backward down the shaft and run out of the building and away from this nightmare. Regroup, think of a different plan. Warn Melinda of everything that had happened. Find Dani.

But she didn't dare. Didn't risk making a sound.

Emily wondered how long she'd have to hide, wondered when they'd believe she'd escaped. Wondered if Rebecca had called the cops.

Had she?

Emily pressed her face to the vent and stared down. Was Rebecca's phone on?

Her phone.

Too late Emily realized she should have been recording what these men had done.

She slowly, carefully, reached behind herself, into her backpack, as Victor Winters walked back over to Rebecca's body.

What happened next happened quickly.

The vent creaked as Emily stretched, and suddenly she was falling. Her body landed on Winters roughly, her side slamming against his shoulder. She bounced down to the floor; he sprawled next to her.

Rebecca's body was under her. Emily's hands pressed in her blood.

Victor Winters was on his knees.

Emily's baton slashed across his face.

It didn't feel like a hard hit, but the blow knocked him back and turned him over. He howled.

Emily scrambled to her feet, rushed out of the room, headed down the hall. She saw the stairwell door fly open and pressed into a doorway. Shadows of men raced past her.

Emily peeked out as they rushed into the storage unit Victor Winters was in. She let them pass and ran to the stairwell. Bounded down the stairs, mask crooked, backpack bouncing. Pushed through the front door and into the night.

Emily had walked into this building with the confidence of a hunter.

She left hunted.

PART THREE

But I Love Her

That woman I got is a liar and a thief,
A scamp and a cheat,
Got no money, and she's missin' teeth,
But I love her.
Oh yes,
I love her!

That man I got is a bully and a brute,
An absolute goof,
Got no money, and he ain't that cute,
But I love him.
Oh yes,
I love him!

We ain't got much, but we got each other,
Even when life gets harder and tougher,
Even when it seems like everything's over,
We ain't got much,
But we got each other!

Excerpted lyrics from "But I Love Her"
Written by Markus Peña and Rebecca Winters
The Complete Markus Peña, Baltimore University Press

CHAPTER

TWENTY-FIVE

Melinda woke and stretched and had a moment's calm before remembering the night before—the revelations from Rebecca, the plea for help from Emily. What she'd learned about Markus, his lost child and broken love. These thoughts troubled her, threatened her resolve like a redirected river rushing toward a crumbling dam.

She welcomed the distraction from Rick's voice downstairs, his inquisitive murmur when talking with someone. She assumed he was on the phone, given his desire (which she never understood) to start work as the sun rose.

Melinda turned on the *TODAY Show*, listened to the television anchors discuss their plans for the upcoming Thanksgiving holiday, went into the bathroom. A knock on the bathroom door paused her, toothbrush hanging out of her mouth.

"Mel?" Rick's voice. "Someone here to see you?"

David.

She took out the toothbrush, stared down into the sink.

"Okay."

That was the only person it could be. David, wondering why she hadn't shown up yesterday, why she was avoiding his phone calls.

This was something Melinda had feared, and she worried it was what she deserved. David and Rick knew each other, but faintly—she wasn't surprised Rick hadn't recognized him. They'd met once in passing, had a genial "male" conversation, friendly and bland and unmemorable, largely made up of deviations of "How are you?" and "What sports do you like?" (Rick liked football and David didn't, so they found no common ground there.) Melinda had wondered what would happen if they came face to face again, the three of them in a room. If she was forced to lie openly to Rick, as David watched her.

She quickly brushed her teeth, tied her hair in a ponytail, left the bedroom, and headed downstairs to the foyer.

It wasn't David.

"Melinda Peña?" the woman standing in her home asked. "Isabel Pike."

Melinda shook the other woman's soft, lotioned hand, still confused. "Hi?"

"Is there somewhere we can talk?"

"I'm sorry," Melinda said. "Who are you?"

The other woman's expression was like a flame about to dangerously flicker at the slightest wind. "I'm an attorney for Victor Winters. I'm here to talk to you about your sister, Emily."

◆ ◆ ◆

The coffee mug was too hot, but Melinda didn't mind the heat. She held the mug in her hands, let the burn slowly dissipate against her palms.

Isabel sat across from her, took a sip from the bottle of water Melinda had offered, wiped her lips dry. There was something about the other woman's mannerisms that was passive yet dangerous, a fisherman's lure floating in the sea.

"What about Emily?" Melinda asked.

Isabel ran her hands through her black hair, which was straight and shiny and seemed a little wet, her dark-brown eyes both wide and sharp. She was attractive, a softly athletic build under her couture black business suit. Enviable skin. Sensual lips.

Melinda felt entirely underwhelming.

"¿Quieres hablar en español?" Isabel asked.

"Oh, no, that's okay," Melinda said. "My Spanish isn't that great."

Isabel nodded, reached into a large Louis Vuitton, the brown checkered pattern bright as if the bag was brand new, pulled out a notebook. Opened it, uncapped a pen.

"When was the last time you saw Emily?"

"What's this about?" Melinda asked back. She wondered if her tone was too guarded. "Why do you want to know about my sister?"

Isabel shifted the notebook, jotted something down. The angle made it impossible for Melinda to see what she was writing.

And then Isabel paused and, to Melinda's surprise, underwent a transformation. The tense pensiveness relaxed. Her forehead softened. She turned from professional to personal, her countenance kind.

"I'm sorry, this job." Isabel closed her eyes, breathed. "You're probably not aware of this, but Mr. Winters is heavily involved in commercial real estate. As his attorney, most of my meetings tend to involve disputes about land development or zoning ordinances. I haven't worked with people for so long. And by people, I mean nonbureaucrats." She smiled.

Melinda instinctively smiled back, glad for the change in tone.

"I'm not even sure why Mr. Winters asked me to take this on, to be honest." Isabel's voice lowered. "It's not my specialty, and it's not like he couldn't afford different lawyers. Or a detective."

"A detective? For Emily?"

"He trusts the police, of course, but wants to conduct his own investigation."

"I'm sorry, about what?"

"We have reason to believe that, late last night, Emily Peña murdered his niece, Rebecca Winters."

I saw Rebecca last night. She was fine.

Emily would never do that.

Rebecca can't be dead.

Those sentences rushed to her lips. Melinda managed to hold them back.

But she couldn't stop surprise from taking over her expression.

And a small part of her realized, like a voice from another room, that Isabel was still writing notes. She'd been writing this entire time, her hand furiously moving even as she passively watched Melinda's face. As if Isabel were two different people.

"Rebecca's dead?" Melinda asked.

"As of last night. Had you seen her recently?"

Melinda didn't know what to say.

There was too much going through her mind. No part of her believed Emily would have done this. But if Rebecca really was dead, who had?

And was Emily okay?

She must be, if Isabel hadn't mentioned her.

But if Melinda admitted to meeting with Rebecca, was there a chance she could somehow implicate Emily? Herself? Did Isabel know more than she was revealing?

And, central to all that, like an arrow striking deep . . . Rebecca had been killed.

Melinda should have been afraid. Instead, she wondered why she wasn't. Her resilience probably had something to do with her family, the way her father had fought battles with and against the city, argued in council meetings, shouted into the phone. There was nothing passive about any of the Peñas, particularly when they thought they were right.

And Melinda knew she hadn't done anything wrong.

And she knew, somewhere deep in her soul, neither had Emily.

Melinda realized her eyes were closed, her breaths shallow. Her fingertips felt like they were scrabbling to hang on to the edge of a cliff. She forced herself to breathe deeply, slowly. Pull herself up. Look Isabel in the eyes.

The other women was still watching her, writing. As if she was tracking every change of expression in Melinda's face.

"I haven't seen Rebecca for years," Melinda lied, speaking heavily. "And I only met her a couple of times, when she was dating my brother, Markus."

Isabel said nothing.

"I still remember her. She was the only woman my brother took seriously. He had a . . . reputation."

"I remember. I was such a fan of his music."

Isabel's words sounded artificial, the kind of statement someone offered when they were forced to make polite conversation.

"Was she still singing?" Melinda asked, hoping to put more distance between herself and the truth.

"I spoke with Rebecca recently," Isabel said, instead of answering. "We had a conversation about her finances. As Mr. Winters's attorney, I also represent his family in personal matters." She crossed out something she'd written in her notebook. "But that's not important to this conversation."

Melinda's hands were in her lap.

"What is important," Isabel went on, "is that Rebecca told me she met with you."

Dammit.

Melinda shouldn't have lied.

And why was she even answering this woman's questions? Isabel wasn't with the police. She had no right to question her.

The thought reminded Melinda that she was prepared for this. As a social worker, she'd spoken with police before. She'd been interrogated, maintained neutrality when it was in the family's best interest. She used to admire her own poker face, her ability to persuade.

Melinda decided she'd answer Isabel's questions, for the sake of her sister, until she found the truth. She'd do what she could to shape the story.

And Melinda wanted to turn the story away from Emily.

She tried to think of a reason to justify her lie and absentmindedly picked up a necklace she'd left on the counter the other night, a no-reason gift from Rick. She was always leaving her jewelry everywhere around the house, was surprised she didn't lose it more often. Melinda played with the simple black string, rubbed her fingers over the swooping gold curve attached to it as she thought.

And saw Isabel glance at her hands, make a note.

"All right," Melinda said. "I did see Rebecca. That's true. But she asked me not to tell anyone."

That professional expression back on Isabel's face. It reminded Melinda of looking into a blank computer screen, the cursor blinking, waiting. "Why is that?"

"She met with me to tell me about her and my brother." Melinda's mind rushed while her words slowed. "About what happened with their relationship. It was private, and she wanted to keep it a secret."

This was a version of the truth, and it gave Melinda footing. Not a lie but not revealing everything.

"There's nothing I don't know about Rebecca," Isabel said. "Can you tell me what she told you? Was this about the pregnancy she had with your brother?"

So Isabel did know everything.

"She told him that her uncle would never accept a child that wasn't fully white," Melinda said defensively. That helped. Gave Melinda a reason for lying, for not being up front with this attorney.

"Mr. Winters is firmly against racism, sexism, or any form of bigotry," Isabel droned, as if this was a statement she'd read many times before. "His businesses employ minorities in a variety of positions, and he's donated to numerous politicians and causes that advocate equality and a fair workplace."

"Sure."

"Speaking of employment," Isabel went on, and she turned a page in her notebook, glanced down, "you work with David Martin, correct?"

"Yes . . . ?"

"In a business that consists of the two of you? And only the two of you?"

"Yes." Melinda was confused by this direction. She set the necklace back down on the table.

"How would you characterize your relationship?"

"I'm sorry?" Her own words were sharper than Melinda expected.

"Are you co-owners of Essentials? Equal partners?"

"I'm sorry, what does this have to do with anything?"

"It's a small but successful business." Isabel's expression was like a shrug. "Mr. Winters is always interested in small businesses, how they're performing. It's part of his Color and Culture Counts initiative, where he awards grants to worthy minority-led businesses."

"David's white."

Now Isabel did shrug. "Just thought I'd ask."

Melinda felt completely thrown off guard.

Which, she realized, was probably what Isabel was hoping to do.

"Did Emily attend your meeting with Rebecca two days ago?"

Two days ago. So Isabel wasn't aware of their meeting last night.

Or maybe Isabel did know about it, and she was going to ask later.

Melinda felt like she was playing poker and half her cards were exposed.

"She wasn't there," Melinda said. "It was just me and Rebecca. I haven't seen Emily for years."

Something inside gave Melinda the strength to meet Isabel's gaze. This was something she was willing to lie about.

"You haven't seen your own sister for years?"

"Our family isn't close. After my mother died . . ." Melinda stopped speaking, wondered why she was telling this woman so much. "I haven't seen Emily for years," she repeated.

"I have on good authority that Emily—"

"No," Melinda said, interrupting her. Riding new strength. "Answer some of my questions now. I've told you a lot because I like Rebecca and I want to help. But you have to tell me why you think my sister had anything to do with this."

Isabel stopped, tapped the pen against her paper.

"That's fair," she agreed. "You haven't seen your sister in years, correct?"

Melinda nodded. Even if Isabel knew she was lying, this was a lie she could later justify.

"Was Emily violent as a child?"

"You're still asking me the questions," Melinda said. "Why do you suspect Emily?"

"I'm sorry. I asked about the violence because we have reason to believe Emily thinks Victor Winters had something to do with Markus's death."

"She does?"

Isabel jotted down a quick note. "Emily seems to think that Mr. Winters was upset enough about your brother's relationship with his niece to murder him years later." Her pen touched paper again. "Were you aware that the relationship between Markus and Rebecca was abusive?"

"Yes."

Isabel pursed her lips. "Can I be frank with you?"

"Of course."

"Victor Winters loved Rebecca like she was his own biological daughter. Doted on her, took care of her. Made sure she never wanted for anything. I can understand why someone could suspect, as bizarre as it seems, that he would snap years after a relationship ended, but he would never have done something to hurt Rebecca. I knew Rebecca, and as you've admitted, you did too. Did she have any anger whatsoever toward your brother?"

"No," Melinda replied honestly. "She should have, but she didn't."

"She loved your brother, despite what he did to her. And Mr. Winters would have never hurt her by hurting Markus."

Melinda said nothing.

Isabel frowned. "But Emily seems convinced that Mr. Winters did this heinous act. And, from what my research has shown, she's not the most . . . stable person?"

"Your research since last night?"

"My research since Markus and Rebecca were first romantically involved. And I have reason to believe your sister calls herself Three Strikes and acts as a masked vigilante."

"Emily is a masked vigilante?" Melinda asked. "Like a superhero?"

"She seems to think she is."

"That's insane." At least, Melinda thought, that was an honest response.

"*Right?*" Isabel agreed, the word emphatic, personal, girlish. "But she snuck into Rebecca's building two days ago, attacked a guard, was caught, and escaped after . . ." She glanced at her notes, grimaced. "Biting off a guard's nose."

"Again," Melinda said, not saying much because she didn't trust her voice, "insane."

"Prior to that, she attacked one of Mr. Winters's distant cousins, a man named Jon. She broke a bone in his back, even came close to paralyzing him."

Well, Emily hadn't mentioned this little bit of information.

"And we have your sister on camera," Isabel continued. "A day before Rebecca met with you."

Something in Melinda faltered. "On camera?"

"We believe she's on camera in a mask entering Rebecca's apartment building. Where she was captured and, subsequently, escaped before the police arrived."

"Oh." Melinda had no idea what to say next.

Isabel kept talking. "There are a few stories online about a masked vigilante named Three Strikes who fits that description exactly. She's been active, from what I can tell, over the past year or two. So you can see why I asked if Emily had any violent tendencies as a child."

"None that I remember," Melinda lied.

"And if she broke into Rebecca's apartment," Isabel pressed on, "and then Rebecca was murdered days later, you can understand why Emily would be a suspect."

"Are you going to the police?" Melinda asked.

Isabel regarded her evenly. "I wanted to talk with you first."

"Thank you. Please, let me try to find her. I mean, she's my sister."

"I may come up with other questions." Isabel offered a pained smile. "It's what lawyers do. Would it be okay if I called you again?"

Melinda gave Isabel her phone number, took her card.

She walked her to the foyer. Opened the door, watched Isabel head to her car, a shiny silver Lexus sedan. Even departing, Isabel had a commanding presence. Head held high, large Louis bag in the crook of her arm, her dark suit almost overpowering the bright morning.

"Who was that?"

Melinda shut and locked the door, turned toward Rick.

"A lawyer," she said. "One of Markus's ex-girlfriends died." The end of her sentence grew weaker as she spoke. Melinda cleared her throat. "She had some questions about it."

"Died? How? Was she killed like Jessy?"

Melinda winced at the memory. "I don't know. I don't know how it happened."

"Was she a friend of yours?"

"Kind of."

"I'm so sorry." Rick touched her arm. "Do you need to talk? I can't believe this."

"I'm okay." Melinda wasn't, but she wanted to clear her mind first. "Markus had a fucked-up life. Everyone close to him got hurt. They're still getting hurt."

Rick waited, as if about to say something else.

Melinda drew in a ragged breath, patted and moved his hand. "Honestly, I'll be okay. I just need some time."

Again, like before, she needed distance from Rick and didn't understand why. But she felt desperate for it.

Until she saw something in Rick's expression, a look rarely there. Doubt.

And his doubt bothered Melinda more than she'd expected. It worried her.

"I'm sorry," she said. "It's just . . . I need to think."

"Okay."

Melinda stood by the door as he walked off, nervously chewing a thumbnail, a bad habit she'd broken as a teenager but one, lately, she'd resumed.

She wanted to talk to Rick again, but first she needed to find Emily.

Melinda went upstairs to get her phone.

"Hey, Sis," Emily said, halfway through her bedroom window. "Who was *that* bitch?"

Chapter Twenty-Six

Emily closed the window behind her. And noticed her sister wasn't exactly excited to see her.

"What happened after I left last night?" Melinda asked. "What happened to Rebecca?"

"They killed her."

Emily told her about hiding in the ventilator shaft, the gunshot, Victor Winters viciously murdering his own man. About hitting Victor in the face with her baton and escaping.

And Emily told Melinda how, after running from the storage building, she had returned to her apartment but made the decision not to go inside. It wouldn't take much for the Winters clan to figure out which apartment was connected to that storage unit. In fact, they might already know. Men could be inside, waiting for her to return.

But her Civic was alone on the street. She glanced up and down the block, looked at the dark buildings on either side. Didn't see anyone watching her. Emily had pulled her keys out of her handbag, slipped in. Started the engine and drove deep into the city.

Emily hadn't let herself think about Rebecca as she drove. She kept her eyes on the cars around her, staying vigilant, even if she wasn't exactly sure where she was going.

She'd arrived at Anacostia Park, pulled into a small lot that looked out to the river. Water sparkled from city lights. Occasional headlights passed over a near bridge.

She shut off the engine. The rear windows of the Civic were tinted and impossible to see in without daylight, and she felt safer lying in the back than the front. She had spent the night in her car's cramped back seat, somewhere in the confusion between asleep and awake. Flashes of violence angrily yanking her out of dreams.

"You really saw her die?" Melinda asked.

"Yeah."

"Are you okay?"

"I think I was in shock afterward, but I'm okay. I just feel so bad for Rebecca."

Something about that didn't seem right with Melinda. Emily could tell she was bothered, as if examining a painting of the sky with the wrong hue of blue.

"Emily, in your work . . . in what you do, have you ever killed anyone?"

"No," Emily said resolutely. "And I never would."

"But you find people and attack them. They *could* die."

"I don't take it that far." Emily realized what her sister was saying. "Do you think I killed Rebecca?"

"You just don't seem that bothered by it. And I worked with people who went through trauma. It's not this easy to recover unless you're still in shock." Melinda paused. "It's hard to tell with you."

"It's not easy," Emily said, heat under her voice. "I felt Rebecca's body, Mel. I had her blood on my hands. And then I had to escape because a pack of murderers were trying to find me. None of this was *easy*."

Melinda nodded. She'd just needed, Emily understood, to see that deeper emotion. To see what, if anything, was under the surface.

To lift the mask.

"I think they know who I am," Emily went on. "The Winterses. That's why I couldn't go back to my apartment. I couldn't take the chance."

"They *absolutely* know it was you," Melinda told her. "That woman who was here? She was Victor Winters's attorney. She said that you were the one who killed Rebecca. And she knows about your . . . vigilante work."

"Really?"

"Yes."

Emily sat on the window seat. She felt small compared to Melinda, frail and childlike.

"They're saying you killed Rebecca," Melinda repeated.

"What do you think?"

"I believe you," Melinda said.

But Emily felt like she didn't.

Not entirely.

Even to Emily, her own story didn't seem plausible.

After all, Emily *had* tried to kidnap Rebecca.

And she *had* assaulted someone.

Many people.

She suddenly felt a darkening sensation, reverberations in her arm from the baton's strikes, the blisters on her palm from its textured grip threatening to pull her out of this conversation, out of this room, away from her sister.

"I feel awful about Rebecca," Emily said, her voice tiny but enough to keep her grounded, to remain. "I'm the one who told her to stay in that storage room. I said they wouldn't hurt her if they found her. And they didn't mean to, it was an accident."

Emily was surprised when Melinda walked over to the window seat, sat close to her.

"Something awful is happening," Emily said. "Markus, Jessy, and now Rebecca. Rebecca was an accident. But Markus and Jessy?"

"Once the cops find out about Rebecca," Melinda told her with forced confidence, "they're going to realize something isn't right about all of this."

"What do you mean, find out about Rebecca?"

"Once we talk to them."

Emily stood, panic inside her like an exclamation mark. "I can't go to the police!"

"Why not?"

"Do you know what I do? Do you know what they'll do to me if I'm caught up in this?"

"Emily, that lawyer told me she's going to tell the police about you. This is a chance to clear your name first. To tell them what really happened."

"You think they'll take my word over the kind of lawyers Winters can afford? That chick was rolling in a Lexus. You think they'll trust anything I say?"

"What choice do you have?"

Emily rubbed her fingers together. She wished she was holding her baton. "Rebecca was right. We're not going to be able to tie any of this to Victor Winters. But I can tie him to the sex trafficking. I just need to find someone willing to talk. That's the key. That's the domino. Push it over, everything else follows. That Dani chick. She's the domino."

Emily could see Melinda considering it.

"Okay," Melinda relented. "If you think that's the best move, then do it. And if you end up needing legal help, I'll see what I can do."

"Thanks, Mel." Emily sat back down next to her sister, wrapped her arms around her, rested her head against Melinda's shoulder.

She wondered if Melinda could feel the need in her hug, the way that, even though her arms were lightly around her, Emily clung.

"Listen," Emily said. "One other thing, and it's really tiny. Not a big deal at all. I left my car in DC and took buses here so no one could follow me. But they're definitely going to be watching your house, making sure you're not in contact with me. So I don't think it makes sense for me to stay in your guest bedroom. You know, somewhere visible. Maybe I take the attic instead?"

Melinda had been nodding as her sister spoke, but she abruptly stopped. Moved away.

"You think you're staying here? With me and Rick? In this house?"

"Aren't those all the same question?"

"You can't stay here!"

"Why not?"

"Are you serious? You're wanted for murder, you . . ."

"Not yet," Emily corrected her.

"You're *going* to be wanted for murder, you're running around as a secret vigilante for some reason, you bit off a man's nose . . ."

"Just part of his nose."

"And I haven't told Rick about you yet."

"Rick doesn't know you have a sister?"

A rough sadness, a loneliness, tugged at her words.

"He knows I have a sister. He knows about you. But he doesn't know about anything that's happened with you. That you snuck in the other night. That we met at the storage building."

"Really?" Emily asked. "You didn't tell your boyfriend about me? That's pretty dishonest."

Melinda nearly shouted. "Dishonest? You're a secret vigilante!"

"Yea, verily. But at least I'm honest about it. Kind of."

Melinda rubbed her scalp, tugged her hair.

"Mel," Emily went on. "I don't have anywhere else to go. I can't go back to my apartment. I can't go to Calvin's . . ."

"Who's Calvin?"

"A guy I've been seeing."

"He doesn't know the truth about you?" Melinda asked. "So I guess you're not completely honest either."

"That's not the point. If I go there and they see me, they'll kill him. And me. You know how rich Rebecca's family was. They'll find me wherever I am."

"So you're going to put me and Rick in danger?"

"That's the thing. They've already been here. And I can trust you. If they come back, I know you'll cover for me. I can't expect that from anyone else. I don't have anyone else."

Emily could tell Melinda was trying to think of other reasons.

"You don't even have to tell Rick," Emily insisted. "I'll just hide in the attic, like in an eighteenth-century novel. All you have to do is bring me food and make sure the window isn't locked. Oh, and your Wi-Fi password. I'm promoting this one dude's release from prison that my company was working on, and I need to send a press release out tomorrow. And also a TV. I don't want to miss my *Housewives*. Do you watch Bravo?"

"Look," Melinda said, "I need to tell Rick. And our attic isn't finished or anything. And there might be a raccoon in there, Rick's supposed to call someone. You can stay in the basement. It's small, but it's all we have. Rick uses the guest bedroom for his office."

"Thank you, Mel," Emily said solemnly. "I promise I'll get this figured out in a few days. It won't take long."

"Yeah."

"Also I need to borrow your more fashion-forward clothes. And makeup. And toothpaste. And a toothbrush. And . . ."

Emily kept prattling on, even as a small part of her wondered why, despite having just learned about it, Melinda didn't seem that affected by Rebecca's death.

CHAPTER
TWENTY-SEVEN

The door to the Lexus softly, firmly closed. The noise from outside disappeared. The leather scent was strong, the panel polished, upholstery unblemished. Isabel Pike didn't take time to savor these sensations from her new car. She went through the Louis handbag on the passenger seat, found her phone, plugged it into the charger.

Scanned messages. Played a brain-teasing game.

After five minutes she left the car and walked back to the townhouse.

Victor always told her to check everything twice.

Melinda's boyfriend answered the door again. And frowned when he saw her.

"Yes?"

Isabel allowed herself an embarrassed smile. "I forgot my sunglasses inside. I think they're just in the kitchen? Would you mind if I came in and got them?"

Rick Walker looked unsure of himself.

Isabel added, "I'm sorry, I'm just so forgetful." She put emphasis on the embarrassment behind her smile. Played the role of a hapless woman needing help.

"Sure." Rick stepped aside. "Come on in."

"Thank you! I always leave my things everywhere." Isabel followed him to the kitchen.

She hoped to see Melinda, wanted to find out if her mood was dramatically different. Experience had shown her that people tended to have an extreme reaction after intense questioning, their behavior unhinged.

Like the time, months ago, when she'd questioned a man who ran a small shipping warehouse and had discovered that the crates he was keeping for Victor were filled with illegal weapons. He threatened to tell the authorities unless he was given a larger cut. Victor was incensed, but Isabel had assured him she could handle it.

She'd gone to the man's home just outside of Georgetown, bordering the river. Talked with him in the yard while his wife and children watched a movie inside. Surprised him by telling him it was fair to expect more money, given what he was storing and the risk of his involvement. He was belligerent at that, encouraged by her passivity, and mocked her offer of an additional 5 percent. Countered with an increase of 200.

Isabel refused and left.

But before she left, Isabel told him to tell his wife and children she'd said goodbye. And named all of them.

She hadn't driven half a mile before he called.

When she returned, he was nothing but apologies and glances back to his family.

They had settled on a 1 percent increase.

Isabel was an expert at nudging someone off the ledge. It was simply a matter of walking them to a cliff and making them look down. Seeing how hard and fast the drop was. Pointing out the rocks below where their body would land.

And having them realize, with a complete and total belief, that you would push them.

But Melinda wasn't anywhere to be seen, which was unfortunate. Isabel was going to ask Rick about her when he suddenly spotted the sunglasses she'd intentionally left behind. He picked them up off the stool.

"Are these yours?" he asked.

"Yes!" Isabel said. "Thank you so much. And would you mind telling Melinda thanks again?"

"Sure."

What a bland, cheerful man, Isabel thought, as Rick walked her out. He probably had no idea how screwed up this family truly was.

They passed the stairs. Isabel heard female voices above.

It sounded like a television.

But she noted it.

◆ ◆ ◆

The drive to Potomac from McLean wasn't long, twenty minutes if the beltway didn't have much traffic. But Isabel allotted herself an hour, because there was always traffic. She'd grown up the daughter of an ambassador, lived overseas for most of her life before her father retired and her family settled in the green, wealthy acres of Potomac. Her father had taken a position as an adviser to the State Department, and her mother became the headmistress of a local private school. Isabel was their only daughter, and both parents were so busy they'd rarely had time for her.

Not that she'd needed the attention. A loner with a proclivity for studying, Isabel easily spent hours submerged in homework. She had her choice of colleges upon graduation and picked Georgetown for both her undergraduate and law degrees. She enjoyed the college life, the small intense classes, the loveliness of the old campus, but never felt at home in the university. Most of the other students came from similarly wealthy families, their parents almost always successful in business or law or politics. Her fellow students were motivated, often with fully formed ideas of the type of career they wanted to pursue. Isabel was similarly ambitious but didn't know which kind of law she wanted to practice. Or what she'd do after graduation.

It was her mother who introduced her to Victor Winters, one of their neighbors in Potomac. She'd invited him over to talk with Isabel about his work.

Victor and Isabel went for a walk. They strolled past the widely spaced estates.

He offered her a cigarette, which she accepted.

"Real estate," he told her, "is a business of hope. Doesn't matter if you're selling a colonial, a condo, or a store."

Isabel didn't say anything.

"Business is people, and people are desire. Doesn't matter what you're selling. At the end of the day, every decision made is desire. You understand that, you'll do well in anything."

"Death is the opposite of desire," she said.

He glanced at her.

"Tennessee Williams."

He flicked ash off the edge of his cigarette.

"Your investment in northwest DC was a good move," Isabel told him. "That neighborhood's been struggling with gentrification. Nearby communities didn't have high-end stores. This ensures no more lower-income housing. Brings in more money. Risky, but it'll pay off."

"You did your homework."

"Always."

With that she'd impressed him. And that made her happy.

But, of course, she'd acted in a way he wanted.

Desire.

There had been an attraction between them, despite their difference in age. Isabel felt comfortable with him, easily intimate, and could sense Victor felt the same. She was too careful to trust him, but it was hard to shake the sense that she could tell him anything.

Isabel even thought, briefly, about telling him her secret.

The time she'd been driving home from school, looking up something on her phone, and her car had clipped a man walking on the side of the street. She'd stopped her car, walked back on the dark quiet road, knelt next to an old man gasping hoarsely, bleeding everywhere. Isabel had stared down at him, fascinated as his breath slowed, his eyes widening and tightening as he tried to see her, tried to talk. Minutes later Isabel had nudged him with her foot to make sure he was dead, checked her car, saw only the mildest of dents on the front bumper. The pavement had done most of the damage. She'd driven home and watched the news the next day.

He'd been a retired owner of a popular local bakery. The community mourned him, the police offered rewards for anyone with information, her mother wept. Isabel had gone to the funeral, spoken with his family, mildly surprised guilt didn't appear. But what had come was a tantalizing possibility of being discovered, of being caught.

Secrecy had spoken to her like a seductive whisper, tickled her neck and earlobe.

When she met Victor, she sensed he understood that feeling.

He offered her a job with his small company after graduation. The salary was exorbitant, but it wasn't only the money. That wasn't the reason Isabel followed him. She'd grown up among rich men and women.

It was the danger.

Something about danger called her, and it was something he could sense, the same way she sensed that his clean hands had been washed of blood. It aligned Victor and Isabel, made them kindred spirits, even if he was at least twenty years older.

It wasn't long before Victor calmly told Isabel the truth behind his practice, how he sold the newly constructed businesses as places where drugs could be made, weapons traded, money cleansed, whatever someone needed. How, even though he'd made a small fortune from commercial real estate, his true success had come elsewhere.

He told her this one morning at breakfast, the sunlight dazzling through his bedroom window.

Isabel had suspected as much. She found it more engaging than problematic, the crimes fascinating in their practical application. And his honesty had completely opened their emotional connection, a river flowing without dams.

Sometimes she wondered what would have happened if she'd had the opposite reaction. Revulsion. Risen from the bed and stalked to the front door.

Would he have let her leave?

More to the point, would she have stayed if this hadn't been a part of his life?

She doubted both. Accepted both.

As they had grown closer, as they became immersed in each other even more professionally and emotionally, Isabel began to wonder if there was, in fact, a line she wouldn't cross.

Once a panicked woman escaped from one of his houses and came to her. Mistakenly ran to his office near the house, found Isabel, asked for help. That was when Isabel first realized he trafficked more than weapons and drugs.

But Isabel had simply called Victor. His men had picked the woman up.

Isabel remembered that woman's eyes as she was taken away.

The desperation.

There was no line.

◆　◆　◆

Victor didn't want her to come inside.

"But you need help," Isabel told him, parked outside his estate in her car. "Your eye."

"The nurse is with me." His voice was deep with grief. Grief beyond pain.

"Can they save it?"

"No." Victor wasn't a man given to emotions, something Isabel admired, and the hurt in his tone surprised her. And, if she was being honest with herself, repelled her a little.

"Are you in pain?"

A ragged breath. "Like never before."

The short sentence surprised her. She'd rarely heard Victor confess to any emotion.

But Victor had loved his niece, and Isabel had noticed the attention he'd paid to Rebecca. The unquestioned manner in which he gave her money (too much money, Isabel thought). The picture of her on his phone, taken at Ocean City's boardwalk, Rebecca's elbows on a wooden railing and her smiling face turned toward the camera. Her music a constant in his home, demos he'd paid to have produced. The favors he'd called in to help her career, until Rebecca had asked him not to. She was good, Isabel knew, but not great.

But she'd never tell Victor that.

"Are they sure they can't save it?" Isabel asked.

"Doesn't seem like it."

"Do you need surgery?"

"After all this is over."

"You sure you don't need me inside?"

"I need you outside."

Isabel understood.

Victor would never give her explicit instructions over a phone, but she knew what he wanted.

Find Emily Peña.

End the damage she was doing.

Isabel was already close to Emily, the dots connecting almost as fast as they appeared, like a constellation of stars blinking to life. Just hours after Rebecca's death, Isabel had confirmed that the storage unit was being rented by Emily Peña—a call to the unit's owner from a cop who worked for Victor provided that information. Isabel had found a picture of Emily online, sent it to Brandon Dawkins, asked if this was the woman who had bitten off his nose. Confirmed. She found Emily's sister, Melinda, through the same cop who'd found out Emily was renting the unit.

No insights from Melinda yet, but they would come. Isabel was just getting started with her.

It was almost time to show Melinda where her body would land.

CHAPTER TWENTY-EIGHT

"Rick? This is my sister, Emily."

Rick was sitting behind the desk in his office, staring intently into a computer monitor. He glanced up, bounded to his feet as Melinda and Emily stepped in and walked around his desk.

Melinda looked for any signs of concern or mistrust, for that doubt she'd seen earlier. But there was nothing other than a smile on Rick's face.

"Emily!" he said. They shook hands. "I didn't hear the doorbell."

"I knocked," Emily told him at the same time that Melinda said, "I heard it."

A moment of confusion, but Rick shrugged it away. "Melinda's talked about you, but this is the first time we've met, right?"

"Yup," Emily replied. "Our family sucks at staying in touch. Like, has anyone heard from Markus?"

"Jesus, Emily," Melinda said. "This is why I didn't bring her around sooner."

"I'm *kidding*," Emily said. "So, Rick, what do you do?"

"I'm a patent attorney."

Emily pondered that.

"Okay," she eventually said. "I can see it."

"Sorry?" Rick asked.

"I had to put it together," Emily explained. "You know, like you're a puzzle and this is a piece I need to fit in? Especially if we're going to be siblings-in-law someday. There's stuff I need to know. What teams do you root for? What's your favorite food? How do you feel about secret vigilantes?"

"Emily's *a lot* to take in," Melinda hurriedly explained.

"I can see that," Rick replied, but gamely. Rather than off-putting, Melinda noted that he seemed to find Emily's eccentricities charming. "I root for the Browns and, um, I like steak. Zorro seemed cool? How's that?"

Emily gave him two thumbs up.

They seemed to be getting along, so Melinda figured she might as well ask:

"Would you mind if Emily stayed with us for a bit?"

"My apartment's being fumigated," Emily said, going with the story she and Melinda had decided on earlier.

"Fumigated?"

"It's full of rats," Emily told him. She nudged Melinda with her elbow. "Get it?"

Rick looked back and forth between them. "Get what?"

"Give us a second," Melinda told Rick.

She took Emily's arm and led her sister into the hallway. Closed the door to the office.

"What's wrong with you?" Melinda hissed. "Can't you be normal for, like, five seconds?"

"I'm nervous! Do you think he likes me?"

"He probably thinks you're crazy."

"I want him to like me."

"He likes you. But can you just be cool? Can you do that? Can you calm down?"

"The odds aren't great, honestly."

They walked back into the office. Rick was standing against his desk, his hands cupping the edge.

"So your apartment is filled with rats?" he asked. "You must live in DC."

"Exactly," Emily told him. "A few blocks from the cathedral."

"I always wanted to live downtown."

"You did?" Melinda asked. This surprised her. Rick had grown up in Ohio, moved to the area to study law at George Washington University, then left DC for a job in Northern Virginia. He'd never mentioned returning to the district.

But now he nodded. "I love big cities."

"It is nice," Emily agreed. "A little noisy, and the rats are a problem, but it beats the burbs. Not very sexy here. No offense, but if I moved here, I'd be drier than Arizona. Probably a good place for kids, though." Emily glanced at Melinda's stomach. "Speaking of kids, are you . . . ?"

Melinda took a step back. "No!"

"I didn't say you *looked* pregnant! I was just asking if you're trying."

"We've talked about it," Rick said. "I mean, we do want kids."

The topic made Melinda uneasy. "Someday."

An uncomfortable silence.

"I hate condoms," Emily offered. "I know I shouldn't, but I do. Actually, it's a funny story . . ."

"So anyway," Melinda said, "Emily would stay in the basement."

"Sure." Rick seemed bemused by Emily, which was the best Melinda could hope for.

"One other thing," Melinda went on, wondering how to phrase it. "Would you mind not telling anyone she's here?"

That puzzled frown returned to Rick's face. "Why?"

"It's just . . . ," Melinda said slowly, trying to think of something. "Her ex is a little obsessed with her, and she's trying to avoid him."

"Mel's right," Emily agreed. "He needs to keep his goddamn distance."

"No problem," Rick said. There was no fear in his face, nothing lurking behind his eyes. Melinda realized she'd never seen him afraid.

That realization was comforting, attractive, like his height and strong build and easy confidence.

"What's this ex-boyfriend of yours look like?" Rick asked.

"Just, like, a guy?" Emily said. "I don't know."

◆ ◆ ◆

"That went well!" Emily told Melinda as they headed to the basement.

"How low's your bar for things going well?" Melinda asked. She'd seen that concern return to Rick's face as she and Emily left his office, that suspicious sense. It was clear something in his trust had been broken. Melinda hoped it wasn't irreparable.

"Pretty low," Emily admitted. "But I appreciate you helping me. And Rick seems nice. Cheerful, maybe a little bland."

Melinda turned on the light. Their basement didn't have much to offer—a tiny family room with glass doors leading to a small patio, a square unfinished room off it, cramped bathroom.

"You can sleep down here," Melinda said. "We have an air mattress, and I'll bring in some sheets."

"This is really nice," Emily told her, surveying the space. "I'll probably take the other room. Sleeping next to the patio doors will freak me out. I don't want to wake up and find some dude staring down at me and playing with himself. You know what I mean?"

"Not really."

"Should I have told Rick that I saw his penis?"

"My God."

"I thought about it," Emily admitted, "but then I would have had to explain the hiding-in-the-closet thing, and it would have been a whole other discussion. But I felt a little guilty, you know, when I was talking with him just now? I kept thinking about it. And that's the kind of thing I think someone deserves to know."

"It's not, it's absolutely not." Melinda stared into Emily's eyes, made sure she understood. "Don't tell Rick anything about his penis. Or think about it."

"We have fun," Emily said, warmly. "You and I. Yea, verily. Maybe someday I can have a secret cave, and you can sit in it and work the computer and talk to me on an earpiece, and we'll solve crimes together."

"No."

"Why not?" Emily whined. "Mel, I could use the help."

"Why not?" Melinda repeated. "Because I don't like your vigilantism and I want you to stop."

"It's my calling," Emily said solemnly.

"Yeah." Melinda spotted her laptop on the couch, picked it up, sat down. "Come here. Speaking of vigilantes, let's do some research."

"Research?" Emily flounced down next to her sister. "Why?"

"That woman who stopped by, Isabel Pike, knew who you were."

"Yeah, I know." Emily looked pleased.

"Why are you happy?"

"I mean, I didn't even pick the name. Three Strikes. I just wanted to beat up some assholes. Next thing you know, I have a following? Like Gandhi."

Melinda opened her internet browser, typed in "Three Strikes" and "vigilante."

Emily slid closer to her sister.

"There," she said. "That article."

"That's not an article," Melinda told her. "It's a Reddit thread."

"Same diff."

Melinda opened the link, scrolled down a series of posts speculating that a masked vigilante was behind a number of assaults in the DC metro region. One of the victims had described the assailant's mask ("Oh, that guy was an *asshole*," Emily put in). The guesses at the identity included police officers and military, both active and retired; public defenders who had grown exasperated at defending clients they knew to be guilty; various local sports figures.

"Is there anything else?" Emily asked.

Melinda found a couple of blogs that mentioned Three Strikes, but only in passing. Nothing more.

"Sorry."

Emily was clearly disappointed. "Well, shit."

There was so much Melinda wanted to ask her sister. Emily had hidden her bruises under makeup before they'd talked to Rick, and this vanishing was how Emily seemed to regard her own actions—what couldn't be seen, didn't matter.

"Articles about you online isn't the kind of attention you need," Melinda told her. "Why are you doing this, anyway?"

"The men I hurt have it coming," Emily said.

"You only attack men?"

"The violent crime index, not to mention sexual assault, lists men as the majority of—"

"I know the stats," Melinda interrupted her. "But you're making yourself a hero here, Em. You sure you deserve to be?"

Emily's lips thinned. "You don't get to decide who's a hero and who isn't, Mel. Not after you abandoned all those women."

"I'm sorry?"

"All those women, trying to start new lives. And you just stopped working with them."

"You mean when I left social work?"

Emily didn't respond.

"Okay, Em, you don't know what I was going through. You don't know what it was like to hear those stories, to keep hearing those stories. To hear what those men were doing to women. To children. To have the dreams I was having."

"Yeah, and, like you said, this was happening to *children*. And you just walked away. You didn't even stop . . . him."

Melinda abruptly stood. Her arms were crossed so tightly over her chest that it was hard to breathe. She had to remind herself to keep her voice down.

"Him? You mean Markus?"

"Yes, I mean Markus. Our own fucking brother hurting and using women, and that's when you left?"

"They didn't want to be helped, Em. Those women didn't want me. You think Markus was the only one who double-crossed me? They did, too, when they went with him."

"So you're blaming them? No wonder you quit."

Melinda was so mad her vision blurred. She touched the side of her head, took a couple of deep breaths.

"How dare you tell me . . ."

"You're not the only one Markus hurt," Emily said quietly. "He hurt those women. And he hurt me too."

The heat in Melinda still simmered, but she spoke over it. "What do you mean?"

Emily's eyes were wet. "There was a time I needed him and he wasn't there for me. You weren't either."

It felt like a giant fist had slammed into Melinda, that same dread she'd experienced when talking to a member of a client's family, often a child, who was about to tell her what her father or uncle or grandfather had done.

"It was before Mom died," Emily went on, "right when he got famous. I went to one of his shows. You know how he was then. I mean, he was always, like, volatile. But after he hit it big, and when he and Rebecca ended, he was just . . ." Her voice faded.

"What happened?" Melinda managed to ask.

Something in Emily changed. Her wet eyes dried. "Like I said, he wasn't there for me. You want to know why I'm doing this? Because *someone* should have been."

Emily's hurt expression hardened.

"So you want to know what happened, Mel? Fine, I'll tell you."

CHAPTER TWENTY-NINE

Emily hadn't been surprised at Markus's success. She'd heard about her brother's work ethic and drive, even though their decade of age difference kept them apart. More like cousins than siblings. But she'd dutifully followed his career, seen him perform, listened to the songs he'd put online, bought his first studio album. Blues for You, the DC-based label that had put out that debut, *Inner Demon*, was small but respected, and the musicians they'd paired him with were fantastic. The songs were a mix of standards and originals but performed sparsely, a lone guitar or infrequent drum or shy horn accompanying his voice.

And that voice. The deep baritone was still present, but now Markus sang brokenly, at times his words little more than a mumble, the songs a form of desperation, pleading.

The *Baltimore Sun* described him as "a preternatural Leonard Cohen with the anguish of Bessie Smith," which was a comparison Emily didn't understand—she had no idea who Leonard Cohen or Bessie Smith were. Pitchfork reviewed *Inner Demon* and called it "the story of a man wandering an emotional hellscape, serenading lost ghosts." Again, no idea. Buzzfeed listed *Inner Demon* in a listicle titled "Music You'll HATE Yourself for Not Listening to Sooner!" NPR caught wind of the album, played snippets on the air, interviewed Markus over the phone. Emily listened to the interview, and her brother was guarded and elusive, especially when they asked him about the anguish that inspired his songs. "What led you to this?" the host asked, and Markus hung up.

He was a little, but not much, more verbose with Emily when she would call him, often because he was inebriated. She wondered if that was why he didn't do concerts, but Markus was evasive when she asked. Instead, Blues for You released videos they'd shot of his recordings. Markus in a small studio, a guitarist next to him, head lowered over the instrument. The videos were put on YouTube and garnered hundreds of views, and then Adele tweeted one of the video links and wrote "Oh my God, I'm ugly crying at this <cry emoji> <heart emoji>!" And the views shot up to millions overnight.

Everything changed.

Suddenly Markus's face and voice were everywhere—his dark, haunted eyes on every website; his music in commercials; Sunday news shows conducting long interviews with him, Markus and the host walking side by side through the streets of Baltimore.

But Emily noticed that so much about Markus, despite the sudden success, seemed the same. Almost as if Markus had expected this. He was nonchalant during his phone calls with Emily, always with that distracted sense despite her excitement. As if nothing ever fully engaged him.

Except Rebecca. Emily had seen them together once when she'd visited him in Baltimore, seen how Markus doted on her, compared to the way he'd ignored every other woman who'd loved him. Emily didn't know what had happened since that time, but his relationship with Rebecca had changed. They'd moved in together, but there was a distance when Markus mentioned her. And he'd only mention her when Emily asked.

"Harold said this is my big chance," Markus told Emily over the phone two months after that Adele tweet, when Emily kept seeing his name and those studio videos on website after website, post after post. "They want to see how I'll do on tour."

"How cool!"

"It's a small club. Couple hundred people, tops. This company they're bringing wants to take me on the road. But they need to check me out first."

Emily went to the show a week later. The club was in DC, a tiny jazz venue called Trading Fours. Emily didn't know it would be crowded and was taken aback at the packed room. She walked inside, spotted Markus at the bar. An older thin man with gray hair poking out over his ears sat next to him. Another man, blond and tall with sharp good looks, stood on the other side.

"Hey, stud."

Emily had walked right in front of Markus, but it was as if he hadn't seen her until this moment. "Em?" Markus blinked. "What are you doing here?"

"Come on," Emily said after a quick hard hug. "You're finally performing in DC, and you think I'm going to miss my chance to see you? No frickin' way." She looked closely at him and sniffed. "Are you already drunk?"

"Mostly," Markus said. "Is this crowd real? Am I imagining it? Does beer make you hallucinate?"

"Yes, no, and no. But I do want some of what you're drinking. Who are these guys?"

"Harold Peterson," the older man said. "Markus's manager."

"Dietrich Anders. Volume Entertainment."

"Cool, cool," Emily said. "I'm Emily. Markus's little sister."

Neither man seemed particularly interested. "You must be proud of your brother," Harold said.

"Oh yeah. But I always knew he'd be a singer," Emily told him. "Either that or, like, a kickass barista."

"Harold . . . ," Markus said. He grabbed his manager's arm. Emily noticed how pale Markus looked, how shaken.

"Let's get you backstage," Harold told him.

Emily followed them through the crowd, leaving Dietrich behind. The crowd parted for them, parted with silence and stares and a few hesitant touches on Markus's back and arm for luck. The three went to a small room, nothing but a couch and a desk with a mirror before it. A guitarist was curled in a corner of the couch, tuning his instrument.

Markus walked in, sank to his knees. Crawled to a corner of the room and vomited.

"Whoops," Emily said. She closed the door.

"Oh fuck," the guitarist put in. "No wonder you missed sound check."

"He'll be fine," Harold told the room. "Just needed to get that out of his system." He knelt in front of Markus, lifted his face up. "What'd you drink tonight?"

"Little bit of everything."

"Yeah," Harold said, looking hard at Markus. "You're going to be okay."

"I'll be okay."

Harold's palms were on either of Markus's cheeks. "You're fucking going to be okay."

"I'll be okay."

"You don't get chances like this twice," Harold said, his voice hard. "You go out there too drunk to perform, there's no second chance. I've seen it happen. No one's going to waste time with a mess at the beginning of his career. No matter how talented he is."

Markus looked like he was about to throw up again.

"Your future's tonight," Harold went on. "You do what I know you can do, your ticket's punched. You go out there like a bitch, and you go back home and might as well never come back outside."

"Harold. I can do this."

"You were fucking born to do this."

"I was fucking born to do this."

Markus began to cry.

"Wow," Emily said. "This is so weird."

"Honey," Harold told Emily without turning to look at her. "Why don't you keep Dietrich company at the bar?"

"Excuse . . ."

"Emily," Markus said shakily. "Please."

Emily left the dressing room, went back to the bar. Dietrich was staring at a pretty brunette wearing something flimsy, but she took her drink and walked away. He turned toward Emily and beamed as she approached.

"Markus okay?" he asked.

"Maybe?" Emily watched the brunette as she passed through the crowd. "I don't know. Either preshow jitters or morning sickness."

"Buy you a drink?"

"Damn straight."

Twenty minutes later Markus was onstage, squinting into spotlights. The lights dimmed, softened to a comfortable glow.

"Okay," Markus told the crowd. "I probably shouldn't have done shots before this."

Emily laughed loudly, but the rest of the crowd didn't know how to respond. A little bit of nervous laughter, mainly silence. DC crowds, Emily knew, were always reserved. It took a moment to warm up.

"Or maybe I should have had a few more?" Markus added.

That loosened them. Laughter rippled through rows of standing people.

"One, two, three, four," Markus said, and the guitarist started playing, and Markus began singing "Round Midnight."

His voice turned to a rasp, every note a pained reach. The song took control of him, the guitarist strumming out a series of slow, low rising notes somewhere in the background. Like Markus had run into the woods and was alone and calling for someone to guide him out.

Emily wondered again what had happened with Rebecca. She hadn't seen her here.

But that was a distant thought because Markus was impossible to ignore.

Watching Markus, Emily realized, was watching two people.

There was the Markus onstage, singing a song he'd probably sung hundreds of times, matching the guitarist's pace, the guitarist matching his tone, the two of them talking to each other in a language no one else understood.

And there was the distracted part of Markus she knew so well, the part she now had a glimpse into. The part of Markus that must be constantly lost in memories. Like someone who'd been in a horrible car accident, and, for nights afterward, could feel the exact sensation of impact. That was Markus, but with emotions. Bathed in emotions, like a weary warrior bathed in blood. And they informed his music, broke his voice into glinting shards others longed to gather. His voice a path of footprints.

It was all in his voice, so much weight that Emily didn't understand how he could carry it, hate and love and fucking and violence all mingled in a room like strangers bumping into each other, lust and loneliness rolling over each other like doomed lovers, desperate fighters.

Applause as the song ended.

Markus kept singing. Emily had looked at him and seen a man lost. Trapped. Pleading for a way out.

◆ ◆ ◆

It happened at the end of the evening.

The show had finished five minutes earlier when Emily stormed to the dressing room, Dietrich walking behind her, talking quickly.

She swung the door open.

Harold was picking his teeth in the mirror while Markus wept on the couch.

"I wasn't trying anything," Dietrich said, and he closed the door behind them.

"The hell you weren't!" Emily exclaimed.

"Em?" Markus asked, looking up.

"What happened?" Harold asked.

"I saw him put something in my drink!" Emily told them. "He tried to drug me!"

"That's not true," Dietrich replied. His voice was calm and deep, as if this was an answer he'd given before. "I don't know what she saw, but I'd never do that."

"Why would I lie about it?"

"In this business," Dietrich said, and he looked at Markus, "women lie a lot."

"I don't even know who you are!" Emily exclaimed.

"The bar was crowded," Dietrich said. "I gave her a drink with my hand over the top, to prevent spilling. She thinks I put something inside."

"Where's the drink?" Markus asked.

"I threw it away," Emily said. There was a break in her fury, a moment of uncertainty. "I was so mad."

"Why would you lie about this?" Dietrich asked her.

"Are you kidding me?" she shouted. "Markus!"

"Listen," Harold said, his hands up, as if that would calm everyone. "I've known Dietrich for a long time. He's a stand-up guy."

"Markus," Emily said again, not shouting now but still urgent. "I know what I saw."

"I don't know, Em."

Emily took a step back. "Are you serious?"

"It's okay," Dietrich told her. He touched her arm.

Emily whirled, her hand rising, faster than even she knew she was capable of, and she smacked Dietrich. The sound reverberated through the room, and Dietrich yelped. Harold grabbed Emily as she lunged at Dietrich again. She was wild in his arms. Markus lifted himself off the couch and bear-hugged them both.

He and Harold managed to wrestle Emily to the ground, held her as she screamed. Harold covered her mouth with his hand, muffling her.

"Calm down!" Harold hissed over and over. "Calm down!"

Then he shrieked.

"Bitch bit my hand!"

Emily squirmed, loosened herself from Markus's clumsy grasp, hurried to the other side of the couch.

She stood there, panting, glaring at the three men.

Her nails must have scratched Dietrich, because her blow had left three cuts on his forehead. He stood next to Markus, Harold on the other side, the three of them breathing heavily.

"Get out, you fucking whore," Harold said, cradling his hand to his stomach.

"Fuck you, you bald, fat, stupid fucking fucker. I hope my teeth give you rabies."

"Get out," Dietrich said, touching his forehead.

"Just get out!" Harold cried. "Cunt!"

Emily looked at Markus.

"You should probably leave," he said.

Emily would wonder, later, if Markus had meant those words the way they sounded. If he actually meant that they needed to look into this further and that wasn't going to be possible, given their emotions.

But it didn't come out that way.

Emily stared hard at the men, especially Dietrich, who watched her with a smile lurking under his expression, those three cuts from her nails across his bleeding forehead.

"The three of you," she said. "I won't forget this, what the three of you did. I won't."

"Your sister is one crazy bitch," she heard Harold say just before she slammed the door on her way out.

Emily walked angrily down the hall, refusing to calm. Wondered if her brother would come after her, console her.

He never did.

CHAPTER THIRTY

"After that night," Emily said. "I didn't see him until Mom died."

"That's exactly how I remember Markus," Melinda told her, anguished. "I feel like I should be sadder about what happened to him. But I can't. And I hate myself for it."

Emily realized her own foot was shaking. She couldn't stop it.

"What you said earlier," Melinda went on. "You're right. I've left people behind. But, Em, that work was killing me. I couldn't do it anymore."

It wasn't fair. Emily knew that.

She hated seeing Melinda suffer, just as much as she hated the thought of those women her sister had left behind.

No. It wasn't fair. And, still, she couldn't help herself.

"There are a lot of people out there," Emily said carefully, "who the Winterses are hurting. The women you used to help . . . women like that are being hurt by them. It was enough that Rebecca was willing to cross her own uncle to stop them. It was enough that Dani tried to find you after Markus was killed."

Emily recrossed her legs, set that shaking foot on the floor.

"We can stop all that, Mel."

But everything about Melinda, from her conflicted expression to the nervous way she rubbed her arms, seemed uncertain.

Emily turned Melinda's laptop toward herself.

"I need to find Dani," Emily said. "Victor Winters will get to me soon. And I'll never be able to hold him responsible for Rebecca's death, or that guy he killed afterward. But I know I can tie him to this."

Melinda nodded, sat next to Emily.

Closed the laptop.

"We don't need my computer," Melinda told her. "We just need to visit a few of my old coworkers."

They went out searching that night. The clichéd image of sex workers hanging out at street corners and waiting for cars to drive by still happened, Melinda explained to Emily, but nowadays most arrangements were made online. Daytime was just as busy, if not more so, than night. It was easier for married men, who made up a good portion of johns, to take an hour off their jobs than sneak away from their families in the evening.

So there was a chance they could find Dani at one of the safe houses or group homes Melinda's former colleagues ran.

"Your car smells so dang nice!" Emily told her as they drove into DC. "And you don't even have one of those tree air fresheners. What's the secret of your success?"

"It's because I don't let anyone eat in here," Melinda replied. "And speaking of my car, wait inside while I talk with people. I don't want someone seeing you."

"I was going to say the same thing," Emily told her. "But mainly because I don't want anyone to see me in this outfit."

She was wearing Melinda's mom jeans and a large sweater, which was dramatically different from the low-cut, tight clothes Emily preferred. She'd been complaining ever since she dressed.

"Okay, look," Melinda said. "I was actually going to donate that sweater."

"Just the sweater?"

"Quiet," Melinda told her. "And stay in the car while I go inside."

"*Fine*," Emily said. "I'll just hang out here, play with my phone. Does Grubhub deliver to cars?"

"No food!"

"No promises!" Emily replied gaily.

She was back to herself, Melinda noted. Emily seemed to flit between two moods. Either serious or irresponsible. And whenever she was serious, it was always about something that involved her past. As if she was trying to piece together memories.

Or craft new ones.

Melinda had seen this before in her work with broken women. So much in their lives was emotionally compartmentalized that their thoughts were broken into fragments, as if different people assumed different roles. And when those roles merged, there was a flash of anger or sadness or violence, a lack of control that often resulted in lashing out.

She wondered what else had happened to her sister.

They slipped into the city. Drove down North Capitol Street, away from the glowing white lights of the monuments, the buildings and road more disheveled the further they went. Finally pulled over and parked next to a building marked DC Comfort.

"You're going to wait here, right?" Melinda asked Emily.

"Uh-huh."

Melinda headed into the building. DC Comfort was a homeless shelter, and the woman who ran it, Eve Peterson, an old friend. Melinda stepped inside, glanced around at the little hallway leading to a large cafeteria, at the line of men and women waiting for beds. Felt the instinctive pull to head over to them, see if they needed help.

"Melinda!" She turned and saw Eve.

They embraced.

"I'll never understand," Melinda told her, their hands cupping each other's elbows, "how you don't look any older."

It was true. Eve and Melinda were approximately the same age, but Eve carried a natural sense of strength. And Melinda knew from experience how difficult it was to do this work and not have it weigh on you.

Some of it was in her style. Melinda's outfits had always been a mix of worn jeans and faded sweatshirts whenever she worked in shelters. But Eve was wearing a long black skirt and high black boots and a form-fitting red sweater. A lovely angular face. Dangling dreads.

"You know that whole 'Black don't crack' thing," Eve said. "Plus my friends are really good liars."

Melinda felt a welcome warmth. Hadn't realized how much she needed it.

"Thanks for seeing me," she said. "I didn't know if you would."

Eve seemed surprised. "Really?"

"I thought everyone was mad at me."

"Why?"

"Because I quit."

"Are you kidding?" Eve told her. "Everyone quits this gig."

"You haven't."

"I started late. I'm sure I'll go into, I don't know, real estate or some shit next year."

They laughed, and the laughter felt good.

"I could talk to you for hours," Eve said. "But not tonight. We should do lunch sometime."

"I'd *love* that," Melinda told her. "And I won't take up too much of your time. Like I said over the phone, I'm trying to find someone. A sex worker who goes by the name of Dani."

"You have a picture of her?"

Melinda shook her head. "She's short, maybe around five feet. Stocky, white, long dirty-blonde hair. Round face, blue eyes. No accent."

"And she's a sex worker?"

"Yeah. She was involved with Markus."

Eve didn't add to that.

"Dani was the person who told me Markus was dead," Melinda went on. "Then she tried to push her way into my home. She was scared."

"Really?"

"I didn't let her in," Melinda said guiltily. "And she left."

"Why are you trying to find her now?"

Melinda couldn't tell her the whole truth.

Just another lie, she thought, in a life suddenly full of them.

"I want to know what she was going to tell me," Melinda said, "about my brother. Would you mind asking around?"

"Of course not."

"Thanks, Eve. I'll let you get back to work, but I have one more question."

"Anything."

"Have you heard of a man named Victor Winters? A real estate developer in the area?"

"No. Why?"

"There's a chance he's involved in sex trafficking. He might be related to all this."

Eve frowned. "I don't know him. Haven't even heard the name."

"He works with a lawyer named Isabel Pike."

The frown deepened. "Her neither. Do you know anything else about them?"

"They're mysteries. But I have reason to believe they're involved in the business."

"So they're rich and dangerous and you're looking into them? Still fearless, huh?"

"Fearless?" Melinda was taken aback. "I quit."

"Yeah, but you never took shit when you were working." Eve didn't give Melinda a chance to counter. "Victor Winters and Isabel Pike. I'll ask around. And, Melinda? Be careful."

"You, too, and I will."

Eve embraced her unreservedly. Melinda was hesitant, still thinking about the half-truths, the complication they brought, especially given how Eve saw her.

She felt guilty hugging Eve.

Melinda had lied to everyone she knew and loved.

Except, strangely, Emily.

◆　◆　◆

That was the first in a series of stops Melinda made. Each time she returned to the car without a lead, but with hope.

"Nothing?" Emily would ask.

"Nothing *yet*," Melinda would tell her.

Emily noted that her sister's mood lifted as the night went on, as if being reminded of her past was helping her. Healing her.

She didn't share her sister's optimism, although she did appreciate her efforts. But Emily began to realize that, even if Melinda's contacts found something, it wouldn't be in time.

After all, she needed to expose an entire criminal operation.

All the Winterses needed to do was find her.

Emily was growing tired of waiting in the car. After the seventh stop, she finished off a packet of Goldfish she'd hidden in her purse, opened the door, and stepped out into the chilly night. Walked down the dark street. A few tents were pitched, sleeping bags sprawled over grates raspily blowing out steam.

Emily thought it would be nice to slip a few dollars into the bags or tents, but she hadn't brought any cash. Then she remembered Melinda's purse was in the car.

She walked back and passed a vacant lot. Noticed a sign:

A WINTERS PROPERTY
COMING SOON

Hello my ragtime gal, Emily thought and walked into the lot. More tents and sleeping bags were scattered around. She made her way through them.

Melinda had told her what she'd learned about the Winterses' development company. How it specialized in strip malls. Promised to make undesirable areas desirable.

"Ugh," Emily had said. "Gentrification."

"I don't know," Melinda told her. "It brings in money and jobs. More money and more jobs mean better schools and services."

"But it feels like the suburbs coming to the city."

"A little bit, yeah."

"Hey." A man interrupted Emily's memory. "Want to make money?"

He was kneeling next to one of the tents.

"Sorry?"

"I could put you to work." He stood. "Ass like that."

"Leave me alone, cabrón."

"Give me a quick taste. I'll tell you how much you can make in a night."

"Go away!" Emily left the lot. Turned down the street.

Headed into an alley and heard him behind her.

When he stepped inside, her foot smashed his knee.

"Fuck!"

Emily stood behind him, wrapped her arm around his throat.

"Do you know a woman named Dani?"

"What?"

"Do you know a woman named Dani?" Emily pushed him toward the wall, her arm still around his neck. Held the back of his hair, rubbed his face hard into the brick.

"Dani? Does a woman named Dani work for you?"

He tried to answer, but she was grinding his lips and teeth into the wall.

Emily yanked him back by the hair, brought the back of his head to the ground.

"I don't know her, I promise!"

His scraped, bleeding face looked like a child had scribbled red all over it.

Emily left him in the alley, headed back to Melinda's Jeep. She calmed her breathing and rubbed her raw knuckles where the brick had bruised them. A plan began to come to her, a hazy horizon turning visible.

She was mulling it over when Melinda emerged from another shelter.

"Nothing?" Emily asked as her sister climbed into the driver's seat.

"Nothing *yet*," Melinda said.

"Listen," Emily told her. "I got an idea. And it's perfect and can't go wrong."

"What is it?" Hesitancy in Melinda's voice.

"I need you to set up a meeting with that Isabel chick."

CHAPTER
THIRTY-ONE

DC's Dupont Circle was always crowded, which was why, Isabel Pike assumed, Melinda Peña had asked to meet her here. Even on a chilly November day, the park was packed. Traffic traveled in a noisy circle as drivers did their best to navigate the stoplights and sudden lane changes. Inside the circle, men and women congregated at the base of a fountain, eating lunch.

Isabel walked over to the central fountain, handbag slung over her shoulder, notebook in hand. Her phone buzzed. She pulled it out of her jacket pocket.

Let me know what she says.

Victor.

Of course, she replied. When can I see you?

Isabel watched the screen, waiting for his next message.

"Ms. Pike?"

Isabel looked up. Melinda was approaching.

"Ms. Peña." She slipped her phone back into her pocket.

"Please, call me Melinda."

Isabel could tell Melinda was waiting for her to offer the same courtesy.

She stayed silent.

"Thanks for meeting with me," Melinda said after the moment passed. She seemed unsure of herself, as if searching for the right words. Or, Isabel thought, trying to remember rehearsed lines. "I wanted to talk to you about Emily."

"That's a good idea."

"Can we talk over there?" Melinda pointed across the park, to an empty bench underneath a bare tree.

"I prefer this one." Isabel indicated a bench next to them.

"Okay."

The two women sat, Isabel intentionally sitting close to Melinda, eliminating any hope for privacy.

"Why did you bring me here, Melinda?" Isabel asked. "What do you need to tell me about Emily? I don't have much time."

As Isabel had expected, Melinda was taken aback. People didn't do well with a sudden deadline, even one arbitrary or artificial. Subconsciously, they responded to the urgency.

"I think Emily is who you said she was. Three Strikes."

"Of course she is," Isabel snapped, continuing the push. "I wasn't waiting for proof. She's a dangerous, delusional criminal."

"I had to find out for myself."

"Then I hope you also found out for yourself that she's the kind of person who causes suffering, Melinda." Isabel used her first name to increase urgency. "The kind who sees violence as acceptable recourse."

Melinda nodded. "I know. And she needs help."

"Help? She killed Rebecca Winters."

"Maybe," Melinda said. Isabel turned wary. That kind of admission should resonate, but Melinda spoke matter-of-factly.

Did she know more than she was revealing?

"Maybe?" Isabel asked.

"I mean, I know she could have. She's my sister, though." Melinda looked at Isabel, as if for empathy.

Isabel offered none.

"So I want to see if you can help me," Melinda said. "I don't know how to reach Emily. I tried calling her, asked friends of hers. No one knows where to find her." Melinda paused. "But I do know someone who might help. A woman named Dani."

"Dani?"

Melinda looked directly at Isabel as she spoke. "I think she was friends with Emily. And she was involved with my brother. Rebecca told me about her."

Isabel opened her notebook, turned it against her crossed legs so Melinda couldn't read what she was writing. "What's Dani's last name?"

"I don't know."

"You only know her name is Dani?"

"She was a sex worker. But I didn't know her back when I was doing social work."

Isabel made a point of not reacting, of continuing to write in her notebook. "Why would you expect me to know her?"

"I mean, you're like a detective, right?"

"I'm an attorney," Isabel corrected her.

"But you said you do a bunch of different things. Like, you handle all of Victor Winters's affairs. Even the nonlawyer ones."

"Are you implying"—Isabel added incredulity to her words—"that Mr. Winters has an association with sex trafficking?"

"No," Melinda said. "I'm just saying you seem good at your job, and maybe you could help me find her."

A miscalculation, Isabel realized. She'd overreacted, risked putting an idea in Melinda's head that didn't belong there. She thought about clarifying it somehow.

Decided it was best to let her comments lie.

"I'm not a detective, Melinda. If I was, I'd have brought your sister to the authorities by now."

"I want to help you bring her to the authorities," Melinda agreed. "I mean, if she really did do something to Rebecca. But I need to talk to her first, and I think Dani is the best way to find her. Dani came to my house, she's the one who told me about Markus. Rebecca told me that Emily had known her."

Something about Melinda's words didn't ring true to Isabel. She turned her notebook to the pages of their first meeting, glanced at her notes.

"You never mentioned this visit from Dani when we spoke the other day," Isabel said.

"I guess it didn't occur to me," Melinda replied. Isabel heard uncertainty lurking behind her words. "I mean, the whole thing caught me off guard."

"So you're asking me to help you find a sex worker named Dani, in the hopes that she can lead us to your sister?"

"She's the only lead I have."

"But she's not the only lead I have. Your sister has coworkers, friends, a boyfriend. Your father lives locally. Your mother had family in Panama."

"I talked to a lot of those people," Melinda said uneasily. "No one knows where she is."

"You talked to your father?"

"Yes."

"About Emily? Recently?"

A pause, so slight Isabel might not have noticed it unless she'd been looking.

"Yes."

"I also spoke to him," Isabel said. "This morning."

"You did?"

She observed the surprise on Melinda's face.

"I called him to ask about your sister. He said he hadn't heard from you in a week. And from her? Years."

214

"Look, I—"

"Melinda, are you hiding something?"

Melinda was rubbing her own wrist. Isabel doubted she even noticed.

"It's not—"

"I thought you wanted to help your sister."

Personally, Isabel found interruptions in conversation annoying, but they were an excellent way to lead someone.

"My father and I don't have the best relationship," Melinda said quietly.

"I'm sorry," Isabel said, although she wasn't. "That's none of my business."

She kept talking before Melinda could agree with that sentiment, try and get an upper hand.

"I cared about Rebecca," Isabel lied. "And I don't know what your sister's going to do next. You understand that, right? The kind of danger she's in?"

Melinda nodded. She was close to breaking, Isabel could feel it.

"Hey, Sis."

Isabel turned.

"Who in the fuck are you?" Emily asked.

Isabel glanced back at Melinda. She seemed just as surprised.

"Emily Peña?"

"Yeah."

"We were just talking about you."

This was completely unexpected. And unless Melinda was that good an actress, which Isabel doubted, she was just as dumbfounded as she appeared.

"What were you saying about me?" Emily asked. Her eyes were impossible to see behind large sunglasses.

"Why don't you sit down?" Isabel asked back. "I'd like to talk with you."

"Nah."

"Emily." Melinda's voice was strained. "What are you doing here?"

"Yes," Isabel said. "How did you know to find us?"

"Heard you were looking for me, Mel," Emily said easily. "Went to your house, saw your Jeep heading here. You didn't see me behind you?"

"I guess not." Melinda glanced back at Isabel, her expression a mix of worry and helplessness.

Isabel ignored her. Turned her full attention to Emily.

"My name is Isabel Pike. I'm an attorney for Victor Winters."

"Oh that fucking guy."

Isabel felt her muscles tense.

"His niece, Rebecca, was murdered. I believe you know something about that."

Emily stared right back at her. "No idea what you're talking about."

"Several of his associates, including a distant cousin named Jon Winters, have recently been attacked."

"Sounds like he's hanging out with the wrong people."

"Emily," Melinda said. "Please."

"It appears all of the attacks were perpetrated by the same woman," Isabel went on. "A vigilante who goes by the name Three Strikes."

"Well, that just sounds awesome."

"Not when it results in someone's death. Or people being maimed."

"Depends on the people, right, Bella?"

Isabel thought about Victor's voice over the phone, the damage to his eye. Anger flashed like lightning. "My name is Isabel. And whoever did this is going to pay, and pay dearly."

Emily leaned over, her face level with Isabel's.

Melinda flinched.

Isabel didn't.

She just stared at her own reflection in Emily's sunglasses. Tried to see through it, and couldn't.

"Or maybe," Emily said, "you should be careful with who you're fucking with."

"I'm not the one in trouble with the authorities."

"I know a bunch of people who'd disagree with that, Bella."

Isabel kept her gaze measured. "Sorry?"

"I know about the trafficking. I know what your boss is doing."

Isabel didn't move. "You don't know anything."

"I know what he's doing and what he did to my brother. Markus was a piece of shit, but he didn't deserve that. Your boss is in all sorts of trouble. And you'd better steer clear unless you want to get dragged down with him."

Fear and anger in Isabel were twisting together, writhing, forming something else.

Hate.

"You've hurt people I know," Isabel said. "I won't forget that."

"I don't want you to."

That hate was like water rising inside of Isabel, drowning her. "You shouldn't test me. You might end up getting the fight you want."

"When?"

"Soon."

"Why wait?"

"Emily," Melinda said, and the terror in her voice woke something in both women. Brought the sounds of Dupont Circle back. People talking, cars driving.

"See you soon, Bella."

Isabel stared at Emily as the other woman walked away.

"I didn't know she was going to show up here," Melinda said, her voice still weak.

"I believe you."

"She doesn't know . . . ," Melinda started, and stopped. "Please don't hurt her."

Isabel still felt that anger but it was leaving, like the receding sound of a smashed cymbal. She took a deep breath, steadied herself.

"She's going to contact you," Isabel told Melinda. "When she does, it's imperative that you let me know."

Melinda picked up her handbag.

Something bothered Isabel as Melinda left, but she couldn't figure out what it was. Like staring at a page with a misspelled word but being unsure which one.

Then it hit her, a realization so sudden and startling that Isabel almost hurried after Melinda. But she thought more about it and reconsidered. Decided to save this clue for when she needed it.

Emily *was* in contact with Melinda, much more than Melinda had admitted.

She was wearing the same black string necklace, with the gold half-loop pendant, that Melinda had been playing with when Isabel questioned her the other day.

CHAPTER THIRTY-TWO

"What the fuck shit were you thinking?"

Emily took a step back from Melinda.

"I think you put an extra word in there," Emily said.

Melinda was pacing in front of the patio doors in the basement. She'd been waiting for Emily to come home . . . after driving home herself and realizing Emily had taken Rick's car to follow her to DC. Without asking him. Or her.

"That wasn't the plan!" Melinda exclaimed. "You weren't supposed to come!"

"I wanted to say hi?"

Melinda sat down hard on the couch, pressed her forehead into her hands. "I was going to get her to find Dani for me."

"She's still going to do that. Probably. Actually, I didn't hear. Do you think she's going to?"

"You can't be this way right now," Melinda said. "You need to be better than this."

"I'm exactly who I need to be right now."

"All you had to do was wait."

"You were on the ropes, Mel," Emily said. "I was watching your face."

Melinda didn't respond. Emily wasn't wrong. The entire meeting with Isabel Pike had put her on edge. She'd felt out of control from the start.

"Something else is bothering you," Emily said. "What is it, Sis? You can tell me, boo."

"The way you talked to each other. The violence. All the lying I'm doing. Everything."

"You're not doing anything wrong," Emily reassured her. "I'm not either."

"And Rebecca died. And Jessy died."

"Yeah."

"And I haven't even talked about this with anybody. I haven't told anyone what I'm going through. I'm scared and I'm angry and I'm sad and I'm lying so much. About everything. I can't keep living like this."

"I get that," Emily said.

The two sisters were silent.

"You'd make a hot redhead," Emily told her.

"What?"

"I went blonde years ago." Emily touched her hair. "It's the best. And I've always thought you'd make a good-looking redhead. I hate gingers, but you could pull it off."

"Emily, what the fuck are you talking about?"

"I did it myself. Bought the hair dye at CVS and did it in the kitchen. We should do it tonight!"

Melinda stared at her sister. "I'm not looking for a disguise. Or to change who I am."

Emily grimaced. "Really?"

"Hey."

"At least buy new clothes?"

"Shut up."

As random as Emily was, it helped a little.

Her sister was good at providing a distraction. For others. And herself.

Emily had always been like this, able to take a failing grade or a punishment from her parents and find some way to soothe it, shift pain somewhere else. She did it too much, of course, to a dangerous level of avoidance and lack of self-awareness. But, right now, Melinda felt it was a better defense mechanism than anything she had.

Still, Melinda wondered how it was possible that so little bothered her sister. Those threats between Emily and Isabel felt like bees hovering, and they stung when she remembered them.

It was sickening seeing two people so eager for violence.

Two people desiring death.

"We'll use the kitchen sink!" Emily was telling her. "It'll be fun!"

Melinda looked at her.

There was nothing but a strange happiness on Emily's face.

Melinda had seen it before.

◆ ◆ ◆

Two years ago Melinda had been smoothing a tablecloth, trying not to act on the sounds of her father sobbing in his bedroom. Every time she'd knocked on his door, he'd asked her to go away. She knew her father's grief had turned into anger at her, anger because the sudden death of her mother had gutted him, left him inconsolable. Seeking answers and, since he couldn't find any, blame.

She'd received the phone call days earlier, the phone in her hands and then on the floor. Melinda standing alone in her silent apartment, a shadow of herself.

She'd never been close with her parents, and that distance from her mother had felt like a slow ache. Melinda wanted that relationship, the intimacy that so many of her girlfriends shared with their moms, a closeness they'd discovered after college, as adults. The daily texts, weekly calls, lunches. But Melinda's mother always seemed controlled by her father. Not in an abusive manner, but a humble acquiescence. She was loving and caring, but ultimately deferred to whatever Frank Peña wanted.

And because Frank was distant from Melinda and Emily, their mother was distant from them as well.

Her sudden death had dug a deeper hole than Melinda could have known. Now that she was gone, Melinda regretted not fighting through her father's resistance, forcing her mother to become her friend, doing whatever she needed, sacrificing whatever stupid pride had held her back. Ever since that phone call, sorrow had informed Melinda's thoughts and actions and words, an almost physical weight pressing her down, suffocating.

She hadn't said much to her father when she'd seen him that morning, could hear the resentment in his hoarse voice, the way he avoided looking her in the face. He kept slipping into his room to cry, until, finally, he refused to emerge.

Instead Melinda sobbed with her two aunts who had arrived from Panama the day before, the three of them in one long, shuddering embrace. The aunts barely spoke English, and Melinda had lost touch with Spanish, but it hadn't mattered.

They helped her set up the funeral reception, framed pictures of her mother placed on a long table in the living room, arroz con pollo and bread cooking in the kitchen, creased and faded illustrations of saints and the Virgin Mary and a long wooden crucifix.

"Melinda!"

She turned toward Markus's voice, surprised by the shout. She hadn't heard him come into the house. One of their aunts yelped.

Melinda's expression tightened when she saw him. The tears she'd wept froze.

"You fucking called the cops on me?"

She glanced at their aunts, the women's eyes and mouths open.

"Let's not do this now," Melinda told him. "This isn't the time."

"You had no right."

She felt a flare of anger in her face, saw he wanted it. And she saw something else through his rage. His inebriation. The slight sway as he stood, the uneven roughness in his words.

"You know what you did," Melinda told him.

"That was my business. Not yours."

Melinda looked at their aunts. "Perdón," she said in her unpracticed Spanish. "Mi hermamo y yo necesitamos hablar. ¿Dame un minuto?"

"Sí, sí."

"They don't have to go," Markus said as they left the room. "Not like you can hide what a massive bitch you are."

That flare again. This time, it stayed. "So the cops came by?" Melinda asked. "Was it at one of your concerts? Did they pull you offstage?"

Markus took a step toward her. "They came to my place. Told me someone said I was paying whores. Gave me a warning."

"A warning? They should have put you in jail."

"That's what you wanted, right?"

"I trusted you! I introduced you to those women to help them! How could you do that to me?"

"How could I . . . ? You tried to have me fucking arrested!"

"If you see one of those women again, I'll do more than try."

"You want that, right? You want my life ruined?"

"You're ruining your life, Markus. Not me."

"You can't stand it, can you?" Markus asked. "I made it, and you're nothing. And you were always the smart one. You were always the good kid. You loved making me and Em look bad. Now you can't stand that one of us is doing better than you."

"What are you talking about?" Melinda asked.

"You couldn't even keep these women safe from me," he said. "You failed in every way."

"Shut up, Markus."

"I'm shitting all over your life, and you can't stand it."

"You're drunk," Melinda told him. "You're drunk, and you're a mess, and you've always been one. And I can see it, and everyone else will too."

"It's killing you, what's happening to me."

"I don't care if you're successful, Markus!" Melinda exclaimed. "I don't want you to fail. Or suffer. You're my brother! But you want to know what I hate?"

"Tell me."

"These glowing reviews and profiles talking about what a great guy you are, how you have this understanding of love? It's such bullshit. You don't know the first thing about caring for someone else. You only care for yourself. You're not even here for Mom. You're here because you're pissed off that I caught you and almost showed the world who you really are."

His hands were fists.

"I know it," Melinda said. "And Emily knows it. And so does Rebecca."

"Mel . . ." The pain in his voice surprised her.

"Stop seeing those women!"

"You can't handle it," Markus said distantly. "They chose me. Mom and Dad chose me. Jessy chose me. Everyone chose me. And now these women are choosing me. Instead of you."

"Those women are hurt."

"They're mine."

She slapped him.

He punched her.

Melinda felt her nose snap under his fist, her tooth scraping his knuckle. Her knees buckled, collapsed.

And suddenly her brother was on top of her, her throat in his hands, her body bent over the table, Melinda scratching his face, one of his hands on her throat and his other hitting her face and chest and stomach and she was on the floor and he was crouched over her and . . .

Everything went away.

She looked up.

Emily stood over them.

She was glaring down at Markus's face, his curly hair firmly in her hand.

Emily's knee rose and smashed his chin. He fell back. He reached up and Emily's fists came crashing down, blindingly fast. It looked like Markus's face was going to break apart, his hands helplessly trying to cover him. And there was a weird light, an excited happiness in Emily's expression Melinda could never forget.

Melinda rose unsteadily, pulled her sister off.

Markus stumbled out of the room. Their aunts were hurrying back in, and he pushed past them, knocking one against the wall. Melinda staggered over to her aunt, helped her up as Markus ran down the hall, past the bedroom where their father was still sobbing, through the back door, into the yard.

Emily walked over to her.

Melinda pushed her away.

She couldn't look at her again, that nightmarish glee.

CHAPTER THIRTY-THREE

Rick smiled at Melinda as she walked into his office and closed the door.

"What's going on?" he asked.

"Do you have a minute?"

"For you," Rick replied, "I have all the minutes."

Good God, Rick was boring, but there was something blessedly simple, even attractive, about his workmanlike approach to life. His easy resolve.

It wasn't that he lacked passion, even if he kept it under the surface. Melinda remembered when a neighbor had once come over because of an emergency, asked Melinda to watch her son while she rushed to the hospital. "My father's dying," her neighbor had said, her face a blur of tears. "I don't want Sam to see him." And Melinda and Rick had found themselves with an uncertain six-year-old for the day.

Melinda had always thought of a child as a ten-thousand-piece jigsaw puzzle she had no desire to remove from the box. She didn't dislike kids, and she and Rick had loosely discussed the idea of having their own someday, but the urgency or longing other women experienced escaped her. In truth, Melinda often wondered whether she'd care if she didn't have children. And deeply worried about regretting her decision, either way, later in life.

She didn't even know if she could have a baby. She'd always thought her body would let her down. She'd had close calls: missed periods with boyfriends, a pair of terrifying months in her early twenties when she was certain a baby was growing inside her. Relationships where sex was constant, long weekends spent tangled in a man's arms and legs. But pregnancy had never happened.

Rick hadn't talked much about children either. Melinda had known he wanted a family someday, but it had seemed like something that would happen in due course, a life milestone along the lines of owning his first car, graduating from college, getting a job, buying a house. So Melinda was surprised at the change in his personality when they played with Sam. Rick crouched on the floor with the child, played with the toys Sam's mother had brought over, chased him in a game of tag that left Sam shrieking. *He's good with kids,* Melinda realized, and she'd felt a pang of sadness, sitting on the couch and watching them, sadness that this enthusiasm and abandon was something she didn't share.

"By the way," Rick told her, interrupting her memories. "Emily said she's dyeing your hair tonight?"

"What?"

"She borrowed my car to go to the store and pick up the stuff."

"Great." Melinda sighed. "Listen, about Emily. I need to tell you something."

"What's going on?"

"What's going on," Melinda repeated him. "Well, this is going to sound sort of crazy, but have you ever heard of, and I can't believe I'm saying this, a vigilante named Three Strikes?"

"I'm sorry?"

Melinda filled him in. She told Rick everything, feeling better and better as she did, like a balloon that had been dangerously close to bursting slowly losing air. She told him how Emily had sneaked into their house, the meetings with Rebecca, their fractured relationship with Markus, the visit from Isabel Pike, the encounter earlier that afternoon at Dupont Circle.

"Emily thinks the Winters family killed Markus," Melinda finished, "and so did Rebecca. But she can't prove it, so she's going to try to catch them on the sex trafficking. At the same time that the Winters family is trying to pin Rebecca's death on her."

Rick was leaning back in his chair, hands behind his head, elbows pointed like the tips of angel's wings. "And you're sure you're not high?"

"I wish."

"You were really with her this afternoon? You saw Emily talking to this Isabel Price?"

"Pike. Yeah. It was awful."

Rick changed his posture, rubbed the knuckles on his left hand with his right, a tic Melinda had first noticed when they'd started dating. "I knew something wasn't right."

"Yeah, but that's sort of obvious about Emily."

"Not with her, although she is strange. I meant you."

"Me?"

"I had a feeling you weren't telling me the truth about something."

"Oh."

"Now I'm almost relieved," Rick admitted. "I didn't suspect secret vigilante, but it's a lot better than anything else I was thinking."

Tears pushed at the backs of Melinda's eyes. She did her best to keep her face composed.

"But I am sorry," he went on.

"You're sorry?"

"Sorry you had to see that," Rick clarified. "That you're being put through all this."

"Rick . . . I lied to you. About Emily. Who she is. What she's doing." Melinda took a moment. "About what I'm doing."

"She's your sister, Mel."

"No! You can't just *understand* this! You need to—"

Rick rarely interrupted Melinda, but he did now. "This isn't the time for guilt," he told her. "You feel bad about lying, but you did what you thought was right. The way I see it, we need to help your sister. Even if she's a little weird."

"*Little's* a charitable word. But I don't understand. You're not scared? These are dangerous people. *She's* dangerous people. And the lying I did . . ."

Rick walked around the desk and embraced her. "We'll be okay," he said. "I promise you. Bad people rarely leave the shadows. There's more of us good people than there are of them. That's why they're weak and why we're strong. And why we'll be okay."

He kissed Melinda's numb lips.

"I love you," he said.

"I can't believe you're like this," Melinda told him. "You're the strongest person I know."

She'd never realized this before.

"I'm not that strong," Rick said. "I just understand why you did it."

Melinda blinked hard, stepped out of his arms. Looked past Rick, through the window in his office to the brown bare tree outside, the neighboring townhouse beyond it.

"Rick, I've been lying to you this whole time."

He nodded. "It's okay."

"Not just about Emily."

And now she finally saw fear in Rick's face. Her words had pushed past his strength, as if, Melinda realized, she was determined to ruin him. And everything he offered.

"Mel?"

Melinda sighed heavily. Dropped the very last precious thing she'd been holding. "I need to tell you about David."

CHAPTER

THIRTY-FOUR

"Emily?" Calvin asked, surprised. "Where have you been?"

"I know," she said. "I suck, I'm sorry." Emily glanced down the hall, didn't see anyone watching her.

So far, Emily hadn't noticed anyone following her since she'd left Melinda's townhouse and driven to DC. Not that Emily was trained to spot a tail, but she'd read a few articles online and remembered something from a spy novel about watching cars three or four vehicles behind her own.

She'd parked a block away from Calvin's building and walked up and down a few different streets. Hid in doorways, her hand in her handbag, holding her baton, waiting to see if someone turned the corner.

Nobody suspicious.

"I didn't know where you were." Calvin closed the door behind her. "I called, stopped by your place. Nothing."

"I'm staying at my sister's out in Virginia." Emily walked over to the living room window, looked out. She didn't see anyone suspicious on the street, no cars loitering in the parking lot. Calvin lived off U Street in a giant apartment building nestled near Adams Morgan, one of the hipper areas of the city, full of cool restaurants during the day, blaring bars at night. Emily understood the appeal of living here. She liked living somewhere that always seemed active, no matter the time. Found that energy weirdly comforting, especially compared to her sister's townhouse in McLean, where everybody seemed to go to bed at 8:00 p.m.

"And you didn't tell me about the new job," Calvin went on.

Emily turned from the window.

"What said who?"

"The job you're applying for with that nonprofit for the Nats? Strikes Out, or whatever? They called, told me I was a reference?"

Emily stared at him. Slowly comprehended what had happened.

Isabel Pike, or her people, had called Calvin to find out information about her. Pretended to be a prospective employer so they could ask all sorts of personal questions.

And they'd gone by the name "Strikes Out."

Which, Emily had to admit, was pretty cute.

"Right," she said. "Sorry, I should have said something. What'd they want to know?"

"The usual. Confirmed your name, phone number, address, that kind of stuff. Then some questions about your work history."

"Which you know nothing about."

"But I lie really well."

"That's all I wanted." Emily smiled as her mind raced.

How had they found out about Calvin? They must have located her employer, probably duped her landlord somehow. Talked to someone at her office and gotten them to name Calvin. Emily had mentioned him to her coworkers before.

Or maybe they were watching her apartment and had seen him when he stopped by. Followed him, found out who he was.

Or maybe Melinda had slipped and said something when she met with Isabel.

Emily would go crazy trying to think of how they'd discovered him. Better to think about the present.

"Hey," she said. "I need to run to that CVS around the corner. Want to take a walk?"

◆ ◆ ◆

She spotted the man with the Winterses right away. Waiting outside Calvin's building. Following them as they headed down the squat brick row houses on W Street.

Emily pulled out her phone, casually glanced at it.

"Give me a second?" she asked Calvin. "It's work."

"Sure." Calvin pulled out his own phone, scrolled through tweets.

Emily stepped into an alcove between houses, put her phone to her ear, waited for the man to walk past.

Then she stepped out, quick-tapped him on the shoulder.

"Hey."

She studied his face hard when he turned, trying to see if there was any reaction, any sense of recognition.

None.

"Can I help you?" he asked.

On second glance, he didn't look like the kind of guy who worked with a secret criminal organization. Glasses, thin tie, weathered slacks. Probably wrote for a DC think tank. Smugly answered *Jeopardy!* questions before the contestants did. That kind of guy. A DC archetype.

"Sorry," she said. "My mistake."

She headed back to Calvin, who was absorbed in his phone.

"Did you know him?" he asked.

"Thought I did."

"What's up with work?" Calvin was still staring down as they walked to the store. "And that Simon Glowalter?"

"You heard about that?"

"You're the one who told me. And then I saw something about it on the news."

"Really?" One of her press releases must have worked, which was a relief. She'd felt a little guilty about her distractions, her cursory attention to her other job.

Calvin slipped his phone into his pocket. "I was telling my mentor about it, and he said he thought for sure Glowalter was guilty."

"Trevor?" Emily asked. Calvin had an FBI agent prepping him for the rigors of the FBI examination, and he referred to him as his mentor, which Emily found unbearably charming.

Calvin nodded. "He said everyone at the office was talking about it the other day, after that news story came out."

"Huh." Unbeknownst to her employer, Emily had taken it upon herself to look into Simon Glowalter rather than risk helping a guilty man leave prison. She'd found his family and home in Winchester, Virginia, an idyllic town about an hour from DC. Driven through long stretches of trees and low distant mountains until she reached the small city. Gone to a mom-and-pop grocery store and struck up conversations with people, asking if they knew Simon, what they thought of his story.

Emily had talked to at least a dozen people that day, at the grocery store and then a bar, and all of them had expressed surprise at Glowalter's arrest. He'd been a churchgoing family man, hardworking, charitable, all the terms Americans typically used to describe someone as morally decent. Emily didn't put any stock in those words, but she didn't come across a thing to discount them. And neither, apparently, had the investigators looking into his case. Or the judge who set him free.

Emily had been pleased at Glowalter's release, enjoyed the virtuous feeling her work brought.

But now, listening to Calvin, she felt amateurish.

And defensive.

"People involved with the case reviewed it," she said. "Even her family said they were fine with his release."

"They didn't say they were *fine* with it," Calvin countered. "They said they wanted whoever killed their daughter caught. And that's probably not going to happen."

"Why wouldn't it?"

"This happened, what, five years ago? The best hope they have, at this point, is for someone to come forward. And if they haven't come forward yet, they never will. Besides, the cops have more current cases to look at."

"So you think he should have just stayed in prison?"

Calvin glanced at her. "I don't mean to upset you. I know New Paths did a lot to—"

"New Road."

"New Road, sorry, did a lot of work on this. And I think they do good work. I'm just telling you what I heard."

Emily tried to soften her annoyance as they reached the CVS. "It's okay," she said. "It's not you. I have a lot of stuff going on. New Paths would be a better name anyway."

She was proud of what the small organization did, fiercely so, but Emily had always considered her work with New Road nothing but a day job, something to pay her bills, give her a small sense of accomplishment.

Her real work was wearing the mask.

And no matter how bruised she'd left someone, no matter how sickened Emily felt after an attack, when a man had been stripped of his confidence and strength and was reduced to begging and his anguished pleas finally broke through her anger . . . she could always return to her work at New Road. Her day job was her saving grace, a necessary good to which Emily contributed. Necessary for society, and for her.

And when it was questioned or criticized, she was shaken.

Without that, what was she?

"Why are we here?" Calvin asked as they headed into the drugstore.

"Red hair dye. I'm dyeing my sister's hair tonight."

Calvin went to pick up some drinks, and Emily headed to the hair care aisle. Examined the dyes, trying to imagine which would look best on Melinda. Looked at her own hair in an overhead security mirror and grimaced. Her roots could use a touch-up.

In the store mirror, she saw the thin nerdy guy.

He'd been walking in the opposite direction, away from her. And now he was in the store.

Emily watched him glance down the aisle, walk to the end.

Near Calvin.

She hurried to the back, quickly and quietly. Pushed open the restroom door. Shoved the stranger inside.

"What . . . ," he exclaimed. She slammed the door closed.

One hand over his mouth, the other flicking her baton open.

Murder in her eyes.

"You know me?" Emily asked.

He shook his head, eyes wide.

"Why are you following me?"

She moved her hand from his mouth.

"I'm buying condoms!" he whispered urgently. "And Doritos."

Emily studied him.

"That's a weird combination."

"My girlfriend is really into—"

She interrupted him. "I'm good not knowing. Victor Winters."

"What . . . winters? Victor? Like *Game of Thrones*?"

"Isabel Pike."

"I don't know where that is!"

Emily peered into his eyes.

"You really didn't follow me here?" she asked.

A knock on the door.

"I'll be just a minute," Emily called.

"Em?" Calvin's voice from the other side. "Did you just shove some skinny dude into the bathroom?"

"Um . . ."

"Why'd you do that?"

"I'm wondering that myself," the man called out.

Emily retracted the baton, dropped it in her handbag. Opened the door. The man scurried past Calvin.

Calvin stared at her, leaning against the doorway, hands in his pockets.

"So," Calvin said. "What's going on with you?"

"I thought he was shoplifting."

"And you jumped him? Don't you think that's a little extreme?"

"Aren't you the one going into law enforcement? I'm doing your job, man."

"Are you?"

"Look, it's my sister." Emily's thoughts were everywhere—the Winterses, Calvin, condoms, Doritos. She forced herself to concentrate. "I told you I was staying with her, right? Some guy's been bothering her. An ex-boyfriend. He's really violent, and she's scared. It's made me jumpy. I'm sorry. I should have said something sooner."

"I get it." Calvin looked around. "Still, we should get out of here before you get arrested. We can go to my place. I'll fix you a Xanax on the rocks."

That almost made her smile. "Give me a second, okay?"

Emily closed the door to the restroom. Bit her lip. Looked at herself in the mirror.

For a moment, she didn't recognize the woman staring back. Eyes uncontrolled and helpless, lips nervous, near tears.

She reached into her handbag.

Looked back into the mirror moments later. Stared into the mask, the three stripes running down it like scratch marks.

She breathed easier. In control.

Emily took off the mask and stuffed it into her bag.

She left the bathroom without looking at herself again.

CHAPTER
THIRTY-FIVE

David opened the door.

Melinda felt like years had passed since she'd last seen him. As if he was from a different part of her life.

David still had the same boyish energy, the cheerful disregard Melinda had once found attractive.

But his enthusiasm dissipated when he saw her face.

"Melinda?"

"Rick left me."

Her voice felt wrung from her throat.

"What happened?"

"I told him about us."

"Oh," David said uncomfortably. "Was he mad?"

Melinda's eyes ached from crying. "I've never seen him like that before. Can I come in?"

He led her to his kitchen, pulled out a chair in the small breakfast nook, gave her a bottle of water.

Melinda pressed her palms against her forehead. A headache was starting, swirling.

"Why'd I tell him?" she asked helplessly.

"Why did you?"

"I was just—I was just tired of lying. So tired of it. But I shouldn't have said anything. It was one time."

David let a beat pass. "It doesn't sound like you're upset that you told him. Sounds like you're upset it happened."

Melinda wiped her eyes.

"Why did we do it?" she asked.

"I mean, you're pretty hot. Me too." David grinned.

But there was no humor for her now. "I don't like me very much."

"It was a mistake," David told her. "That doesn't mean it's who you are."

"What defines us better than mistakes?"

"Everything else." David reached over, placed his hands on hers. Days ago that touch would have stirred something. Now it was nothing but comforting. And barely so.

She moved her hands away.

"My whole family is like this," Melinda said. "Self-destructive as hell. My brother was an abusive drunk who brought his own death on himself. My father's pushing everyone away and living in depression and isolation. My sister's going to get herself killed. I just sabotaged my own future."

"What about your mother?"

"She died of a stroke, so her body pretty much self-destructed," Melinda said bitterly. "Another one of us killing ourselves."

"That seems like a reach."

"Rick was so hurt," Melinda said. "I've never seen him like that."

"He kicked you out?"

"He left. I asked him if he wanted me to go with him. He said no."

David watched her carefully. "Are you going to try to get him back?"

"I don't know if I can. I don't deserve him anyway."

"Do you want him back?"

Melinda's instinct was to say yes, of course yes, she loved Rick. And that was true. But there was a small hesitation inside, like a feather floating, that gave her pause.

There had been doubt.

Melinda had always wondered if Rick was what she truly wanted. If her questioning was a natural thing, if everyone in love had it. If doubt was human and permanent.

Was she really in love, that full, complete, total, give-every-thing-away love?

A married girlfriend of hers had once had a yearlong affair. When her girlfriend confessed it to her therapist, the therapist told her that, throughout her life, she'd always encounter people who were better matches for her than her husband. Melinda had remembered that, the way it dispelled the notion that there was one soul mate out there, someone perfect for you.

And so maybe that's why she would always doubt.

Was this what love was supposed to be?

"Melinda?" David asked again. "Do you want him back?"

"I don't know . . ." Her sentence trailed. "Maybe I wouldn't have done it if Rick was right for me. I've never been the type to cheat. This was my first time."

"I think if Rick was the right person for you," David said gently, "you wouldn't be here now."

"What do you mean? I'm not here because I want—"

David held up a hand. "I meant you'd be going after him."

"Oh."

Melinda hadn't thought about that.

"Or I'd give him his space," she offered weakly.

"Maybe."

"It's a lot to deal with," Melinda said. "My sister is staying with us. People are dying. We don't know when we—"

"People are dying?" David asked sharply. "What?"

"I told you my brother was killed. And his best friend was too."

"Jerri?"

"Jessy. And now his ex-girlfriend, Rebecca."

"Who's killing all these people?"

As helpless as Melinda felt, despite her need for honesty, she still guarded her answer.

"We're not sure."

And she hated it, this guarded feeling, this sense of shoving honesty away.

"What the *fuck*?" David said, and stood. "Melinda, what's going on with your life?"

His mood change was so abrupt that it surprised her, almost shook her from sadness. "It's not me. I'm not involved in any of this. It's my sister, and—"

"The sister you're letting stay with you?"

"Yeah."

"Aren't you scared?"

"Not really."

But David was, and it was a fear Melinda had seen before. The same fear that had been in Jessy's face, almost panic. As if he'd heard a gunshot and was waiting, midflinch, for the bullet to land.

And now Melinda wondered if she should be frightened, too, but fear simply wasn't something her family trafficked in. Markus had been too drunk and dumb to care about the trouble he was courting. Emily was too crazy. Melinda, too selfish.

All three of them, she thought, too self-obsessed.

Rick had become the constant in her life, the only person she'd refused to abandon, despite her own actions and guilt and doubt. And now he was gone. And she was the reason why.

Everyone had been right about her.

"Can you leave, Melinda?"

Shaken from her thoughts. "I'm sorry?"

240

David put his hands out, a gesture either pushing or pleading. "I don't want to be caught up in anything."

"David, you're not in danger."

"I'm already worried about Rick coming by and kicking the shit out of me. And now this?"

Melinda's mind flashed back to Rick calmly telling her, just hours ago, that they would be okay. That there were more good people than bad in the world.

And she looked at the fear consuming David.

She'd never truly recognized Rick's courage until today. It was something she'd taken for granted.

Like, Melinda thought, his love.

CHAPTER THIRTY-SIX

The passenger-side window of the Lexus rolled down. Dani stepped forward, tentatively leaned in. Regarded Isabel Pike warily. Glanced into the empty back seat.

"This for your husband or something?" she asked. "Both of you? You didn't say in your text."

"Get in," Isabel told her. "We're going for a drive."

"I don't go for drives," Dani said.

"You do with me. I know James. You and I need to talk."

Dani tensed at the name of her pimp. "You're a cop?"

"Who I am isn't important to you," Isabel said. "What I'm going to tell you is. Get in."

Dani did, reluctantly. Isabel smelled alcohol on the woman, the smell overwhelming her car. Held back a grimace.

"You're paying for this, right?" Dani asked.

Isabel didn't answer. Dani kept her seat belt off as Isabel pulled away from the corner, keeping an eye on the congested, constant traffic around her. Rosslyn bordered the edge of Virginia and DC, a forest of glass office buildings and apartments and hotels, a commercial developer's concrete dream. It was gray and underwhelming and depressive, and Isabel understood completely why Victor had targeted it for both of his businesses.

"I know you're not a cop," Dani said. "No cop can afford a ride like this."

Isabel ignored her. "You knew Markus Peña."

"Yeah," Dani said uncertainly.

Isabel didn't like her, but the immediate revulsion wasn't from the sex work. That didn't bother her. Much. It was the alcohol, how it reeked of desperation. Weakness.

"What about Markus?" Dani asked.

"There are questions about his death. Some of the people asking questions may come to you."

Dani clutched her seat belt. "They think I did it?"

"They think you have information about who did."

"I don't!"

"That doesn't matter." Isabel knew it was important to keep her voice calm, confident. Present someone with worrisome news, but give them something to cling to.

"I told you that I know James," Isabel went on. "I can make your debt to him disappear."

"How?"

It was a common scam, one of the fundamental practices in pimping. Place someone in debt, and they were tied to you. And if you could conflate that debt with loyalty, the way some pimps did, the victim would be tied to you forever. At most, they'd feel a remote sense of unease. But they'd remain.

"I need you to contact one of Markus's sisters. Melinda Peña."

"I'm not sure I know her," Dani said carefully.

Isabel knew she was lying but understood why. "You do know her. I want you to leave a note at Melinda's house asking her to call you. When she does, you're going to tell her you're on the run and scared. Set up a time to meet with her. And then tell James when and where the meeting will be."

"That's it?"

They were rounding the block, getting close to the apartment building where Isabel had picked her up. "Once the meeting happens, you're free."

"That's all I have to do? Ask Markus's sister to meet with me? And then I'm done?"

Isabel nodded.

"James promised me before that I'd be out," Dani said. "But then he wouldn't let me go."

"He's not promising you anything this time," Isabel said. "I am. Drop the note off tomorrow."

"What do you want it to say?"

The room was so dark that Isabel couldn't see Victor. He was just a shadow sitting in a chair on the far side of the bedroom.

The distance hurt.

Isabel wanted to tell him it didn't matter, that the loss of his eye wasn't something she cared about. But she knew better than to try and comfort him. That approach repelled Victor. He had to heal on his own.

The loss of his eye. The loss of his niece.

"Where are we?"

There was no pain in his voice. His tone was firm. A sign that he was recovering. She was grateful.

"Dani will drop the note off tomorrow. And tell James when a meeting's scheduled."

"Why not grab Melinda now? Use her to bring out Emily?"

Victor always did this. Quizzed her, made sure Isabel knew every step, so thoroughly that nothing was left to chance. Went over every detail until the plan was a dog-eared book in her mind.

"I can't guarantee Melinda can find Emily," Isabel told him.

"You mentioned the necklace."

"There's a chance they have identical jewelry. Not uncommon for sisters."

Victor mulled that over.

"So Dani sets up this meeting," he said. "Says she's worried the people who killed Markus are going after her. And you think Emily will just show up?"

"Emily's clearly watching Melinda. I'm hoping she'll find out about the meeting, follow her sister to it. The same way she did when I met with Melinda."

A memory of that meeting in Dupont, a taste of the hate Emily roused in her, like a sour candy in her mouth.

Isabel cleared her throat. "Emily thinks Dani will tell her you're involved in sex trafficking. And that she can use that to go to the authorities."

A soft scratching sound, rough but pleasing. It broke through her anger, brought out something else.

"Are you rubbing your chin?" Isabel asked.

"Why?"

"I like it when you do that."

Isabel knew Victor would ignore the admission.

But she'd needed to say it.

"I still think you should send some killers to Melinda's house," Victor said. "Draw her sister out, put a bullet in them both."

"That's not what this calls for," Isabel told him, saying the rebuke carefully. "If you want Emily, then we have to bring her to us. We can't find her, she runs too well. But we can make her run in our direction."

"What about her sister?"

"We'll let Melinda know that if she tells anyone what we did to Emily, then her father's next. And after him, her boyfriend. Keep the wound fresh whenever she thinks about it."

"Wounds heal," Victor said. "Give it a couple of months, then kill her too."

That scratching sound again.

And there was that hurt, that lonely hurt.

Isabel closed her eyes, even though it was already dark.

CHAPTER THIRTY-SEVEN

Dani gripped the crumpled note in her pocket as she walked down Rosslyn's long cold streets, high buildings on either side, the road crowded with cars. She was too distracted to pay attention to the men staring at her from their driver's seats as they lingered at red lights, almost as if they weren't conscious they were watching her. Like they were gazing out at land they owned.

Dani was used to those looks. She ignored them, lost in thought.

She didn't trust Isabel.

But this felt like the only chance she had.

Dani would never be free of what she owed James; that debt would never be erased. She barely made enough to cover her rent and food, not to mention her truck payments and a pair of insurmountable credit card bills. Often Dani felt like her debt was a giant chasing her, his footsteps smashing the land.

She didn't know if Isabel could really free her from James, give her a chance to start over, but it was worth a shot.

Her life was better now than it had been, but Dani still hoped for escape, that chance to make an honest break. She'd been doing this for almost a decade, and, yes, her life was better . . . but she wondered if that was because she was used to it. Used to poverty and loneliness and callous men and the lingering threat of James.

Her first pimp, Frankie, had taken her away from a lot of pain, from experiences like the one that had happened when she was fifteen, and she'd stuck with him. With Frankie, she'd followed a set schedule. Made a little more money. When someone wanted to hurt her, they had to ask him first—something Frankie made sure the men knew, and it was a rule they almost always followed. Dani didn't have to worry about getting paid because the men didn't pay her, they paid him.

And then Frankie had been replaced by James, and it was the same thing. Except that James worked for more dangerous men than Frankie ever had.

It was always the same thing, and she was never going to make enough money to leave. Dani knew that, but there was a part of her that clung to the hope she could, that she'd be able to do something else, like those stories of people who switched jobs and became teachers or lawyers or doctors. But Dani didn't have the money. Or time. Or faith.

She reached her truck, slid into the driver's seat, turned on the engine, waited for the cabin to warm. Connected her Bluetooth and listened to Markus sing a slow, low, rumbling version of "Key Largo," nothing but his voice and a violin sometimes accompanying him. Markus's sound like the night, the violin an occasional breeze.

Dani typed in the directions for Melinda's house. Thirty minutes. She scowled at her nearly red gas tank; then her mood lifted when she imagined buying a beer while the tank filled.

Dani pulled out of her space, slipped into a break in the line of cars. Drove away from Rosslyn and deeper into trepidation, the sense that she was heading toward something irreversible.

But what choice did she have?

Outside. She had to stay outside of whatever was happening with this terrifying Isabel chick and Markus's bitchy sister. Something was happening that was bigger than her. Dani knew that and knew that the only way to make it through was to stay distant. She'd fucked up before, gone to Melinda's house after Markus died, needing something . . . a reminder of him, a way to share the sadness overwhelming her. And found nothing there.

She'd hoped for empathy, ended up sprawled on the sidewalk.

Dani had expected more from his family. After all, Markus had been one of the only ones to treat her well.

Most of the time.

She remembered their first dinner at Aldo's, a swanky restaurant in Baltimore's Little Italy. None of those men had ever taken her to dinner.

"So you're a singer?" she'd asked him.

Something was on his mind. Markus answered without looking up from his phone.

"That's right."

"I don't think I've heard any of your songs."

Now Markus looked up at her, as if incredulous. But he grinned. "No?"

Dani wondered if she'd offended him. "Sorry."

"Who do you listen to?"

"I listen to anything," Dani said, even though she didn't. "You ever heard of that old band Rare Essence? Lately I've been into them."

"You like that go-go mix, huh? The Chuck Brown vibe?"

"Who doesn't?"

Another grin.

"DC girl?"

"One of the only ones born there."

"And one of the only ones doing honest work."

"Speaking of that . . . ," Dani asked, "why'd you bring me here?"

"To Aldo's?"

"I mean, *me*. I always wonder about guys like you. I looked you up online."

"But didn't check out any of my music?"

"I was in a rush." Markus was still smiling. Dani went on. "It's not like you have to pay for ass." She took a bite out of a piece of bread. Garlicky and soft and gentle in her mouth. It tasted so good that it nearly brought tears to her eyes.

"Why'd I bring you here?" Markus put his phone back into his pocket, took a moment before he answered. "Because I assume there's no bullshit with you."

"I get—"

The waiter came by with two menus. Markus glanced sharply at Dani. She stopped talking. After they'd been told the specials and the waiter had left, Markus nodded. She resumed.

"I get that. No bullshit."

"So why do *you* do what you do?" he asked. "You like the no-bull-shit approach too?"

He took a sip of wine; she did the same. It was a liquid jewel in her mouth. Dani kept it there for a moment before she swallowed.

"It's more that I like the money."

"Not a fan of the work?"

Dani smiled. "Not all guys are like you."

It was a practiced line, one she always used. The planting of a notion, an attempt to make a man think of himself as kind and com-passionate so he'd follow that role later.

A safety measure.

But Dani already felt safe. Perhaps it was the fancy restaurant, or because he was a public figure . . . although she'd been with athletes and actors and politicians and knew they weren't different from any other men.

But there was something more to tonight, something in the open way Markus had treated her, a vulnerability she noticed. In his smile. Behind his smile.

A shadow of hurt.

After dinner Markus drove them to his condo overlooking the harbor, and they finished a third bottle of wine as they listened to his music. They sat on the couch and kissed, and she led him to his bedroom. It was a night of falling asleep, waking, losing themselves in each other and falling asleep and waking again, exhausting and lovely. Dani nearly broke a promise to herself that had been easy to keep, to never let herself come with a client, even though she felt the shuddering start, her arms suddenly clutching him, almost surrendered to the sensation until Markus cried out the name "Rebecca" and his face fell to Dani's shoulder and he wept. Her feeling was suddenly gone, like an unseen door in a house closed. But she did hold him.

They saw each other again, two nights later.

Dani learned everything about Markus. Studied him online, rather than the quick scan she'd done earlier. She listened to everything Markus sang, nearly memorized his Wikipedia page, read through mentions of him on social media (he had accounts, but she could tell someone else posted for him). She was more cautious that second night, more reserved, until she sensed her hesitation was losing him.

There was a Rebecca somewhere in his past, long ago or recent, and Dani knew she needed to be her. To have something this other woman did, some element that would give her control.

But she was hesitant as she tried to study Markus and saw his snarling anger emerge. So Dani had risked giving more of herself, but not too much. Had hoped she didn't lose him.

A car horn blared.

She'd been listing in thoughts, the way that always happened when she listened to Markus's voice.

The road to Melinda's townhouse was an exit away.

Dani turned off her music and wiped her eyes.

Markus had been so much more to her than he realized. He was escape, the hope for escape.

She would tell the new girls she met in her business to find something like this, to try and become some man's fantasy, because the only thing men wanted was fantasy. She told them to exert some control, make that control part of it, even though you never had control. Dani told them what had happened to her at fifteen because, desperately, she never wanted it to happen to them. That time when she'd been driven to North Carolina to work near an area of new construction. The sleepless nights of men lined up outside her room, sore and burning mornings, nauseous afternoons, and then those nights of endless men standing outside, shuffling back and forth, waiting their turn. She'd glance at them through the crack in the window, hoping to see when the line ended, hoping the nervous ones would decide not to go through with it.

But they had all gone through with it.

She told those women to never work the construction sites or military bases or anywhere else where groups of men gathered and no law was nearby. Not that the law would help them, these women.

Some of them listened to her. Not all.

And that was the other place Dani's money went. Because sometimes those women returned to her, broken and desperate. And Dani would give them whatever she had. She couldn't help herself, even if she needed the money she gave them.

Sometimes she had blamed her generosity on being drunk and careless.

Sometimes she had told herself that she was going to end up with Markus and this little bit of money wouldn't matter. Because then money wouldn't matter.

But now Markus was gone. That hope was gone.

She parked her truck across the street from Melinda's house.

Took the note out of her pocket.

This was all she had left. Her last chance to leave.

And all Dani had to do was deliver it.

CHAPTER THIRTY-EIGHT

"What's the letter say?" Emily asked Melinda. They were in Melinda's basement, Melinda on the couch, Emily sitting cross-legged on the coffee table. Which would normally bother Melinda, but she had too much on her mind to care.

"It's not really a letter," Melinda said. She gave the paper to Emily.

they said your looking for me

im going to the cops but want to talk first

call me

Dani

A phone number was written below her name.

"What a crap haiku," Emily said.

"It's not a—"

"I'm kidding," Emily went on. "It's a trap."

"A trap?"

"Mel," Emily told her. "I told that Isabel chick I'm looking for Dani two days ago. Now Dani wants to meet? They're setting this up. And I'm insulted. They should have just come here, guns blazing."

"Wait, what?"

"Relax." Emily scratched her arm. "They can't kill us right after Markus's death. Not both of us. It'd be way too suspicious, especially once word gets out Rebecca's dead too."

"So what do we do?" Melinda asked, unease rising in her. She held a throw pillow against her chest, her chin denting it.

"Oh, I'm totally going to this meeting. You go ahead and give Dani a call, set something up."

"But you think it's a trap!"

"Yeah, but they're giving me what I need. Putting it out there, waiting for me to walk right into the noose. They have this bait, and, if I don't act on it, they'll just throw it away."

"You don't know that."

Emily shrugged. "It's what I'd do."

Melinda pressed her chin deeper into the pillow. "The conversations I've been having. My life is insane. I should be running away from all of this. Back to Rick."

Emily reached over and touched Melinda's leg. "Now, wait a dog-gone minute, Sis. You're going through a lot of shit lately, and you're not seeing things clearly. Rick left. You feel bad about what happened with David. Rebecca and Jessy are dead. I accidentally erased *90 Day Fiancé* from your DVR. It's a lot."

"And also Markus."

"Him too!" Emily exclaimed. "Forgot about him. Anyway, what I'm saying is you have so much stuff running through your mind that it's got to be a mess in there. You can't see clearly. It's a tornado of pain."

"I basically just feel really sad."

Emily frowned. "Don't mess up my metaphor. It's a tornado of pain. Which is why it's a good thing that I'm here. I can guide you through this."

"Em, I just want my life back."

The frivolousness in Emily paused. "What do you mean?"

"I miss what I had. Even if I wasn't sure about it, I miss it."

"You mean Rick?"

"I wasn't unhappy."

Emily studied her. "That's a low bar."

"Have you ever been in love?"

"No."

"Then you don't know. Maybe what I had is enough. Maybe it's what everyone has. Maybe it's what Mom and Dad had."

Emily considered it. "Dad's a total prick, but Mom did love him. Go figure."

"All I know for sure is that Rick deserved better."

"He did," Emily agreed. "You're right."

"If I didn't think it was going to work, I should have been honest."

"No one's honest," Emily said. "Rick probably had his secrets too. Check his browser history. I guarantee you'll feel better. Like, I found out Calvin's really into German women." Her face darkened. "Like, really."

"This isn't about the type of person he was, Em. It's about the type of person I am."

"You fucked up, Mel," Emily told her. "It's true. But if you knew it was wrong to leave him, you'd be running after him. He's gone, and you let him go."

David had told her the same thing.

"I don't know."

"It's not like you got caught," Emily went on. "You made a choice to tell him. Yeah, you felt guilty, but his happiness should have outweighed that guilt."

"That seems wrong."

"It was the right choice in the wrong situation. We've all been there."

Melinda stared at her sister. "I hate when you're deep."

"I *know*! I don't like it either. But you can trust what I'm saying. And you can trust me on the Wintersessessess. I don't know how to make it plural."

"Maybe," Melinda said again.

"This is the only play we have," Emily insisted. "If I can find Dani and get her to tell the cops about what the Winterses . . . is that right? If I can get her to tell the cops, this ends. All I have to do is find her. And they're dangling her out there. You have a chance to do what's right, you take it."

You have a chance to do what's right, you take it.

Melinda thought about what Emily had said.

"Sometimes I think about Markus," Melinda said quietly, "and I still get angry. I think about him, and it's like I feel how mad I used to get when he was alive, like I can't see straight. Like I'm going to black out in rage. That I'm going to do something I can't forgive myself for. Sometimes I even wonder if I was sleepwalking and went to his apartment and killed him myself."

"What?"

"I know that's crazy." Melinda looked at Emily uncertainly, unable to hide her worry. "But after seeing what those women I helped went through, and the nightmares I had, and then these moments of anger, it just . . . it just seems like, maybe I did? I'm scared of myself, Em. And I'm scared of the direction I'm going in. Maybe it's who I really am. Turns out we're kind of a violent family." She tried to smile, failed. "Maybe I need a mask."

Emily watched her sister and, more than anything, wanted to reassure her, to tell her she had nothing to worry about.

But she couldn't.

Part Four

A Song for Killers

I died beside you,
Inside you,
Despite you.

I touched heaven from hell,
Tried to pull myself up but fell,
Despite you.

You held me inwards,
Showed me blues are for killers,
Warmed me those winters,
The victor,
Despite you.

And though I'll never be whole,
The way you bought my soul,
Oh, this toll I owe,
I'm miserable,
Because of you.
These killing blues.

Excerpted lyrics from "A Song for Killers"
Written and recorded by Markus Peña

CHAPTER
THIRTY-NINE

Dani disconnected the phone. Handed it to Isabel. Isabel put the phone in her purse. She'd destroy it later.

"Am I done?" Dani asked.

"You'll be done after the meeting with Melinda."

"You really just going to let me go?" Dani asked moodily.

"Why wouldn't I?" Isabel was genuinely curious.

"Everything comes with a cost."

Isabel regarded her thoughtfully as Dani stared at the floor.

Isabel still didn't like her, the other woman's existential resignation and the constant, unwavering smell of alcohol. But that was a perceptive comment.

"The only cost for you," Isabel told her, "is lying to Melinda."

"Markus didn't mention her much. He didn't talk about his family." Dani bit her lip. "Can I ask you something? You're saying I'm done after all this, right? My debt's paid? I don't have to work for James anymore?"

Isabel nodded.

"Can it be some other girls too?"

"Some other girls?"

"Some girls I work with. Can what they owe be paid off too? If I do this?"

There was no chance. "How many others?" Isabel asked.

Hope in Dani's eyes. "Six of us?"

That would never happen, but Isabel knew she needed to pretend it could. Needed to give Dani the illusion that she had some power. Some value.

"Six is too many."

"Four?"

"Three."

"Okay." Dani accepted it, a grateful smile on her face. "If I can save some others, then I'm okay with lying to Markus's family."

"Give me their names, and I'll talk to James."

"They don't all work for James," Dani said. "Is that okay?"

Isabel's expression was nonchalant but, underneath that cool, thoughts swarmed like a shaken beehive.

If Dani thought Isabel could help other girls, then Dani must suspect Isabel's reach extended beyond James. She must have a sense Isabel operated, or was involved with, a network. Isabel thought she'd been careful. Thought she'd put enough false leads and multiple tracks to lead anyone with questions elsewhere.

But maybe too many people were dying.

Correction.

Too many of the *wrong* people were dying.

Isabel had learned long ago that a sex worker's death went unremarked. A john might ask questions, but not many, not when they had to hide what they were doing from their families. They might be sad but, a day later, those johns were with someone else.

"Why do you think I can help these women?" Isabel asked.

Dani waved her hand around the guest room in Victor's estate, the room Isabel had locked her in. "You're rich, right? You're, like, a DC lawyer, and you have this place, and the food and drinks you're giving me are, like, expensive-people shit. And you said you're paying off James. You're all the way loaded."

So there was a chance, Isabel realized, Dani had jumped to an assumption.

Dani just thought she was wealthy. She had no idea who Victor Winters was, no sense that she was actually being kept under lock and key at his house. She assumed everything belonged to Isabel.

"I can pay for your freedom," Isabel said, "and I can see about those three other women. In fact, give me all their names. Maybe I can help."

"Thank you," Dani said warmly.

These were important names, Isabel knew. They were likely the only people in the world who would care, days from now, that Dani was dead.

CHAPTER FORTY

The door lock clicked as Dani walked back to the bed. She sat on the mattress for a few seconds, fidgeted, then stood and walked over to the stocked minibar across the room. Poured herself two glasses of wine and carried them back to the bed.

Dani had never been in a bedroom like this. It was probably the size of her entire apartment and then some, and that didn't even include the closet or bathroom. Windows looked out onto long grassy fields, a fountain, a gazebo, a distant road with cars occasionally driving by. Too far away for the sound to reach her.

The windows were fixed in place. Dani had tried lifting them when Isabel brought her here last night, Isabel having surprised her at the gas station while Dani sat in her truck as the tank filled, her hands nervously playing with the bottle cap on one of the Millers in her lap. There wasn't a threat or coercion, just Isabel suddenly at her truck window, somberly asking Dani to step outside. Telling her she still needed her help, promising that she'd pay off James, but only if Dani would come with her.

"Listen," Isabel had said. "I won't force you, but I will say that if you want James out of your life, if you truly want the chance to start over, you'll come with me now."

Dani had hesitated.

"Or don't," Isabel said, "and find a different way."

Dani had left her truck parked across the street from the gas station, ridden to this mansion in Isabel's car. Isabel didn't speak and didn't listen to music, just kept her sharp eyes on the road.

A secure black iron gate opened for her. They drove down a long road, a humongous home growing more and more visible as they wound around curves.

"You live here?" Dani asked.

An assenting sound.

Dani had been terrified that first night, locked alone in this room. She drank greedily from the bar and tried the windows and the door, inebriated and stumbling. Restrained herself from shaking the handles, trying to break through the wood or glass. Isabel had taken her phone.

She'd turned on the television, watched reruns of old sitcoms, the same shows she'd used to watch when she was a girl and her mother would leave her at night in their small cold apartment. Those were her earliest memories, waiting and watching shows about people comically confounded by problems Dani was too young to realize. And the commercials. The endless commercials.

Dani had loved the commercials.

She'd stared at the depictions of cheerful lives in bright rooms, green grassy yards where excited shaggy dogs tumbled after tennis balls and families laughed together. A pretty mother in a comfortable kitchen marveling at bright-blue dishwasher soap. A young eager girl piling with her soccer team into a sparkling silver minivan. People dancing in happiness because of a sale at a clothing store. The promise of riches Dani didn't have. Riches that extended far beyond money.

When Dani remembered those days of early childhood, it was a wave of nights spent alone while her mother was out, staring lost into the television. Nibbling on a Pop-Tart or sipping milk from the thermos she'd left her, Dani peeing in her Pull-Ups because she was too scared to go down the dark hallway to the bathroom.

Waiting for her mother to come home. Waiting for the promise of those commercials to someday be realized.

But it wasn't all lonely or scary. There were the times her mother would surprise her by staying home, watching television with her. Reading with her. Playing with toys on the floor. Turning their apartment into an imaginary kingdom or house.

She never remembered waking without her. Not once.

Maybe that was why, Dani thought, she wanted to take care of her friends.

She didn't trust Isabel. But if Isabel was telling the truth, and if she released Dani after whatever Isabel needed next, then maybe she'd actually honor her promise. Pay off the debts of those other women.

And if Isabel was lying?

Then Dani would find a way to run. Find a way to escape her and the Winterses.

The Winterses. Dani had almost slipped, seen the flash of concern across Isabel's face, the careful way she'd asked, "Why do you think I can help these women?" But Dani knew exactly who Isabel worked for. Had known for a while. Remembered once when Markus had woken up next to her, late at night in his apartment. Dani had been squinting up at her phone. Turned it off when he sidled next to her.

"Everything okay?" Markus had asked.

"Work."

"They wondering where you are? You know I'll cover you for the whole night. Tell Frankie I got this."

"It's not Frankie anymore. Frankie left."

"Where?"

"No idea. Said it's not his choice."

"What do you mean?"

She was used to this curiosity from men about her business, like the men were tourists, glancing at her from inside a bus. "Some guy named James is taking over, that's what Frankie told me. He works for some dude named Victor Winters, even though Frankie told me not to tell anyone that. So don't say anything."

Markus had been rubbing Dani's back.

His hand stopped.

Something had provoked him. Something beyond curiosity.

"You know him?" Dani asked.

Markus stayed awake the rest of that night, first seething, then writing, then, near dawn, sleeping. Saying the name *Rebecca* in his dreams, like he always did, but differently. Not with sadness, but rage.

He woke and drank and, in a teary panic, finally told Dani who Rebecca was, their relationship, the baby. Her family. His torn heart.

Then Markus finished the bottle, quickly fucked Dani, wrote some more, fell back to sleep.

Dani looked over the pages Markus had written as he slept, his body facing the opposite direction with his knees pulled up and his arms wrapped around himself, curled like a sleeping shrimp. Markus fiercely hated for anyone to see his work before it was recorded, and Dani saw only the title before he started rustling:

"A Song for Killers."

And now she didn't doubt that the Winterses had killed Markus because of Rebecca. She figured Melinda was probably asking questions about her brother's death, and she'd be next.

And so Melinda's death would be Dani's fault.

That wasn't an easy cross to bear. Dani felt its weight as she sat in the giant bedroom, as she waited for the wine to blur her worry.

But if she was going to sell her soul, at least she'd save her friends.

CHAPTER FORTY-ONE

"So I want to say I'm sorry," Melinda finished. "I should have been there for you more than I was."

Frank Peña gave his daughter a hard stare, then set his cane against his recliner. Hobbled over and embraced her roughly, like he was collapsing and Melinda holding him up. His goatee tickled her.

"Okay, Dad," Melinda said. "That's a little tight."

Frank relaxed the embrace, stepped back. Still held her arms. "It's just what every parent wants to hear: *I'm sorry, Dad, I was wrong.*"

"I didn't say I was—"

"Just let me have this, Melinda."

"Fine."

He smiled at her. It felt like the first time Melinda had seen her father smile since she was a little girl, a welcome contrast to the lines unhappiness had etched in his face.

"I'm sorry for raising my voice the last time you were here," Frank told her.

Melinda noted that he wasn't apologizing for *why* he'd raised his voice. But even this apology was a step forward for their relationship.

Melinda indicated the television set.

"Wizards winning?"

"Hell no." Her father made his way back to his recliner, gently stretched out his leg on the ottoman.

"That's okay," Melinda said, settling on the couch. "I could use some consistency."

Her father had been a basketball fan all her life. She remembered the faded Bullets T-shirt he'd worn on weekends, and then the Wizards shirt after their name change. His disappointed groans at the television, game after game, season after season.

"What brought you here?" he asked. "That Rick going to call to get my blessing?"

For a moment, Melinda had no idea what he was talking about.

Then, grief.

She'd tried to contact Rick over the last day, relentlessly, left voice mails and sent text messages and emails. Would have driven to him, anywhere, if she'd had any idea where he was. But Rick was avoiding her.

Melinda didn't blame him. She should have reached out earlier. Run after him. Even if she doubted their future, Rick deserved more.

But Rick wasn't something Melinda could talk about with her father. The loss was too raw. She didn't want to cry again, not right now.

And she couldn't talk about the other feeling clawing around inside her. Melinda was scared of what was going to happen to Emily because Emily, like Markus, seemed destined to be killed. The meeting with Dani was tomorrow night, and Melinda kept thinking of Emily's certainty that it was a trap.

And if it was a trap, she doubted Emily could outmaneuver it.

Melinda gazed at her father's hunched figure, thought of the moment of peace her apology had given him.

No, she couldn't tell him anything.

"I felt bad about our fight," she said. "I'm tired of fighting with people."

"Most of my life has been spent arguing," he replied.

"That happens when you're an elected official."

She saw his pride at the words "elected official," light shining on his face. Frank tried to downplay it, but Melinda knew how proud he was of his public service.

"Some of those fights were worth it," he admitted. "Ours wasn't."

"No," she agreed.

They watched a Wizards player hit a teammate in the face with an errant pass.

"Do you regret fighting with your brother?" he asked.

Melinda held back her first reply.

"I regret a lot that happened with Markus," she said evenly.

Her father looked over at her, about to argue; then he settled for a small sad smile. "We should just leave that there, right?"

"I think so."

But he couldn't. "It was impossible for me to see all of you clearly," he said. "I don't know if that makes sense. This isn't right, but I always felt like I was friends with Markus and not you and your sister. Especially as he became his own man, someone so different from me. I was never as determined as he was."

Melinda could disagree but didn't. She remembered the long hours her father had spent in meetings, the thick documents he'd brought home over the weekend. The way he tirelessly educated himself on legal or governmental issues he hadn't been trained in. He'd been a model of determination, one each of his children followed, in their own way.

"And Emily was such a joker," he went on. "She'd get in trouble and joke her way out of it." He paused. "I suppose that worked, because she's been out of trouble for years."

That was the closest Melinda had ever come to actually choking.

"You and I, though," her father went on, after her coughing fit. "Maybe you and I are more alike than different. Always butting heads. Always trying to take care of everyone."

Crazy the way he saw his children. But Melinda supposed every parent had this blindness, their need to see things a certain way. Maybe it had something to do with the task of parenting, how the failures of their children reflected in themselves.

Melinda's phone buzzed.

"Expecting a call?" her father asked.

"Yeah. Give me a minute."

She pulled out her phone and walked into the dining room.

"Melinda," her friend Eve Peterson said urgently. "We need to talk."

CHAPTER
FORTY-TWO

"This place looks just as gross in the daylight," Emily said to Melinda.

"Don't say that inside," Melinda replied.

"Well, yeah."

Privately, Melinda didn't disagree with Emily. She hadn't seen the graffiti etched on DC Comfort the other night, the illegible tags and half-covered swears, done only for desecration.

And, unfortunately, it matched the rest of the exterior. Garbage on the street, crumbled stone steps. Iron bars loosely hanging over broken windows.

And the gleaming US Capitol up the street.

People often spoke of the concept of "two DCs" in regard to the separation of the monuments and politics from the rest of the city, but that was a falsehood. There were dozens of personalities within the neighborhoods: the wealthy aloofness of Georgetown; the transient workmanlike nature of Capitol Hill; the vibrant, stubborn resistance of Anacostia; the late-night atmosphere of Adams Morgan; the resilient uniqueness of Petworth; the enthusiasm of Dupont Circle. Its history had been endlessly documented, but the true story of Washington was only beginning to emerge.

"You going to spend all day staring?" Emily asked. "Let's go in, I'm cold."

The cafeteria was nearly empty. A couple of volunteers cleaning up for the night. Men shouting in the distance as they unloaded a truck. One sleeping on a chair in the corner.

The door at the far end of the cafeteria opened. Eve walked in.

"How does she look so put together?" Emily asked, gazing at Eve in wonder.

"No idea," Melinda said back, and then Eve was hugging her.

"Melinda," Eve said warmly. "Thanks for coming."

"I'm Emily," Emily offered. "Mel's sister. Okay, how are you so hot? Mel looked like a zombie when she was doing social work."

If Eve was surprised by Emily's bluntness, she didn't show it. Just smiled. "Thanks? I wear a lot of makeup."

"And you dress *beautifully*," Emily said. She turned to her sister. "Mel, do you see how she dresses?"

"Shut up," Melinda told Emily. "Thanks for calling me, Eve."

Eve's smile faded into seriousness. "She's in back."

Eve walked through the cafeteria. The sisters followed her. The cafeteria led to a small hallway with doors on either side. Eve opened one, stepped into a room about the size of a small guest bedroom, maybe fifteen feet square. Chairs were stacked in each of the corners, a table folded flat against one of the walls. A woman leaned against another wall, staring into her phone. She looked up when Emily, Eve, and Melinda walked in.

"This is Lena," Eve said. "Lena, this is Melinda. We used to work together. And this is her sister, Emily."

"You're looking for Dani?" Lena asked.

Straight to the point. Melinda appreciated it. "Do you know her? We think she might be in trouble."

"With the cops?"

"Not exactly." Melinda wasn't sure how much she should reveal.

But Emily didn't share her concern. "Have you heard of a guy named Victor Winters? Big bald white dude? Runs girls all through the region but keeps a low profile. Works with a lawyer, this chick named Isabel Pike. She's real hot but super bitchy."

Lena seemed to appreciate the direct approach. She offered a slight smile.

"I don't know them."

"How'd you say Dani does?"

Melinda was taken aback. She'd expected to do all of the talking, to use her training when speaking with Lena. But Emily was a natural. Had completely broken through whatever defenses Lena had, and earned her trust.

Melinda wondered if she'd have been able to do the same. If something inside her would have resisted reaching out, that sense of connection she used to have now frayed.

"Dani works for Victor and Isabel," Emily answered Lena, "or probably does. I've been looking into this dude for a while now. I almost got him connected to some real shady human trafficking–type stuff."

A slight narrowing of Lena's eyes. "You're a cop?"

"Hell no," Emily said. "This is a hobby."

"Uh-huh." Lena seemed like she was thinking something over, then shrugged. "The thing is, I really haven't heard of him. Or her. But if Dani's in trouble, I want to find her. There's a new girl I know who could use her help. So I called Dani and never heard back. That's not like her. I'm starting to worry."

"You know any other way to get in touch with her, other than her phone?"

"I went to her place with a friend. No answer. Like I said, if she's in trouble, then we want to help."

"Why?" Melinda asked.

Lena turned toward Melinda, as if she'd forgotten she was there. "She'd do it for us," Lena said plainly. "When I started out, Dani took me in. Gave me a place to stay, told me who to watch out for. She's like my big sister. I'm not the only one who feels that way."

Melinda was surprised, both by the revelation of Dani's character and because it was something she hadn't recognized. Their only encounter had been brief, but Melinda had judged her immediately. And selfishly kept her at bay.

Had she invited Dani into her townhouse, as unorthodox as such a move would have been, Melinda might have realized there was more depth to Dani. That she wasn't just scared and belligerent and drunk.

"I'll keep Dani safe," Emily was saying. "I promise. But you can't tell me anything about Victor or Isabel?"

"If they were players here, I'd know. So would she." Lena indicated Eve. "They're either not involved, or they're too deep."

"What's that mean?" Emily asked.

"The deeper you go," Lena explained, "the less names you know. Or want to know."

"Why?" Melinda asked, and she glanced at her sister, noticed that distant look in Emily's eyes. A shadow passing over her sister's face.

Eve answered her question. "Because you don't want those people to know you."

To know you.

Melinda felt like the deeper she was going, the more she was discovering about herself.

Regardless of what she wanted to find.

CHAPTER FORTY-THREE

She'd do it for us.

Lena's words, her simple testament to her friend Dani, echoed in Emily.

Emily had stayed in DC after the quick meeting with Eve and Lena, and she'd convinced her sister to head home without her. Told her she'd call an Uber.

"What about the Winterses?" Melinda had asked. "What if they're watching?"

"Who are they, the NSA? It's not like they have every single thing in DC under surveillance. I'll be fine."

Still, before Emily went into Calvin's apartment building, she circled the block a couple of times. Made sure no one was watching the doors. Waited ten minutes in case someone followed her into the lobby. Walked up and down the hall when she reached his floor.

"You up?" she asked, when Calvin opened the door.

"Emily?" Calvin glanced back into his apartment.

"Wait, do you have someone here? Why'd you look back?"

"I don't . . ." Calvin needed a moment to recover. "Were you coming by tonight?"

"It's cool if someone's here," Emily told him. "I mean, we're not exclusive. You know, boyfriend and girlfriend. Going steady. Wearing each other's promise rings. Carving our names in our forearms. At least, not both of us."

A smile. "No one's here. Come on in."

He closed the door behind her. "I had this vision of some topless chick holding bedsheets to her chin," Emily told him. "I wouldn't have cared, except she was really pretty. In my mind."

"No topless chicks here," Calvin said.

"Not yet."

A surprised laugh. Calvin must have been watching television and reading. Some version of *Law & Order* was on TV, and a book was open on the couch. She glanced at the title. *The FBI Way.*

"Do you want to order dinner? Or watch—"

Emily interrupted him. "I'm tired of waiting."

"For what?"

Emily took a breath. She was surprised that she was nervous. Fighting was so easy for her, but this made her hesitant. She was a twenty-eight-year-old woman, and her nerves were reddening her face.

Causing her right arm to tremble.

Emily hadn't slept with someone for three years, and that last time had been a drunken rush in the back seat of a car outside a bar, people slapping the hood as they walked past. Emily didn't even remember that guy's name or face. And before that, sex had been only occasional in her life, men she'd met on online matchmaking sites, a couple of dates at most. No relationships since college.

No one she'd cared about since college.

Emily crossed her arms over her chest, her hands at her waist. Fingers nervously rubbing the bottom of the shirt.

"What are you . . . ?" Calvin started.

She lifted her shirt over her head and dropped it to the floor.

"Okay, never mind," he said.

Emily actually felt like she breathed easier without the shirt. And Calvin's reaction helped. She kept her gaze on his face, on the excitement in his widening eyes and mouth. Reached back and quickly unsnapped her bra, pulled off the straps, let it fall next to her shirt.

Confidence grew. She unbuttoned her pants and wanted to step out of them seductively, but they were tight around her ankles. She had to hop around a little to finally get them off. Calvin didn't seem to mind.

Emily stood in front of him, in nothing but her underwear, her fingertips just inside the waistband, feeling her smooth skin.

"Is this too much?" Nerves had hoarsened her voice, but she liked it.

"Yes, but pleasepleaseplease don't stop."

Emily pulled down her underwear and stepped out of it, now wearing nothing, watching his eyes trying to take all of her in.

She felt flush with excitement and control and didn't want to be the only naked person in the room much longer.

Emily climbed onto Calvin's lap, loosened his belt, then his pants. Pulled him free from his briefs and kept kissing him, their hands between their bodies, touching everything.

They clumsily fell to the floor, pressed together, his body on top of hers. Her legs loosely wrapped around his waist.

His arms on either side of her head. She kissed his neck, shoulders, lips.

Emily wanted to be as close to Calvin as possible, but it felt like something was keeping her away. An imaginary door rattling, threatening to open. She closed her eyes to concentrate, to let Calvin run through her mind and emotions, but that imaginary door suddenly broke open, and all Emily saw were the men she'd hurt, their anguished cries rising over his.

◆ ◆ ◆

"I think you gave me a concussion," she announced.

Calvin laughed as he lay next to her. "Me?"

"I think I gave myself a concussion," Emily corrected herself. "We should have stayed on the couch."

"Yeah," Calvin agreed. "I have no idea how we ended up across the room."

"That was *a lot* of pent-up emotion."

"It's kind of weird, right? First times are usually . . . not like that. You okay?"

"Okay?"

"You were crying at the end."

"No, I wasn't."

Calvin didn't pursue it.

Emily slid out from under his kitchen table, sat up. Glanced around the apartment, her scattered clothes. The living room was like the wreckage of a boat tossed by rough waves.

"Jesus," Calvin said.

"What?"

"Your legs." He touched the purple bruises on her thighs. "What happened?"

"I just bruise easy. Working out with weights, resting them on my legs." She walked over to her shirt, pulled it on. Her bra wasn't there, and Emily wondered if they'd kicked it under the couch. She made a mental note to find it before she left.

Calvin was watching her. The steadiness of his gaze made her uncomfortable.

"New Road's CEO sent us an email about Simon Glowalter," she said. "Now that he's been found not guilty, they're officially reopening the investigation into his wife's death."

"I heard," Calvin told her as he climbed out from under the table. "I hope they find something."

"You sound like you don't think they will."

"I don't."

Emily quickly pulled on her underwear and pants, sucked in her stomach to buckle them. "Do you think they'll find out he really did it?"

"Maybe," he said. "But there are investigators who always believe they caught the right person. No matter what."

"Because they can't admit they were wrong?"

Calvin spoke plainly, without argument. "Because they stand by their work."

Emily ran a hand through her hair, trying to untangle it. She thought about what Calvin had said, decided not to argue.

She walked over to the wall next to the TV. Peered at a framed photo of Calvin and his mother, she wearing a dress blues police uniform. Calvin back in high school, standing awkwardly, but smiling.

"This is a good picture," Emily announced.

"I should probably get a better one." Emily saw him in the picture's reflection, watched him pull his briefs and jeans back on. She'd always enjoyed watching a man get dressed. "I just like that one. I liked that day."

"Were you two close?"

"Always."

Emily stared back into the picture, wondered why she couldn't look away. The same feeling she had whenever she saw someone beautiful and was determined to learn exactly what drew her eyes.

But this wasn't about what she saw, Emily realized. It was what she felt.

The way beauty provoked admiration.

Longing.

Sadness rose, a polluted cloud of it, threatening to choke her.

Calvin deserves better.

She longed for her mask.

"Anyway," Emily said, turning away. "Sorry I interrupted *Law & Order*."

"I'll just see it tomorrow morning. Or tomorrow afternoon. Or evening. It's on a lot." Calvin never stopped watching her. "You're leaving?"

"I need to go."

He walked over, shirtless. Touched her shoulder.

"Did I do something wrong?" Calvin asked quietly. "Is that why you're rushing out?"

"Oh." A flush of emotion. Those fucking tears welling again. "It's not that. It's . . ." Emily didn't know what to say. "I bought a pet fish, and I need to get home and feed him."

"What?"

"I don't know why I said that. I don't have a pet fish." The tears dissipated. "I do want one, though."

"You're so strange." Calvin fidgeted. "I have this weird feeling I'm not going to see you again."

Emily headed to the door. Pushed her feet into the shoes she'd kicked off minutes earlier. "Why would you say that?"

"Just a feeling."

Emily had never seen Calvin so sad. But her urge to leave was overwhelming.

She hated herself for it.

"Look, Calvin," Emily said, her backpack slung over one shoulder. *Shit,* she remembered, *my bra.* "I wanted this. I'm happy we did it. I want more with you."

That tension broke. "You sure?"

"I'll see you again soon. I promise."

At the time, Emily meant it.

CHAPTER FORTY-FOUR

Melinda let her sister sleep.

She'd stayed awake until she heard a car door slam close to midnight, until she heard Emily unlocking the glass patio door, sliding it open. She'd gone downstairs to see her. They'd talked about Calvin as Emily turned the couch into a bed. Talked about their father as Emily changed into shorts and a T-shirt. Talked about Markus as they lay in bed, staring up at the ceiling. Talked about their mother as they fell asleep next to each other.

Melinda woke to a cold, dark day, her sister snoring next to her. Overcast skies threatened icy rain or hail. She went upstairs, realized it was near noon. Melinda wasn't hungry, but she made a sandwich for herself, melted cheese over bread in the toaster oven. Turned on the television.

She'd been watching TV for an hour when Emily came up the stairs.

"You like these shows?" Emily asked. She pulled a Coke out of the fridge. "House flipping?"

"Not really, because I get tons of ideas about what I want to do with our house, and then I remember that our HOA gets mad if we have a tree that grows, like, bananas instead of oranges."

"Don't want you getting too ethnic?"

"Exactly."

Our house.

Rick still hadn't returned her phone calls.

"I'm glad you're here," Melinda told Emily. "It's been nice."

"Me too," Emily replied. "I kind of thought we'd end up killing each other, but now I'm wondering why we spent so much time apart these last few years."

"I guess we had our own things going on."

"You were getting a new job," Emily said. "And a new life. Meanwhile, I was seeking a path of vengeance and destruction. Not really the kind of thing you can dish about over coffee."

"That wasn't it," Melinda said. She was about to take a bite from her sandwich but, instead, set it on the plate. "That day of Mom's funeral, after what happened with Markus . . . I kept my distance."

"I avoided him too," Emily said.

"I mean from you."

Emily picked up Melinda's sandwich, took a bite from the uneaten end.

She covered her mouth as she spoke. "Why me?"

"I saw something in you when you were hitting Markus. It was scary. And ugly."

"You mean when I was saving your life?"

"If I hadn't pulled you off, I think you might have killed him." Melinda put her fists between her knees. "It was one of the worst things I'd ever seen."

"Worse than what he was doing to you?"

"I think so."

Emily took another bite, spoke as she chewed. "You're making me feel real unappreciated, Mel."

"I'm sorry, I'm just being honest. I felt like I wanted away from everyone in our family. Even you."

"And now?"

"And now I'd be a wreck without you."

"Same here," Emily said. She drank, crumpled the can. "I'm sorry you saw me like that."

"It's okay," Melinda said. "Not everyone is built for that kind of stuff."

"No," Emily disagreed. "Everyone is. Including you, Mel. If something happens to me, you'll need to do what I'm doing."

"What?"

"It's easy. You just follow police reports of domestic violence, then beat up the guys that don't get arrested."

"Emily, there's no way I would do that. Or could."

"All you have to do is hit people with a baton," Emily said. "And you get my mask! Or you can make your own. You could call yourself the Slob."

"Okay," Melinda said. "You're irritating. And I'm not going to become some masked vigilante, and you're not going to die."

Emily leaned across the counter.

"It doesn't matter if Three Strikes is me," she said intensely. "It just matters that she's someone."

Melinda didn't know how to respond.

Emily slid back into her chair. "Think about it. But I have to ask you something else."

"What?"

"Should I get a fish?"

The sisters spent the day indoors, watching television, talking about nothing and everything.

It started raining again as evening grew closer, as darkness overtook the sky.

As the meeting with Dani drew near.

◆ ◆ ◆

Melinda left and locked her car, walked toward the empty house in Silver Spring.

She didn't know where Emily was. They'd stopped at a traffic light a few blocks back, and Emily had slipped out of the car.

They hadn't said much on the drive. Hadn't even said goodbye as Emily closed the door.

There was the possibility, of course, that this meeting was exactly as it sounded. Melinda desperately hoped that was the case as she walked toward the house. Maybe Dani really did just want help. She'd found herself in trouble and needed someone to turn to. Melinda would refer her to Eve, and Eve would refer her to the police. Victor Winters would be exposed, and the danger Emily was in would disappear. Markus's murder would be put to rest. Maybe it would even help their father.

The front door was unlocked. Melinda stepped into the living room of an unfurnished split-level house. Peeling white walls, scratched wooden floors. A small staircase leading to a second story, an entrance to a kitchen across from the living room.

"Dani?"

A moment after Melinda called her name, Dani stepped out from the kitchen. She had the same loss in her eyes Melinda had noticed when Dani came to her townhouse, as if she was in a haze of alcohol, or fear, or both. Melinda felt her training kick in, the way it always did when she saw someone suffering.

"You didn't bring your sister."

A man's voice.

Emily had been right. The trap was sprung.

Victor Winters stepped out from the kitchen. Melinda had seen a photo of him online, but Victor was bigger than she'd expected, a massive presence dwarfing Dani, like a mountain the other woman was too timid to climb.

A bandage covered his left eye. Otherwise, his skin had a smooth, untouched quality.

"You're Victor Winters?" Melinda asked.

He stood behind Dani, his hand on her shoulder, covering her entire shoulder. "Where's Emily?"

"I don't know." Melinda had talked back to dangerous men before, refused to allow them entry into safe houses or shelters when they were seeking women, testified against them in court. And she'd been scared but comforted by the fact that there were layers of law protecting her. Comforted by the fact, as Rick had reminded her, that bad people rarely confronted authority.

But there was a difference with Victor.

The men she'd spoken with always had a trace of fear in their words, in their behavior.

Victor had no fear. He acted like he'd never known fear.

"You don't know where Emily is?" he asked.

Melinda shook her head. Reminded herself that she was partially telling the truth, which made the lie easier. Like when she'd lied to Rick once, told him she loved working with David rather than telling him she might be falling in love with David.

Except she hadn't loved David. She'd loved Rick.

Melinda's thoughts were everywhere. Fear scattered them like wind through leaves, made it impossible for her to focus.

"I really don't," she told Victor.

Victor's free hand covered Dani's other shoulder. He squeezed. Dani's expression creased in pain. Her knees bent.

"I don't!" Melinda said, alarmed. "Please!"

"Looks like there's a lot you don't know about your own sister," he told her.

"Maybe." Melinda tried to get on firmer ground. "I'm just here to help Dani. That's it."

"You want to help Dani, give me Emily."

"I don't have her."

"Then you're not going to be much help."

He squeezed again, and Dani crumpled. His fingers turned white, pushed into her skin. She cried out, eyes clenched, grasped at his hands. It looked like scrabbling at a stone.

Melinda barely realized she was walking toward them. She was just watching Dani's tortured face, her cries filling her mind, and suddenly Melinda was pulling Victor's hands, trying to free Dani. But his fingers were entrenched in her shoulders, dug deep, curled around her clavicles.

Melinda almost cried out for Emily to help her, to come free this woman. She thought about her phone, about calling the cops. And knew she wouldn't dial a digit before Victor stopped her.

Victor was staring down at Dani's head, his one eye impassive.

Melinda saw the bandage covering his other eye.

It wasn't a hard hit from Melinda, more of a push than a punch. But it was enough. Victor shouted, let go of Dani, raised his hands to his face. Stumbled back to the wall.

"Come on," Melinda said to Dani. "We need to go."

Dani tried to rise, wincing, arms crossed over her chest, hands rubbing her shoulders. She was in too much pain to understand what Melinda was telling her. Melinda wrapped an arm around the other woman's waist, pulled her to the front door.

They made it only a few steps before Melinda felt Victor's hand on her arm. Then she felt herself propelled back, deeper into the living room, sailing then stumbling into a wall. She fell to her knees and looked up.

Looked up at Dani's face.

Victor's giant palm was over Dani's mouth. Blood soaked the bandage on his eye, leaked in a thin stream down his cheek.

"Where's Emily?" he growled.

"I don't know!"

"Don't tell him," Dani managed to say.

Victor kicked Melinda's leg, and she fell. His boot planted squarely on her chest, pinned her to the floor like her body was the base of his statue.

He turned Dani's head down, the woman helplessly staring at Melinda.

In the movies, a broken neck happens in a quick, deft move. A sudden turn of the head.

But that's not what Victor did to Dani. He turned her chin to the right, her shoulders to the left. Kept twisting as her arms and legs punched and kicked, as that trickle of blood dripped off his chin. Victor pulled as Dani screamed into his palm, as the bones in her neck tightened, as her legs lifted. There was a pop, and then a grinding sound, like someone's teeth rubbing together.

Dani's head was turned so far it was almost facing Victor. Her hands flailed, slowed.

His boot lifted off Melinda's chest. She scrambled back to the wall, breathing hoarsely, crying.

Victor dropped Dani to the floor. Her hands reached out blindly, without any sense of control.

Victor's boot crashed down on her head. The impact lifted her entire body. His boot came down again. Again. Victor didn't stop, even as Melinda rose to her feet, rushed to the front door.

The door suddenly opened. Emily was there. Scanning the room under her canvas mask. Taking in Melinda's face, a surprised pause when she saw Victor and Dani in the corner.

Melinda wanted to fall into her sister's arms.

But she stopped when Emily yanked someone into view.

Isabel Pike.

Emily had one arm around Isabel's chest; the other held a knife to her throat.

"Hey, Vic," Emily said. "How's the eye?"

Victor turned toward Emily, seething. Dani's head was flattened, a crushed balloon.

"She saw me in the car," Isabel said calmly. "I'm sorry."

Melinda was stunned at how nonchalant Emily and Isabel were in front of the remains of Victor's fury. It reminded her of parents refusing to acknowledge a child's tantrum.

Melinda couldn't look at Dani, even though everything in the room seemed to be centered on her body, as if all of them would have to go to it at some point, as if they were in a labyrinth and Dani's body was the Minotaur. Seeing her felt unavoidable to Melinda, a spirit turning her head, forcing her to look.

"You wanted me," Emily said. "I'm here. And you're going to jail for murder, you gross monster."

"He didn't kill your brother," Isabel said, her tone still detached.

"He killed Dani!" Melinda's voice was high and uncontrolled, nearly a scream.

"No one saw it happen," Isabel replied. "And no one's going to care about her."

"My sister saw it," Emily countered. "And she's not afraid to tell everyone."

Actually, Melinda was terrified. Panic was seizing her, a numb iron taste filling her mouth. That room she'd always imagined, hidden behind a locked door—now she was inside it. A room of horror, of the violence of murder, the bloodlust in Victor's eye, the determination in his hands. The room held images beyond what humans should see.

That's where the secret room existed, Melinda realized. Beyond boundaries. And that's where Victor lived. That was why he exuded authority. Those who made and rewrote the rules of humanity wielded a terrible, incomprehensible power.

"Emily," Melinda said urgently. "We need to go."

"We will," Emily told her, watching Victor. "Soon."

There was another fear in Melinda, and it came from Isabel. She was too calm with the knife to her throat, too relaxed.

Emily held the knife but, Melinda now understood, Emily was the one in danger.

Isabel and Victor had more planned.

"You killed Rebecca," Emily said. "I saw it. And I can prove it."

Victor's fists tightened.

"We didn't kill your brother," Isabel said, her tone still maddeningly unconcerned.

"Then who did?" Melinda asked.

"Your sister," Isabel told her.

To Melinda, those words would have been insane, as believable as if Isabel had suddenly announced that the earth was flat . . . except for the sudden stillness in Emily's body.

The way the room went silent, like a single sucked-in breath.

"What are you talking about?" Emily asked, the knife point pressing into Isabel's neck. "You killed him because he wrote a song threatening to expose Victor."

"We know about the song," Isabel said. "Dani told us. We wouldn't have cared."

"You killed him because of it," Emily insisted stubbornly. "You . . ."

"We knew," Victor interrupted her. "And we made sure Jessy Taylor didn't release it." These were the first words he'd spoken since he'd murdered Dani.

Isabel's eyes lowered.

"You killed Jessy!" Emily said triumphantly. The mask kept turning back and forth between Victor and Melinda. "See? I told you."

"We did. It's okay, Isabel." Victor looked at Melinda, and it was as if she couldn't look away. "This is the time for truth."

"Mel," Emily said. "I think we need to go."

Melinda desperately wanted to leave, but something felt wrong, loose. She wanted to run and leave all this behind, but it felt like there was light shining from behind a rock somewhere, and she needed to dislodge that rock.

And then it rolled away.

"The song," Melinda said. She turned toward Emily. "How'd you know about Markus's song?"

"What do you mean?"

"No one knew about that but Jessy and Dani and them. Jessy told me about it. But I never told you."

"I mean, I don't know. We can figure that out later."

"Emily, did you kill Markus?"

"Mel, no."

But Melinda knew. Knew it as if Emily had admitted to it instead of lying.

And Emily could tell. Her body slumped.

"You know what Markus did to those women," Emily said.

Melinda felt sounds coming out of herself she'd never heard before, unchecked grief and rage. She saw red, she saw nothing, she saw everything.

It was too much, the breaking point.

"Mel," Emily was saying. "Please. It was an accident."

And suddenly, it was all gone.

These three people, determined to die. Determined to kill.

Melinda wanted no part of it.

"I'm leaving," Melinda said. She walked to the front door, past Emily and Isabel.

"Mel, I'm sorry," Emily told her.

Melinda didn't answer. She opened the front door, felt the cold air, the slick rain. The world outside of that hellish house. A new world waiting for her. She didn't know where she would go, but she knew Rick would be there and Emily wouldn't. Markus wouldn't. Victor and Isabel wouldn't.

She made it down the steps, to the sidewalk, before she felt instinct pulling her back.

As angry as Melinda was, as distraught and empty, she couldn't leave Emily.

She turned, walked back up the steps, stopped before the front door. She was about to open it and paused. Felt the rain on her face, the cold night.

She'd do it for me, Lena had said of Dani.

Melinda opened the door and stepped back in hell.

Emily, Isabel, and Victor were in the same places, unmoved.

"Mel?" Emily asked, strained. "Why'd you come back?"

"For you," Melinda told her decisively. "We need to leave. Let her go and come with me."

"You should have left," Emily said.

Melinda pulled her phone out of her pocket. "I'm calling the police."

She meant it as a threat, but no one seemed concerned.

"You should have run," Emily told her. That fear was unmistakable now. Blaring. "You had the chance, even if some of them are waiting outside."

"Who?" Melinda asked.

"Drop the knife," Victor said to Emily. "And I'll let your sister live."

"What . . . what are you saying?" Melinda asked Emily, fingers paused over her phone. "I don't understand."

"Promise me," Emily replied to Victor, ignoring her sister. "Promise me you will."

"You won't believe me," Victor told her. "I understand that. But I promise you. If your sister keeps her silence, she'll stay alive."

"I don't understand!" Melinda cried, the phone forgotten.

"Here's how it'll work," Emily said to Victor. That fear was still there, shaking her voice. "You leave me lying here, next to Dani. Put a hammer in my hand or something. Leave a gun in my other hand. Pin Dani's death and Markus's and Jessy's—shit, anyone else you want, JFK or whatever, on me. That's enough to throw everything off you, right?"

Victor rubbed the dried blood on his chin. The trickle from his bandaged eye had stopped. "Should work."

"We have a deal?"

"Emily," Melinda asked. "What are you doing?"

"Yes," Victor said.

Emily looked at Melinda, let the knife fall to the floor. "We're not alone," Emily said. "They told me when you left."

And then the men came.

Down the small staircase, through the kitchen. From the front door. Pairs of grim men, not saying anything, a dozen standing as silent and attentive as soldiers.

It all occurred to Melinda in a second. What Emily was doing. What was going to happen.

"We walked into a trap," Emily said.

Isabel picked up the knife, touched the side of her neck where a spot of blood had blossomed like an angry rose. She took Melinda's phone from her numb hand.

"I wish it wasn't just a gunshot," Isabel said to Emily, her voice low. "I wish I could cut you a thousand times."

Emily didn't respond.

Victor walked forward and took a gun from one of his men.

"Wait," Melinda said. "Please. You don't need to do this. Emily will confess to everything and go to jail. She'll say anything. Right?"

No response from anyone.

Melinda looked at Emily desperately. "Right?"

"I'm ready for this," Emily told the room.

"Can I just . . ." Melinda felt like she was looking at a rushing river and searching for a way to cross. "We can think of something else. She doesn't need to die. Please. Please! This can all be forgiven. No one has to suffer anymore. This can be forgiven."

"My God, shut up," Victor said.

He shot Melinda in the face.

Chapter Forty-Five

The men led Emily to a car. There was no resistance now. There was no humor.

Nothing but steps to the end.

The thoughts running through Emily's mind kept coming to a sudden stop. Stopping at Melinda's blood on her hands, Emily's hands pressed against the back of her sister's head and face, trying to stop the blood. Trying to push it back in. To push back time.

Emily hadn't been able to breathe when the men had yanked her to her feet. Couldn't breathe until rain splashed on her.

A hand on her shoulder guided her into the car's back seat. The way Emily remembered seeing a cop do it in some movie or television show. A distant part of her understood. Victor had the law working for him.

Everyone and everything worked for him. Life and death followed his whims.

Isabel knelt next to the car door.

"I'm getting my thousand cuts," she told Emily and lifted her hand, showed her a knife. "Tonight."

Isabel waited for a response, seemed disappointed when one didn't come. Tried another tactic. "You got your sister killed."

Silence.

Isabel sighed. "In case you try to run."

She plunged the knife into Emily's thigh.

The blade cut deep, tore through jeans and flesh and shock until it scraped bone. Emily screamed and grabbed at her leg, and her body bent over the wound.

She was in too much pain to notice the car door closing. Stretched her body out, arched it, trying to find a way that the wound wouldn't hurt this much.

When her eyes opened again, Emily felt like she'd emerged from somewhere deep underground. Her head was against the window, and the car was driving, and tears and snot and spit covered her face.

Her fists pressed down over the cut, as if she could block the pain. It seemed to work. Barely.

A man sat next to her. Another drove the car. She couldn't tell if someone was in the passenger seat.

"You remember me?" the man next to her asked. Her handbag was in his lap.

A bandage covered his nose.

The car jerked slightly, and Emily shouted as pain tore through her leg. The man peered at her.

"I remember you," he said. "I've been looking forward to this."

Emily mumbled something.

"What?" he asked, and leaned close.

Emily smashed her forehead into his bandage.

He shrieked and pushed her. The man driving shouted. The car suddenly jerked to a stop. The other vehicle following smashed into them, pitching everyone forward.

The bandaged man had hit the back of the passenger seat. He hunched forward, held his head in his hands. The driver fought off an airbag.

Emily pushed open the nearest door. She saw her handbag on the floor, grabbed it, and fell onto the street.

She stood and fell again. Could barely put weight on her leg.

Car doors. Shouts.

Emily forced herself to stand, hopped to the side of the road. She had no idea where she was. Shadows of trees bordered the street.

Emily limped into their darkness.

She didn't realize she'd been standing on a hill until she was falling, the dark ground rushing up.

CHAPTER
FORTY-SIX

It was as if an animal had overtaken Emily, an inner being controlling her. Guiding her up from the rain-soaked ground, leading her through the trees. The need to run from predators.

She limped through an impossible path of unsteady ground and tugging branches, one hand in front of her, the other pressed to her thigh, desperately pushing away pain.

Emily fell forward, hit her head on something, tried to stay awake. But surrendered.

She came to moments later, blearily stared into a fence. Lifted herself up and realized she was just outside someone's backyard.

Emily pulled herself over the fence, through the soul-wrenching pain of her wound dragging over wood. She hobbled under a deck, shivered as rain poured down through the slats.

Muffled voices.

Emily couldn't stay here. Couldn't risk being discovered, the cops called. Victor and Isabel had the cops. They had everything.

Emily pulled herself deeper under the deck, covered her mouth to quiet her cries as her leg scraped rock.

A door opened, and those muffled voices cleared. A dog trotting down the steps above where she lay.

Emily stayed still.

She closed her eyes and her sister's blood spilled into her hands.

The dog sniffed above her.

Melinda sat in the kitchen, watched TV. Smiled as Emily came upstairs.

Should I get a fish?

"What?" a boy shouted from somewhere. "George, come on!"

The dog scrambled up the stairs.

The patio door closed.

Emily pulled herself out from under the deck. Finally removed her mask. Stumbled to a gate and forced it open.

Those men would be searching for her.

Emily kept walking, stepping gingerly, one hand pressed to the row of fences bordering the neighborhood. She reached a gap between fences and crept forward. Peered down a quiet wet street.

Saw something a few houses away.

A For Sale sign.

Which might mean an empty home.

Emily used her baton to smash a basement window of that house. Slipped inside, into a den. Hobbled to a leather couch and lay down.

Piano music from upstairs. Eerie, tinkling keys. Markus singing. No. Markus screaming. Screaming as the keys shrilly beat faster and faster.

Emily woke. Dragged herself off the couch, clutched her baton.

Opened a bathroom door. Stumbled in and sat on a closed toilet. Pressed her hands against her forehead.

Remembered Melinda's face when she'd realized what Emily had done.

Why'd you come back for me, Mel?

Emily took off her clothes, peeled her jeans off her leg, tearing the cloth from where it stuck to the knife cut. She stepped into the shower and watched as her blood turned the basin red.

Afterward, she covered the wound in bandages from her backpack.

The closets upstairs were empty, but the washing machine and dryer were working. Emily washed her clothes and sat in the laundry room, naked and dazed. Melinda and Markus appeared and disappeared in wide-awake dreams, like when they were children playing hide-and-seek.

Emily thought back to the last time she'd seen Markus.

She'd never been to Markus's new apartment, hadn't seen him since the disastrous afternoon of their mother's funeral. But when she stepped into his living room and saw the harbor-view windows, gleaming leather furniture, shiny black piano, and pristine hardwood floors, all that was momentarily forgotten. He still lived in Baltimore, but it was nothing like the apartment she'd visited in Fells Point. His new condo was in the Inner Harbor, on one of the top floors of one of the tallest, shiniest, newest buildings in an area known for constant tall, shiny, new buildings.

"Holy hell!" Emily had exclaimed. "This is where you live? And you're not the butler?"

Markus closed the front door behind her. "I don't have a butler."

"Motherfucker." Emily walked over to his couch, and her hands glided over the soft black leather. "I mean, *Darién* slaps, but I downloaded that album for free. I felt bad about that until now, because clearly you don't need the money."

"You downloaded my album for free?"

"Okay, I didn't feel *that* bad about it."

"Yeah, I didn't think so. You want something to drink?"

"Water, but just so I can see what kind of fancy SpongeBob-killing plastic bottles rich people use."

Markus walked over to the kitchen. "They're glass," he said. "I'm trying to keep SpongeBob alive."

"I'm a little disappointed, honestly." Emily drank from the bottle he gave her. "Also, this just tastes like water."

"What'd you think it'd taste like?"

"Like French-kissing an angel. You can use that line for an album title."

"Thanks?"

"You drinking anything old and expensive? Like an actual bottle of wine Jesus changed over from water or something?"

"I don't drink anymore."

"No?"

"Well, there's been a lot of times when I don't drink anymore."

There was a sadness to Markus she hadn't expected, a solitude.

Emily walked over to the window, stared at Federal Hill in the distance, the waving American flag, the stone cannons pointed toward the city.

It was clear that Rebecca wasn't here. Emily had been able to tell the moment Markus opened the door. That was the difference, she thought. The loneliness.

"Why are you here, Emily?" Markus asked.

She kept staring out the window as she spoke. "You remember that guy Dietrich?"

"Dietrich?"

"He was at your concert in DC. A tour manager or something?"

"You mean Harold?"

She vigorously shook her head. "Not the old guy. He was younger. Maybe between our ages."

"I don't, sorry."

Emily turned toward him. "You were super drunk, so okay. But he slipped something in my drink. I saw it and tried to say something, but you and Harold told me I was lying. We all got into a big fight."

Emily could see her words tugging at his memory, a hazy picture filling in.

"He was arrested last week," Emily went on. "For the same thing. Slipping drugs in some girl's drink."

"That's awful." Markus paused. "But I still don't remember him. If it helps, we went with a different touring company."

"It doesn't *help*, Markus. He tried to rape me."

Her brother shifted uncomfortably. "But he didn't."

"That's not the point. If you'd taken me seriously, Dietrich might have been arrested that night. Who knows how many women he's hurt since then? Or how many he hurt before?"

"Em, I'm not proud of a lot of the things I did. I know I made mistakes. That was a big one. I'm sorry."

She stared at him.

Markus stared right back.

Emily walked over to the grand piano. Touched a white key, and a high B chimed.

"I remember listening to you play in the morning when we were growing up," Emily told him. "It was so pretty. And you were so determined. Every single morning."

"Hey, Emily," Markus told her. "I am really sorry that I didn't believe you. I should have heard you out. I . . ." His voice stopped, turned hard when he spoke again. "Don't touch that."

The tone switch surprised her. "What?"

"Those papers." Markus indicated the sheet of lyrics she'd picked up. "I'm working on that."

"Is it a new song?" Emily read it. "'A Song for Killers.'"

He walked over, yanked the page out of her hand.

"It sounds like it's going to be weird," Emily observed.

"Yeah, well, it's not finished yet."

"Is it because of Rebecca? Is that why the word *Winters* is jammed in there?"

"You never shut the fuck up, do you? Jesus."

"What happened with her?"

That anger Emily remembered sharply crossed Markus's face.

"She's gone," Markus said. "She left me."

"Because you keep sleeping with trafficked women? Some girl-friends are really picky about that."

"I never slept with anyone else when I was with her. She was my soul, the light and the dark."

"Ew."

"Em . . ."

"So what happened?" Emily walked over to a framed album cover hung on the wall, one of Markus's four albums. The one she'd recently listened to, *Darién*. She'd read the story about it online, how Markus visited Panama quietly, without fanfare. Stayed with their mother's family for a month, toured the city and the country. Titled this album about a region in Panama considered untamable.

"She left me," Markus said. "That's what happened."

"Yeah, but why?"

Silence.

"You going to try to get her back?" she asked.

"I can't. Her uncle, this guy Victor Winters, stopped by and told me that if I came near her again, he'd fill me with bullets."

Emily turned away from the album cover. "All because he doesn't like jazz?"

"It was more than that."

"Victor Winters." She pointed to the page in his hand. "I get it now."

"He's involved in a lot of bad shit."

"Let me see that again." Emily reached for the page.

"No," Markus said. "Stop."

"No? Stop? What am I, a dog? Chill the fuck out."

Something had happened. That moment of communion gone. "You're in my house," Markus said, "and you'll do what I tell you."

"Whoa," Emily replied. "Have we met? 'Do what I tell you'?" She snorted. "Yeah, you adapted to money real quick."

"Shut up."

"Remember Mom's funeral? When Mel said you were sleeping with the women she was trying to help?"

It was inevitable that the funeral would come up. Markus and Melinda and Emily would always relive that afternoon, return to it when they saw each other. The one time they had each been utterly, inescapably honest. Their true selves.

Nobody would ever know them the way they knew each other.

"You still doing that?" Emily prodded.

"Why don't you get out of here, Emily?"

"Holy shit, you are! You're still paying those trafficked women!" Emily roughly pushed over the small end table his papers had been resting on. "All this money, and you can't buy a fucking ounce of decency."

"You don't even know me."

"Let's see . . . a women-beating drunk who sleeps with abused women and no amount of money can ever change him. Is that close?"

Markus's fist hit the side of her face, soft skin and wisps of hair and part of her ear pressed against his knuckles.

Emily was on her hands and knees.

"Get out," Markus told her. "Don't make me do it again."

Emily felt like she was glowing as she rose.

"Do it again."

"Emily . . ." Like all those men, all those other men she'd targeted, Markus didn't understand what was happening. Didn't realize what he'd brought upon himself. The world had belonged to men like him, and they'd walked over roads made of the souls they'd shattered. Blind and confident and unaware that, underneath them, those wounded souls were rising.

Emily touched her cheek and smiled.

Markus took a step back.

Her fist smashed his throat.

He fell to his knees.

Markus couldn't make a sound when Emily reached for him.

Afterward, Emily sat on the floor, her back against the couch, panting. Markus was lying on the carpet, his legs protruding from the other side of the couch. He reminded Emily of the Wicked Witch of the East after Dorothy's house crushed her.

"Well, I think we resolved some stuff," Emily told him. "How about you?"

Nothing.

"Fine, stay the strong silent type. But it can't be good for your machismo to get your ass kicked by your little sister. *Soundly.*"

He didn't respond. She didn't care.

"So here's what we're going to do," Emily went on. "You're going to cut out all the sex workers. Not that I have anything against sex work, but Mel told me these are women she's trying to help. Women forced into the trade who want a way out. That's the first thing. You're cutting that out and dating, like, Rashida Jones or someone. I *love* her. Second, this abuse shit is going to stop. You so much as harm a hair on Rashida's head and I'll make this beating look like a massage. Third, you're going to apologize to Mel. You're going to say these words: *Melinda, I was wrong, and you were right, and I'm so sorry, and I'm not saying this because Emily practically beat me to death. Also, I'm going to give you money to buy nicer clothes.* Got it?"

Still no response. Emily reached behind herself, used the couch to stand. She was surprised at how sore her body was, especially because, aside from that first punch, Markus hadn't landed another blow.

Then again, Emily had been fighting a lot. Ever since she'd started wearing the mask, violence had become her second skin. She imagined herself as a snake, the outer layer constantly shedding Emily away, revealing something else underneath.

She walked over to her brother, limping a little.

And then she saw him, and the limp was forgotten.

Markus's head was perched against the protruding brick hearth of the fireplace.

Emily was on her knees and trying to pull him toward her, but the back of his head had broken open, the brick's edge lodged inside.

When she pulled him free, a current of blood splashed out.

She dropped him and ran to the bathroom and locked the door.

Emily was unaware of how much time passed, how long she stayed in the bathroom, sitting on the floor in the small cramped space between the toilet and the wall. She remembered playing hide-and-seek as a child, when she sometimes found a spot so good that she felt like she could stay there for hours, all night, years. That was how she felt now. As if she wanted to remain in this space forever.

She hadn't killed Markus.

That was her primary thought, first and foremost. She'd never killed anybody. Her first few fights had been sloppy, but those men were alive. Beaten and left with envelopes of photos around them documenting their abuse, but alive when the police arrived.

She was not a killer.

She'd punched Markus, and he'd fallen, and she'd turned before he'd landed. Raised her arms triumphantly, Ali celebrating a knockout. Then she'd settled down next to the couch without once looking at how he had landed. She'd just assumed they were done fighting.

She wasn't a killer.

Emily opened the bathroom door.

She wondered if it would be dark outside, if she'd been in the bathroom for so long that the day had slipped away. But sunlight still shone through the condominium's bay windows; the red-and-blue sail of a boat glided across the water.

And Markus was in the same spot she'd left him.

She wasn't going to call the police. Emily decided that immediately. If the police came and she was arrested, the publicity and story and the trial would destroy her family.

And it would stop her from helping those who needed her. That's what she told herself. Emily needed to keep doing what she was doing, her new calling rescuing women, her careful use of violence.

But her fingerprints and DNA were everywhere, and the mysterious death of Markus Peña would certainly warrant an investigation.

Emily's mind moved quickly. Unless she *did* call the police. Tell them she'd discovered her brother's body and tried to move him. And accidentally contaminated the crime scene.

Her brother's body.

Those three words stopped Emily cold, brought her hand to her chest.

It wasn't possible that she'd killed him, that he was even dead.

The taste and smell of vomit were in her mouth and nose, and suddenly she threw up on the carpet. Emily threw up and wept and screamed into her fists, pulled her hair until it nearly ripped from her head, wrapped her arms tight around her body and squeezed. Her fingernails pressed deeply into her sides.

She was overwhelmed, in a dark place like a tunnel, and at the other end of the tunnel was a yellow flashing light. Panic, threatening to rush toward her.

I didn't kill you! Emily screamed into the void.

You killed you.

The yellow light vanished.

Emily sat up, wiped her mouth with her arm. She was panting and still crying, but the world inside and around her was settling, a shaken snow globe set down.

Emily could see again.

There was a path. It was hazy, but appearing. A path where she could report her brother's death, which was sort of like doing the right thing, and keep her father and sister away from the truth. Markus's death would be hard enough, maybe impossible, for her father to accept. Melinda would be troubled. And Emily would be sad, but not guilty. She hadn't meant to kill him.

But maybe she had.

Emily had killed Markus.

Emily had killed Melinda.

Emily had killed Emily.

Her clothes tossed in the dryer.

"I wanted to die for you, Mel. Why'd you come back?"

No answer, and there would never be, and Emily sat naked in the laundry room, still wet from the shower, shivering.

◆ ◆ ◆

She peeled off bandages, replaced them with the last ones from her handbag. Her leg ached, but the pain had dulled.

The blood hadn't disappeared from her washed jeans; rather, one leg was a different color from the other. But it was night and too dark for anyone to notice.

She drank water from a faucet, thought about Melinda and fought back a sudden, violent nausea. The loss was overwhelming. She kept thinking there was a way Melinda could still be alive, that there was some way to save her.

Emily understood she was in shock from the pain and the loss but, soon, that numbness would recede.

Soon she'd want to die.

And now there was nowhere to turn anymore, nowhere safe. If they couldn't find her, she knew Victor and Isabel would go after her father. Or Calvin. They'd cut her leg and might as well have cut it off, because she couldn't run any farther.

There was only one thing Emily could do, because she couldn't risk anything happening to anyone else.

She'd tried to trade her life for Melinda, and now she'd do the same for her father and Calvin.

Emily hoped Victor and Isabel would accept her offer, because the trade was uneven.

It was more than her life was worth.

Chapter Forty-Seven

The Uber dropped Emily off outside Victor Winters's mansion in Potomac.

Actually, Emily didn't know if the property qualified as a mansion. Wasn't sure what did. But it had a gate and a metal fence and a long, winding drive that led to a large, sprawling house in the distance.

Close enough.

Emily limped around the property, looking for an opening in the metal fence. She didn't find one and hadn't expected to. But she didn't spot any cameras, and the neighbors were too far away to see her as she pulled herself up over the high fence and dropped ungracefully to the other side. She tried to land on her good leg, but her other foot touched the ground first. Fire rushed from her right foot to her thigh.

Emily collapsed, hurt leg bent, hugging her knee as tightly to her chest as a mother protecting an infant. Her teeth so tight she felt like they would grind themselves into dust.

Finally, the pain receded. Finally, she stopped moaning. It took a few minutes for her to stand again. Emily brushed away tears with her coarse sleeve.

She limped up the long lawn toward the house, like an infection relentlessly approaching a heart.

She wasn't sure if the lawn was as large as it seemed or if her halting pace made the trek more arduous, but the walk felt endless. As if the house was some distant wink of a star in space.

There was an inevitability to it, Emily realized. Like her life had been a path destined to end young. Her father had always said that Markus wasn't meant to live a full, happy life. And he hadn't. In the end, neither had Melinda. Neither would she.

Emily was on her knees again, her hands and knees, at the thought of Melinda. Her face in the wet grass.

Emily had been supposed to die. Not Mel.

Markus and Emily were the ones to rush into mistakes. Melinda never should have returned to that house for her, shouldn't have been the one who suffered Victor Winters's wrath. Melinda should have been spared. Married Rick. Lived on beyond the disgraces of Markus and Emily, had children, kept a watchful eye on them to make sure they didn't turn out like her siblings.

Emily pulled her adjusted handbag off her shoulders. Unzipped it. Wiped the wetness from the grass off her face and slipped on the mask, the harsh straw taste of canvas against her mouth.

The front door of the house was at the top of a curved driveway. Emily recognized Isabel's Lexus parked to the side.

She limped past it, headed to the front door.

Rang the doorbell.

The doorbell had a camera attached to it. Through her mask, Emily stared into its silent eye. She wondered if they would simply call the police and have her arrested, pin the deaths of her brother and sister on her. It'd be a sensational story, a masked vigilante arrested for the deaths of her own siblings. Evil and insane, like those mothers who killed their own children. The public and the media would want her blood.

And she would give it.

It was what she deserved. Emily deserved to have her evils paraded before the world, to have her father disassociate from and eventually disown her. To be a pariah even in prison, where, likely, her eccentricities would approach a level of craziness she could no longer control. Emily Peña, the masked psychopath, the relentless killer.

The door clicked.

Emily was so lost in her thoughts that she barely realized she'd opened the heavy front door and shuffled inside.

It was only when the lights turned on, the glare blinding, that she snapped fully awake.

Emily was in a great hall, heavy wooden double doors behind her. Marble staircases with round shiny banisters curled up in front of her on either side. Doors seemed to be everywhere, on this floor and the next level up. Emily felt disoriented, the way she often did when entering a mall or an amusement park, so much to see and all of it overwhelming.

Isabel Pike's voice:

"We're surprised to see you here."

Emily turned to the right, saw Isabel standing in one of the doorways, her hands clasped behind her back. She had a freshness and life to her that exhausted Emily. Like Emily was stumbling to the end of a marathon Isabel had finished an hour before.

"Victor and I were just having dinner."

Isabel kept her hands behind her back.

"Follow me." Isabel turned and passed through the open doorway behind her. Her hands were empty.

Emily did as she was told, glancing up the stairs as she walked. There was a graveness to the house, the solemnity of a tomb.

She thought of Melinda. Tears clotted under her coarse mask.

Emily stepped into a dimly lit dining room. Isabel sat down at the end of an oval wooden table, the legs carved with ornate symbols, moons upon stars. Victor sat at the other end, his back to Emily.

He didn't turn to face her. Just kept eating.

"We've been looking for you," Isabel said. She picked up her fork, hunted through a salad until she found a small tomato. She stabbed it, picked it up, bit into it.

"I know," Emily replied.

"Where'd you go when you ran out of the car? I'm curious."

"I found a place to hide."

"And then?"

"And then I hid."

Victor still hadn't turned around.

"There's no reason to keep secrets anymore," Isabel reprovingly told Emily. "And no reason to keep the mask on. Why don't you take it off?"

Emily ignored the request. "Why'd you kill my sister?" she asked. "And not me."

"She talked too much," Victor said. He resumed eating.

"Why did you come after us?" Isabel asked. "Did you expect to frame us for your brother's death?"

"Markus's death was an accident," Emily said. "But I knew what you were involved in."

"And you were going to pin his murder on us? With no proof?"

"I knew what Markus did to Rebecca. You were going to kill him at some point. You and he have both done a lot of terrible things."

"So have you," Isabel said.

Emily's leg was starting to ache, from either the long walk or tension. She shifted her weight.

"Framing us never would have stuck," Isabel told her. "Why don't you take off your mask?"

"I want you to leave everyone I care about alone," Emily said. "I want to trade my life for them."

That smile stayed. "Emily," Isabel mused. "Why do I dislike you so much? Maybe it's because I could understand Melinda. There was a decency to her I respected."

"Don't talk about her."

"Without you, she'd still be alive. There's no decency to you." Isabel set her fork down, wiped her mouth with her napkin. "You caused your sister's death. Who knows what all this will do to your father."

Burning tears blurred her eyes. "I never said I was a good person."

"Neither did anyone else. Melinda died seeing you this way. Seeing your truth."

Emily didn't know what to say.

"That's why you wear that mask, isn't it? You can't bear to look at yourself. See yourself how everyone sees you."

"I have helped people," Emily said unsteadily. "There were people being hurt. I stopped that."

"No," Victor said, without turning around.

"You threw sand in the ocean," Isabel told Emily. "That's it. That's what it all amounted to. Sand in the ocean."

"I *did* help people."

Isabel pushed back her chair, stood. Picked up her steak knife.

Turned it over in her hand.

"You killed your brother and your sister."

At her words, Emily felt like a giant fist was squeezing her.

Isabel walked toward Emily, the knife at her side. "I want to cut that mask off your face," she said. "I want you to look me in the eye."

Emily took an uncertain step back, tripped, caught herself on the wall.

Isabel was getting closer.

"I don't need to prove anything to you," Emily said.

"You can't live with yourself," Isabel said, her voice low, menacing. "You can keep the mask on, and you can die with it on. Because, Emily, you're going to die tonight. If you don't, your father dies tomorrow."

Emily's back was hard against the wall.

"Here's what will happen," Isabel went on. "You're going to take this knife, and you're going to plunge it into your heart. Or your father dies. There's no escaping that. You're right, you're not a good person. But you can do one good thing. Give up your life for him."

Emily felt trapped, confused, like she was looking through smoke, blinding and choking and eternally dense. "I'm sorry."

"He'll lose his children, but he'll gain his life. And you can be the one to do it, without him ever knowing what happened. Anonymous. Behind your mask."

Isabel held out the knife.

Emily took it and stabbed Isabel in the shoulder.

The smoke had cleared.

Isabel shrieked, stepped back and fell, her hands over the knife. She crawled toward Victor.

"Or," Emily said, unsnapping her baton from her pants, "I could just kill you both now."

Victor exploded from the table, the chair he was sitting in flying back, knocking Isabel to the side and Emily out of the dining room. She stumbled back into the great hall and, disoriented, ducked into the living room, a massive room with a fireplace big enough for a person to walk into, giant rectangular windows showing the grassy grounds of the estate, a mix of modern furniture and artwork spread throughout.

Emily's leg ached. She grimaced under her mask, one hand on the floor. She looked up and saw a blurry shadow rushing toward her. Scrambled to the side.

The pain in her leg from the scramble felt like a dog gnawing her skin. Emily staggered back to one of the large windows. Victor was in front of her, standing in the only doorway out of the room. The doorway that led to the entranceway and the front door.

Isabel appeared at his side, walking unsteadily, the knife still sticking out of her shoulder like a bone jutting from skin.

"You fucking whore," she said, her words icicles.

Victor tossed a chair out of the way and reached for Emily.

Everything, to Emily, suddenly seemed to be happening in slow motion. The chair airborne, sailing into a far wall. Isabel clumsily walking, her legs awkward as she clutched the knife in her shoulder, as if she was made up of two different bodies, above and below her waist. Victor's snarl as he lunged.

And within that slowness was the stone, that violence that lived in Emily. Like the violence was her soul, hidden but now emerged. The same as Markus's music, as Melinda's charity.

Emily smashed the baton against Victor's wrist as he reached to her, swinging it with all her force.

The hit didn't even slow him.

His entire hand encompassed her face, and he lifted her and drove her down.

The back of Emily's head hit first, and then there was nothing.

Darkness.

A train in the distance, wind through a canyon. Sounds distant, coming closer. The taste of her canvas mask. And then the shrill scream of pain.

Emily opened her eyes, couldn't see. She pushed but couldn't move whatever was on top of her. Her hands struck out wildly, and she grasped Victor's arm, felt his hand still over her face, lifting her head and driving it back down.

"No!" someone shouted.

The giant palm rose. The room was crooked. Emily blinked, but it stayed crooked. Isabel was on her hands and knees in front of her.

"No," Isabel said again. "My turn."

She pulled the knife free from her shoulder, crying out as she did, staggered back to the wall. Emily crawled back but couldn't stand.

Isabel glared at her, the knife in one hand, grunting and sucking in a hoarse breath.

"I'm going to kill you," Isabel rasped. She ran toward Emily.

Emily tried to stand, couldn't. She lifted her arms.

Isabel cried out and tripped, arms flailing, and fell down. She rose up to her knees, staggered.

The knife was buried in her stomach.

Isabel fell forward again. Stayed still.

Silence.

"Oh shit," Emily said.

An animal roared from somewhere in the room, a sound she would never forget. Victor grabbed her. His hand was on her waist, his fingers gripping her hips, almost like they were indenting the bone. She struck at him with her baton, and he grabbed her arm with his other hand.

He squeezed her wrist. The baton clattered to the floor.

"You're not using that again," Victor hissed. He drove her down, Emily's body slamming. She crawled forward, and he grabbed her leg and pulled her back, and she was almost sailing through the air.

And then her hand in his, almost gently.

His foot stepped through her elbow.

That's what it looked like to Emily, her arm in the air, and then his foot behind it and through it and everything smashing down to the floor. Her pain was beyond pain, so deep and terrible that Emily felt like she was blinking and breathing in different dimensions of being, and she hoped one was death. Release.

She was lifted, arm protruding like a broken branch. Victor's face in front of hers.

A weird smile on his face, the kind of mischievous smile a cruel child has when it's torturing an insect.

"I'm going to crumple up this mask," he told her. "While you're wearing it."

His fingers pressed into either side of her head. Pushed deep.

Emily felt like her skull was going to crack, and perhaps it was. As if his fingers were going to meet, their tips touch. He smiled deeply, wide shadows lengthening behind him.

"Please," Emily told him as pain and darkness covered her.

"Please do it."

The darkness and shadows grew. Those shadows dancing, black and red swirling as Emily felt her skull start to crack open.

Those shadows, black and red and light, flashes of light. Explosions of sound.

Glinting knives.

Victor's hands loosened. Emily stepped back, slipped, fell hard. Stayed down. Gazed up at the shadows as she touched her bruised head, the shadows turning into three women, the women like witches dancing around Victor.

He roared, reached out blindly.

Collapsed to a knee.

The women surrounded him, their knives rising and falling. Victor's rage turned to cries, fear, helplessness. Still the knives rose and fell, until he was on the ground. Until he was silent.

One of the women helped Emily up. Half carried her out of the living room, to the great hall, to the front door.

"I'm sorry about Dani," Emily told Lena, her voice choked, the words climbing rocks.

"Me too," Lena told her. "But you should have waited for us."

"I didn't want you to have to do that."

"They wanted to. For Dani."

Lena opened the front door, led Emily to a car.

Eve Peterson stepped out of the driver's seat. Grimaced at Emily's broken arm. Helped her sit down and buckled her seat belt.

"Thank you for coming," Emily told her raggedly. "After Mel, I . . ."

"This wasn't what Melinda would have done," Eve replied. "But Victor Winters wouldn't have spent a day in jail."

"I didn't mean for her to die," Emily said. "I didn't."

Eve wiped her eyes, started down the long winding driveway to the gate. Glanced over at Emily, her bruises, the blood running down her leg, her ruined arm.

Emily's tears came like a storm, one that leveled everything in its path, until even the ground was torn apart.

CHAPTER
FORTY-EIGHT

Two Weeks Later

Federal Hill in Baltimore gave the mistaken sense that it overlooked the entire city. It did provide a wonderful view of the Inner Harbor, of the iconic Domino Sugars sign, of some of the city's celebrated neighborhoods. And it was a popular place for picnics, for watching fireworks on the Fourth of July or New Year's Eve. For reflection.

The hilltop was one of Emily's favorite spots in Baltimore. She could see the condo Markus had lived in from here, in a high building that overlooked the harbor. She and Markus had come here once, back before Rebecca, when he first moved to the city.

But now she ignored the view and read an article in the *Baltimore Sun*.

Police stated that no leads have emerged in the deaths of commercial real estate developer Victor Winters and his associate and legal counsel, Isabel Pike.

Since the assault, a number of anonymous sources have informed both this paper and authorities that Mr.

Winters, primarily known for several commercial real
estate projects in and around the district, was a major
fixture in trafficking circles, focusing on drugs, weapons, and people. Although none of these claims have
been verified, DC police have announced an investigation into his businesses, Winters Holdings Inc.

A dog barked, startling her. Emily glanced up at a young woman
dragging some type of hound away, its bloodshot eyes staring balefully
at Emily.

"Hello, dog," she said and resumed reading.

"It's too big a coincidence to ignore," commented
Detective Matt Ignatius. "His niece was killed last week,
her ex-boyfriend [the singer] Markus Peña was murdered last month. Something's going on, and we're
taking any leads or accusations very seriously."

Both Mr. Winters and Ms. Pike were pronounced dead
shortly after authorities arrived at the scene.

She saw him walking toward her, the sun behind him so her eyes
could only make out his silhouette. But she knew who it was.

Rick Walker sat on the bench next to Emily.

Neither of them spoke as she folded the newspaper closed. The task
took Emily a moment, given her arm sling and cast.

"I keep thinking about what I did," Rick finally said.

"What'd you do?"

"I left her."

"You were coming back."

Pain in his face. "How do you know?"

"Because she wanted you back. She would have done anything to keep you."

"Really?"

"My sister loved you. That's what I wanted to tell you. That's why I called."

Emily thought about those words after she said them. And wondered if they were true.

She'd told Melinda that if she had really loved Rick, she'd chase him. Melinda wouldn't be content to let him go, to accept his decision. Emily had told her that the necessity of a lie outweighed the virtue of truth. And Melinda, in her confused, uncertain state, had believed her.

But that advice, Emily now realized, was better suited for herself.

For who she was.

A living lie.

"I just—I just needed some time when she told me what happened with her boss," Rick was saying. "I needed to think. I didn't know this was going to happen."

No one could have known this was going to happen, Rick.

No one could have known Melinda was going to die instead of me.

"It's not your fault," Emily said, and her voice quieted as she spoke. "Melinda followed bad advice. She should have done what was in her heart. Melinda's instincts were always to help people, to stop anyone from suffering, but she got hurt doing that. So she shied away from her instincts. Stopped listening to her gut."

Emily's broken arm ached.

"But Melinda never told me anything bad about you," Emily went on, and Rick looked away from her, down to the cold dry grass. "She would have gone back to you, and she would have realized how much she loved you, and I know you would have taken her back." Emily's words finally felt honest. "And then Mel would have accepted love. I think she needed to be loved by someone she'd abandoned, or who had abandoned her. I think she needed to understand forgiveness."

Emily hadn't thought about any of this before, or at least not this coherently. And she wondered if this was why she'd called Rick. She'd wanted to give him answers, but maybe there was something else she needed. Something only he could offer.

"I promise you, Rick," Emily finished, her voice still quiet. "This wasn't your fault."

"Is it yours?"

Rick turned away from the grass, looked her in the eyes. Emily had expected tears, but saw only anger.

"What?"

Rick gripped the backrest of the bench. "Is this your fault?"

And that's when Emily noticed the cop on the far side of the hill. Walking toward them.

"Melinda told me about you," Rick said. "About who you really are."

Emily subtly moved her good hand closer to her handbag.

To the retracted baton inside.

"She did?"

"Three Strikes." The two words nearly spat out. "I've read about you online. They say you uncovered the whole Victor Winters crime operation, the same operation that killed your brother, that murdered Melinda when she learned the truth. Everyone who knew what was happening with those Winters people died. Except you."

Something snapped inside Emily, but sadly. For the past two weeks her soul had felt like a dead tree, its branches slowly falling away.

The cop had stopped walking, was checking his phone.

"Melinda would be alive if you hadn't been here," Rick told her.

"You're probably right," Emily said, the small sentence heavy. "But Mel made her own choices."

Mel, why'd you come back?

"You got her killed."

Rick's face was close to hers. She felt the anger of his glare, the heat of his breath.

"I don't know why you do what you do," he went on. "I don't know a thing about you. But I bet you thought you were doing something good. And even after all this hell you've left us in, you'll just keep going. Because you think you should. Because you think you're important. Because you think you're more important than anyone else."

"Stop!" Emily said, her voice loud enough for the cop to look up.

Now she faced Rick, faced his fury.

"Mel saved my life, and I didn't want her to, but she did. I'm not more important than she was."

"What you're doing—" Rick began, but Emily talked over him.

"You think you can make me feel worse by telling me what I already know? By making me face some truth that I already have to accept every second? I'm already in hell."

The cop was close to them. "You okay, ma'am?"

A beat passed between her and Rick.

"I'm good," Emily said.

They sat in silence as the cop walked off.

They stayed sitting in silence as the winter sun cast a faint warmth, as tourists wandered through the harbor pavilions on the other side of the water, as hundreds of cars took people on hundreds of different paths, as a pair of children played and shouted and climbed over those old cannons forever pointed at the city.

Rick stood, gazed down at her.

"I'm sorry," Emily told him.

"I hope you burn," he said.

And he left.

CHAPTER FORTY-NINE

"I don't know what I did wrong," Frank Peña said. He stared at the television, slumped in his recliner. The television was off, and the room dark.

"You didn't do anything wrong."

"I buried two of my children in a month."

"They just—they crossed bad people. That doesn't have anything to do with how you raised us. You were good."

"You were all so different. I know the three of you didn't talk." Frank lifted his thumb to his lips, bit the knuckle. Closed his eyes in a failed effort to fight back tears.

"I knew Markus wasn't a good man," Frank whispered. "I know what he did. But I loved him so much. My boy . . ."

Emily stayed quiet.

"And Melinda?" he asked plaintively. Waited for an answer. None came. "Melinda deserved better."

"Markus had that side to him," Emily said. "That dangerous side. Melinda didn't. But she did try to help."

"She did help," he said.

There was a numbness to her father Emily found impenetrable. Of the children, she'd had the most distance from their parents. Either Melinda or Markus, she felt, would have been better in this situation.

Emily walked over to the end table.

"You sure you know what to do with this little guy?" She peered into the tank. "He's a betta, a Japanese fighting fish. They need to be kept alone, but they're beautiful."

Frank leaned to his side heavily. "Emily, I'm not in the right mind to take care of anything."

"I'll take care of him until you're ready. Come over a few times a week to feed him, change the water. Read him a bedtime story. What are you going to name him?"

He looked at the fish, its red fins swishing as it swam through the small tank.

"Darién."

Emily didn't have a reply. She just kept staring at Darién as the fish flicked its tail and darted away.

Frank turned on the television. Emily wondered what to say next. Then the television distracted her.

"Hold on," she told him as he flipped through channels. "Can you keep it here for a second?"

A reporter was talking to an elderly couple. The reporter was young and tall and blonde, her face with a sharpness and intensity that reminded Emily of a hawk. The elderly man and woman were small by comparison, huddled, the way people who had lived lives together seemed formed of the same clay.

The graphic on the bottom of the screen read "Simon Glowalter's Parents Discuss Their Son's Release."

"I worked on this," Emily told Frank.

"What do you mean?"

"My company, the organization I work for, fought for Simon Glowalter's release."

Frank stared at her. "I didn't know that."

"Yea, verily. We really should talk more."

They both turned back toward the television.

"We feel robbed," Simon Glowalter's mother was saying, her voice rough at the edges. "Robbed of five years of our son's life. Robbed of the chance to grieve Cheryl's death with him, whom we loved a great deal. He was our son, and she was our daughter."

She paused.

"And we had both of them taken away from us."

There was resolve to her last sentence, a hardness in tone. She might appear older and frail, but her spirit was steel.

"How did you help them?" Frank asked.

"Well, it wasn't so much me," Emily said. "I just do the marketing and PR stuff. But the organization I work for, you know, they make sure people who are sent to prison by mistake don't stay there."

Emily couldn't remember ever discussing her job with Frank.

"That's good work," her father said.

Emily stayed with her dad the rest of that afternoon, the same as she'd done for the past few weeks since Melinda's funeral. There was little conversation between them other than grief. But it was conversation. And they both needed it. They clung to each other's words like they were hanging on to the edge of a cliff.

She was slowly recovering.

He wasn't, but he would.

She'd make sure of it.

Emily headed back to her Civic and climbed inside carefully, habit keeping her from using her healing arm, now in a light cast. She pulled out her phone and didn't have any messages.

Calvin had stopped trying to reach her. Emily supposed she should feel grateful, since he'd finally done what she'd asked, but a part of her had hoped he'd find and confront her. Even though she'd texted him and expressly said, "I'm sorry, but I can't do this. Please don't find or confront me." Calvin was full of questions, and Emily wished she could give him the answers he wanted.

But he was entering the FBI Academy next year, and their paths couldn't be more different.

Besides, if Calvin knew her, really knew her, Emily figured he wouldn't want her anyway.

There's no home for killers.

She drove out of her father's neighborhood and headed back toward DC.

But she turned off on an old road before she hit the interstate and followed that road past faded stores and small houses, through the side of town that hadn't been remade. The old side that hadn't changed.

She pulled over, turned off the engine. Took out her canvas mask and slipped it on.

The waking dreams, those moments of overwhelming memory, were gone. That distress had been shaken free, like a rock from a shoe. The cries from the men she'd hurt were forgotten. Emily could remember their faces and the fights if she tried to think about them but, strangely, the sound was gone. As if she were watching a movie with the volume off, and it was a movie that starred someone else.

Her only vivid, violent memory was of Melinda. Her sister's head in her lap, her blood, her beautiful face. That memory was grief and it was sorrow and it was rain.

Emily climbed into the back of her Civic.

She needed to make sure that the bound and gagged man inside her trunk was still unconscious. She didn't know his first name, just his last. Dawkins.

He was asleep.

And missing the end of his nose.

She pulled down the back seat, checked Dawkins and his restraints.

Emily kept the mask on, although he was unconscious and she still had a few miles to go before she reached the abandoned farm where she planned to question him. Where she planned to start finding all the men who had been there when Melinda was killed.

She closed the back seat, returned to the front, restarted the engine. The drive turned shadowy as the passing headlights of other cars eventually disappeared, as broken traffic lights blinked, as dormant streetlamps refused to shine. Even so, despite the dark, she kept her headlights off.

Emily knew exactly where she was going.

ACKNOWLEDGMENTS

The mystery-writing community is so close knit and supportive that any writer, a few books in, can write pages and pages of acknowledgments. Fortunately for you, any writer a few books in should know the importance of brevity. I'll keep it short, I promise.

I honestly can't thank the team at Thomas & Mercer enough. Jessica Tribble Wells is every writer's secret hope. There's no better champion or more thorough editor, and she understood exactly what I wanted with *No Home for Killers*. Every suggestion she made was one that I eventually, if not immediately, accepted. And the rest of the team at Thomas & Mercer has been truly wonderful. Thanks to Sarah Shaw for her guidance, Carissa Bluestone for her publicity expertise, Jeff Miller for his tireless work on a truly superb cover, and Rachael Herbert, Elyse Lyon, and Stephanie Chou for their comprehensive edits. You're all a dream team.

And I wouldn't have found any of you if it wasn't for Michelle Richter. There's no one in publishing whom I owe more than Michelle. Thanks for sticking by me all these years and for your unwavering belief. I'm indebted to you for life.

I've been fortunate to work with wonderful people in PR and marketing, and Gretchen Crary with February Media is one of the best. Thank you for the Zoom meetings and phone calls and the fantastic advice throughout this process. And a special shout-out to designer Penny Blatt for her help with my revitalized website.

Sometimes meeting your heroes isn't a bad thing, and I was lucky that my heroes took the time to act as early readers for this book and its proposal. Special thanks to Jennifer Hillier, Eliza Nellums, Sarah M. Chen, Elizabeth Heiter, Alex Segura, Kathleen Barber, Tara Laskowski, and Carrie Callaghan.

I was also aided by expert fact-checkers for various elements of *No Home for Killers*. Much love to Yenny Lucero for her work in making sure that my terrible Spanish (I know, Mom) was correct, to Sara Jones and Ayana Reed for their advice about music, and to both Kayla Quinn (whom I met through the wonderful writer James D. F. Hannah) and Joy Hart for their knowledge about social work. Of course, any mistakes that escaped scrutiny are my own.

I also received help from graphic artist Angela Del Vecchio—visit my website for a look at her rendering of Emily's mask.

As you read through these acknowledgments, you'll get the sense that the crime fiction writing community is a lovely one, and it's made even better by people like Kate and Dan Malmon, Kristopher Zgorski, Dru Ann Love, Oline Cogdill, Torie Clarke, and Tom and Marie O'Day. And crime fiction writers are indebted to organizations like Crime Writers of Color, Sisters in Crime, PitchWars (check out my mentee Sian Gilbert's upcoming novel!), ITW, and MWA. DMV writers, in particular, are tirelessly supported by book festivals such as Gaithersburg Book Festival, 1455 Literary, and Suffolk Mystery Authors Festival; publications like the Washington Independent Review of Books; stores like One More Page and Loyalty Books; and colleges including George Mason and Marymount Universities. This list isn't meant to be exhaustive, just a starting point for readers who want to discover the wealth of resources this area has to offer.

Of course, all the love to my family, to my far-flung relatives, to my parents, to Nancy and Noah.

No Home for Killers meant so much to me. I hope it did to you, as well. Thanks to you, now and always, for reading.

About the Author

Photo © 2019 Marian Lozano Photography

E.A. Aymar is the author of the thrillers *They're Gone* and *The Unrepentant*, which both received critical enthusiasm from publications such as *Publishers Weekly* and *Kirkus Reviews*. His other thrillers include the novels-in-stories *The Night of the Flood* and *The Swamp Killers* (in both, he served as coeditor and contributor).

His column Decisions and Revisions appears monthly on the Washington Independent Review of Books. He is a former member of the national board of the International Thriller Writers and, for years, was the managing editor of The Thrill Begins, an online resource for debut and aspiring writers. He is also an active member of Crime Writers of Color, the Mystery Writers of America, and Sisters in Crime. He runs the Noir at the Bar series for Washington, DC, and has hosted and spoken at a variety of crime fiction, writing, and publishing events nationwide.

He was born in Panama and now lives and writes in and about the DC/MD/VA triangle.